OF LOVE
AND GUILT

OF LOVE
AND GUILT

PTG MAN

M. WITHNAIL PRESS
SYDNEY, AUSTRALIA

Copyright © 2014 by **PTG Man**

All rights reserved. Without limiting the rights of the copyright reserved above, no part of this publication may be reproduced, stored in or introduced into a retrieval system, or transmitted, in any form or by any means without the prior written permission of the copyright owner.

The scanning, uploading, and distribution of this book via the Internet or via any other means without the permission of the publisher is illegal and punishable by law. This is a work of fiction. Names, characters, places and incidents are the products of the author's imagination or are used fictitiously. Any resemblance to actual events, or persons, living or dead, is entirely coincidental.

"No man is an Iland . . ." Epigraph (John Donne). *For Whom the Bell Tolls*. Ernest Hemingway, Random House UK Ltd. 1994.

"O[h] for a life of sensations rather than of thoughts!" *Letter from John Keats to Benjamin Bailey*. "Beauty is truth, truth [is] beauty . . ." *Ode on a Grecian Urn. Poems of John Keats*. John Keats. Penguin Books, 2009.

"My Baby Just Cares for Me." Walter Donaldson and Gus Kahn (lyrics), 1930.

"Oh how I yearn to see Norman again, with his red hair, and his book of poetry stained with the butter drips from crumpets." Paraphrased from "Withnail and I." Bruce Robinson, HandMade Films, 1987.

Cover photograph Che Guevara painting on wall in old Havana, Cuba © Martin Applegate, Dreamstime.com; All section illustrations from Shutterstock – Cuba Stamp © astudio; Whale © Jef Thompson; Cigar © lineartestpilot; Bamboo © Veyronik; Sprayer © RetroClipArt

M. Withnail Press

A Very Human Place. -- 1st ed. 2016

ISBN 978-0-9874316-4-6 PRINT
ISBN 978-0-9874316-1-5 EBOOK

CONTENTS

Prologue   11

Tell Me About Your Childhood   15

Tell Me About Your Time In Cuba   93

Tell Me About The First Time You Found Her   165

Keep A Diary   183

> *Love is the seed in you of every virtue,*
> *and of all acts deserving punishment.*

Dante Alighieri. *The Divine Comedy*, Purgatory XVII, 104-105.

Prologue

Tom finished his life as a farmer, potato and manioc mainly, sometimes tobacco. Of course, it wasn't his chosen profession, but for the last five years or so, it had filled much of his time. I think it's true to say he was a farmer by accident, but he was certainly the wealthier for it.

It was strange, but I had been thinking of him when the package arrived—wrapped in tattered butcher's paper, tightly bound with string, and covered in stamps of butterflies. The parcel came with a letter of introduction, written in a floral penmanship that is seldom seen these days. It started with gentle condolences that tried to soothe but didn't. Tom had died in his sleep some months ago, an autopsy revealing a heart attack. It was unexpected but peaceful, the letter said. The day before, he was tending the manioc he had helped to plant. He was fifty-seven.

"Dear Hymie, I am sending you Tom's manuscript," the letter said, "because I don't know what to do with it. I'm not sure you will either, but I didn't want it to sit in a cupboard or be tossed away. Of course, it's your job to know what to do with such things, and you were his closest friend. Next to her, of course." It was signed Juan Carlos Rebelde—a man I had never met but heard so much of. A man these pages will throw some light upon, though from a fickle source.

I folded the letter back in its envelope and looked out of my window at an oak that pushed against my neighbor's fence. Left to itself, this tree would outlive us all—my kids, perhaps my grandchildren, even little Sarah. As I gazed at the oak, the thick of the leaning trunk, a warm glow rose from my insides and up to my chest. I was happy. For we all want to die in the arms of someone we love—though it usually doesn't figure that way.

But in Tom's case, I knew it had.

Hyman L. David 2018

Original Letter (Author's Note)

Dear Juan,

Well here it is, my assignment, collated into something with at least a little bit of structure to it, although it's as fragmented as you would expect. And I must thank Leonardo for his proofreading skills. What a multi-talent he is! He wanted to add some illustrations, which I thought was cute. He even showed me some preliminary sketches. You'd like them. Not quite caricatures, yet they capture some of the people as they really are. But not all of course, and I can't draw to save my life, so imagination will have to suffice.

The calluses on my hands are flattening. Between writing and Estelle's hand cream, they really don't have any other fate. I miss them, though. Sometimes the dirt was so ground in that, no matter how hard I scrubbed, they looked like big black warts. What else do I miss? You? I can see you laugh, but I'm not sure whether I do. Still, we will be friends, of that I have no doubt. Is 'friend' the word you would use? 'Partners' might be better. Would that make you more comfortable? Something for you to mull on, then. Oh, and my limp has gone. I went jogging along the Malecón this morning. No pain whatsoever. I've made a plan to try and keep fit. I think you'd approve.

So what do I have now? I'm sitting at my desk on the upstairs floor, in my quite spacious bedroom, at the level of my neighbor's balcony across the road, which I must say is occupied by two attractive women—cousins, I think. I've started a new project, set away from this place; Havana is too intense for me now, but I don't really want to talk about it. It's far too early.

It was funny reading my assignment over. I had forgotten some parts. And I challenged you a bit with my one secret, I think I called it. A secret best kept, but c'est la vie. Nevertheless, this secret was not to challenge you as much as protect myself. That guilt of mine always rears its ugly head. What did Saint Augustine say; repentant tears wash out the stain of guilt? Well, maybe he was right, because I've never repented. And I never will. And that stain sure isn't coming out, no matter how hard I scrub.

So, against the good Saint's advice, I was wondering whether I could take you up on that offer of yours a bit sooner. You see, farming has been difficult for me to escape. Maybe it's age, I'll be fifty pretty soon. And I've written quite a lot, most of my adult life, and I want, in the time remaining, something very different when I wake up. And when I go to bed.

So, I guess what I'm saying is, I want to try again. For longer this time. And if it doesn't work, try over. And again. Until it does.

Best to you,
Tom Peters,
Jan 7, 2011.

Tell Me About Your Childhood

Her name was Heather, Heather Jones. A strange name for a Chinese girl living in the western suburbs of Sydney. I guess her family wanted her to fit in for, as I look at my old school photo, she was the only Asian girl in my class. And from my distant memories—granted, now washed with a sepia gouache—perhaps the only Asian girl at school. Nevertheless, whether she was or wasn't really doesn't matter. What matters is I was in love with her.

The photo I'm looking at was from 1971, class 4A, from Crepundia South Primary School. Black and white of course. I'm there in the upper row, taller than I remember, the only boy with his shirt buttoned all the way to the top. I was said to be a very neat boy—as in tidy. The only other physical feature worth noting was that I was skinny, something that persisted until I reached my early forties, and that I had hair like spun gold. That sounds a somewhat narcissistic comment, as if I were a pompous dandy, but don't jump to conclusions. My hair, while naturally blonde, was really dyed with sunshine mixed with many hours in chlorinated water. I was a swimmer, you see, and trained most days.

In the photo I'm standing next to David Bean—"Beany" as we called him; since the fad of the day was to add a "y" or "o" to the end of a name—either first or second, whatever worked. He was my best friend—only counting the boys. He stands with his hands in his pockets, slouching a bit with a hint of a grin, as cool as you could be at nine. He was, too—great at every sport, especially league and cricket, an open batsman and bowler, but never boasted. He had ginger hair and a face that splattered with freckles, leaving just glimpses of pearl-colored skin.

Danno is standing on the top row but further away—with a giant smile. I remember him as a pretty-boy and the photo confirms it—feminine, with pencil thin brows and lips, dark hair and eyes, and a tiny button nose. Rydges sat plump with the short boys on the floor, cross-legged, arms straight clasping his knees, though he still managed to slouch.

I scan the girls, all-beaming. Sepia memories glisten. Pigtails were obviously the fashion then, all tied with ribbons, some as large as dogs' ears. I pick out the girls I liked, but at this moment their lips remain mute, since at school I nearly always hung with the boys. I strain to remember more, but only whispers of events unfold.

So, at least for now, let's get back to Heather. She is on the second row from the top, just below me, taller than the other girls. As tall as me. She stands upright with smiling almond eyes. Her ink-black hair is parted in the center and wound back in double plaits that curl from behind her ears and rest at mid-arm's length against her chest. Her dimpled cheeks, puckering like shallow eggcups, are of light bronze, and her lips, thin, of Georgia peach.

As you can see, there are no sepia memories when it comes to Heather. They flash in vivid color.

* * *

"How high can you piss?"

Danno had set the mark, arching his back to gain maximum distance—the highest splash shining against the metal trough.

"Beat that," he said.

Beany stepped up to the metal grate, pushing a stream two hands above Danno's mark. He sauntered down, satisfied with the result. Cool as.

"I can't beat that," Rydges said, "I pissed only ten minutes ago."

"In your pants I bet," Danno said.

Rydges pulled a face and wilted back against the brick wall, his gray shorts tight against stout flesh. The others, like mine, were baggy around stick legs. Rydges seemed always in retreat—quirky, insecure, but not quite timid. Murky images bleed—perhaps his portrait will become more colorful as the pages turn. But I certainly liked him.

"Go on, Tommy," Rydges said, "show'em what you did the other day."

I moved over to the far left of the trough, took out my willy, and started a quick dance down the full length of the rattling grate, singing out each letter as I splashed a perfectly etched signature onto the metal. I turned to see Beany hunched over with laughter. It was that easy to get the coolest kid at school to be your best friend—just write your name in piss. I see his face clearly, his teeth sparkling through freckled cheeks, shaking his head. He rarely laughed—or at least I don't remember him laughing—except when I pissed my name.

"You're such a rat-bag, Tommy . . . we better get to class."

The lunch bell had already clanged, and we, like always, were slow to move. We sprinted over the treeless asphalt, Rydges hobbling at the rear, then climbed the few steps into the white timbered building that housed two or three or four classrooms. I remember the paint always seemed to be peeling off the siding—like the bark off a eucalypt.

We entered our room in single file in the order we arrived—Beany, Danno, myself, then Rydges. I wasn't fast on the land, but never came last when Rydges was around. On a warm summer's day the scent of Perkin's paste would have filled the space, its creamy blancmange a favorite dessert with some of the kindergarten kids. Well, if you build a spoon into the lid of a pink glue container, surely you expect some to eat it? Paired students sat behind timber desks on timber chairs with comfortable curved backs; couples separated from their neighbors by a small corridor that left ample space for a roving teacher. One wall had large bright windows that peered into the playground of asphalt, while the other walls seemed stuck together with white wrinkled paper that dripped with color. Ahead lay a fat olive-green chalkboard.

"Nice you could join us, gentlemen," Miss Quinter—who would become Mrs. Brydon before we left for high school—said. I'm in year three now, so about eight.

I moved to my desk, but something seemed muddled.

"Don't you like our new arrangement, boys?"

"Miss?"

"I've separated you and David for the time being."

"Why, Miss?"

"Because, I'm the teacher."

I stood alone in a sea of gray and white uniforms.

"Your seat is over here now, Tom . . . where I can keep a better eye on you."

I focused on the empty spot at the front of the room, with my bag tucked under the chair. The rest of the students twisted to look at me, except the one seated next to my bag. I cannot see this student's face—only her pigtails. *Her* pigtails.

Understand, all of the students are paired with someone of the same gender. Except, from this point on, me.

"Come and sit next to Heather," Miss Quinter said.

A grimace smeared over Beany's face as I dragged my feet to the empty chair, the eyes of gray and white uniforms following each step.

I sat down and turned a glance at my neighbor, who kept her stare ahead. I don't think she was happy about the arrangement either, and she had done nothing to deserve it. Miss Quinter hovered just feet in front of us—I had to tilt my neck high to look at her. I don't mind sitting in the front row of the pictures for a few hours, but it was going to be hard to keep my neck up for the whole day. I looked up and down and remember feeling trapped in a cage surrounded by unfriendlies, like those geese Mum kept on about that were force fed to make brown muck on little squares of toast. So I sat there and searched for a means of escape.

But it never came.

* * *

My mother told me some years later that my teacher sat me next to Heather to quiet me down. I do recall giggling a lot in class, mainly with my mates. I remember churning in all directions on my chair. And I so remember the label of 'immature' that pestered like a blowfly throughout my school days—both primary and high. How old are you, act your age, don't be so immature. As I type these words it seems to me the most pointless uttering that can be made to any kid. We are who we are, and if immature best describes us, so be it. So unless the expectation is for a child to act without a tinge of impulse—which would require restraint fastened like a straitjacket—I would propose a ban on the use of the word. At least by all teachers.

I don't remember much of the early days, sitting next to Heather. I guess I just accepted my fate. My next vivid memory was asking a loan of a pencil from her—it may have been the first time I spoke to her. I just assumed she would say no. I remember her turning her head, biting her lip, and giving a little nod. Then she handed me a shiny case full of Textas and pencils licked with rainbow colors. Not even Beany would have given me such an open slather—I reckon I could have taken two. But I only took one, a soft gray that had been shortened by much sharpening. I remember not saying thanks, but I think the gesture of taking the smallest met with her approval, because she flickered a smile before turning her almond eyes back to the chalkboard.

And I sat with a warm feeling in my guts, not understanding why.

*　*　*

Tell me about your childhood, you said, my dear Juan. Such an open-ended question makes it a hard task, although I suspect I know what bits will interest you the most. I assume you don't want a tome, and my sometimes faithful public—although 'public' may be too vast a word for the intimate clique that reads my stuff—would surely object if I produced a Churchillian epic.

I have pinned my school photo against the bed-head, so when I need inspiration I flip over and study the gray and white smiles. Billy enlarged the photo for me—he's such a sweetheart. So . . . four rows of kids, boys cross-legged on the floor, the tallest standing at the top, and the girls sandwiched in the middle. They're all happy, aren't they? They're certainly all beaming, most with Luna Park smiles, so they must be happy, at least for that moment. I know I was happy. Life was candy then, buttered raisin toast, fairy bread, and scraped knees that healed real quick. There was nothing dark. Nothing heavy. Just fun.

This must be so. You can see it in their eyes. How could the cameraman catch all these smiling faces at once, if sadness was amongst us?

It is late, my writing takes me well into the night. I chew into the cold empanada, the last on my plate. Boisterous neighbors suddenly cry out Spanish from the window of my room—the sound of mojitos spilling onto the street can be deafening in Havana.

What do you want from me, Juan?

What can I give you to satisfy your need?

I mold the wax balls that sit in a saucer at my bedside and seal my ears. Perhaps I'll let the drug of slumber play with the gray and white smiles for a while—who knows what insight might awaken.

Who knows?

* * *

In the summer, the days were long.

Not too far from school, a rocky bush-land sprouted, its crevices hidden from prying eyes—a boys' heaven really. We dropped our bags at Beany's place and set off to our hidden spot, kicking at trash from fallen gums along a track that seemed to serve no purpose but to amuse nomadic boys like us. Rydges, as usual, trailed behind and shouted up to wait. But we kept on, car noise slowly rising as we neared our spot.

The bush retreated into a wall of sky, a semi-circle of boulders marking the edge of the cliff. Below, the highway flowed—a straight drop of at least a hundred feet. We sucked in the dry air, our mouths parched, for we always forgot to bring water.

Rydges finally arrived panting. "Why'd you . . . run off? I thought . . . I was lost."

"We've been here stacks of time. And we're at the top. How could you get lost?"

"I think I saw a snake. A brown."

"Come on, Rydges, you said you wanted to go first, didn't you?"

"You bet."

He moved up to the boulders, crouching behind the largest. Next to his knees sandstone rocks the size of fists and larger nested—our ammunition.

"We're running short," Beany said, "we have to bring more next time. So you better aim right."

Rydges took the smallest rock in hand, one that couldn't do much damage. "You lot tell me when to throw. If I miss, it's your fault."

We moved over to the edge to allow full view of the traffic—it must have been peak hour. Usually we reserved the smaller stones for cars, leaving the boulders for trucks and buses. From the distance we were at, there was no real aiming involved, we just picked the busiest moment, then tossed and hoped.

"Now!"

We held our breath as the pelted rock sailed, hung at the peak of its arch, then fell—bouncing on the road just a car length from a swerving Valiant. We dropped behind the largest boulder and out of sight.

"Wow, did you see her move?" Beany grinned. "She nearly shat herself." That makes twice I remember him smiling—pissing and chucking rocks at cars. "Tommy, it's your turn."

I peered through the gap of the boulders, confirming the Valiant had moved on, then grabbed the largest rock—the size of a melon—and stood high at the edge of the cliff.

"A truck buster!" Beany loved how I always took the fattest rock on offer. Maybe I could extend his smiling count to three.

The faceless traffic flowed steadily on the highway. In time, an old two-ton ice-cream truck hove into sight around the bend, two hundred feet from the base of our spot, spluttering charcoal fumes from its red-striped hood. A stream of vehicles cramped behind it, leaving clear road in front. I started to swing my arm in a slow pendulum motion, then increased the arc until my knuckles were at face level . . . and released.

When a truck buster was tossed, we never followed its trajectory, instead we fell behind the boulders and listened—our gasps restless above the traffic.

After ten seconds or so of silence, Beany peeked over the boulder. "Looks like a miss, Tommy."

We stood, not bothering to wipe the sandstone crud off our knees.

"I reckon we should throw the lot," I said. "That'd do the trick."

"Probably would," Rydges said. "But then we'd be out of ammo."

"Rydges, why don't you go and get some rocks," Danno said.

"Why don't you?"

We muddled through the options, the sun moving lower in the sky. Beany shot next without a strike. Danno followed, and we thought he might have hit the tire of a car, but weren't that sure. Then . . . "Fuck!"

I don't know who shouted it, but it wasn't me. I turned to see a tattooed arm slice between the green, no more than ten feet behind us. Then a leg, and saw the boots heavy and large.

The blue whale tattoo struck out—its tail thrashing in the bush.

"Fuck . . . run!"

We darted away without aim, scraped through the green-brown heat, branches hanging, hindered, not sure of the direction, a scratched record of rasping breath, crunching undergrowth—the eye of the whale, small and piercing—grazed legs and arms, never slowed. Never looked back.

After a point, I ran alone. I remember being very alone.

A frayed timber fence came sudden out of the bush, obstructing the way. I slid fast along its breadth, finding other fences, different but still impenetrable, shoulder to shoulder with no gaps. Finally, a couple of palings had been torn from one, rusted nails poking out. I squeezed through, tearing my shirt, skin, and entered a yard breathless. An aged swing-set sat in the center, a rusted sculpture sunken on a bed of high paspalum, I think I can see the swing, hear the sound it could have made, old metal against old metal, the sound of the junk of my childhood. But the swing was vacant, so I sped across the grass towards the cement path that flanked the house, then up to the street that opened in welcome. And kept on running.

I can hear my breath.

The blue fins flapping their chase.

And the blue eye searching.

The journey back to Beany's took a while, a long stretch through streets that were strange to me. Suburban streets can be a labyrinth at that age, a directionless wander deep into unknown territory. I finally entered Beany's backyard to find them sprawled on the lawn, holding cups of yellow drink. On approach, Beany handed me his, which I gulped without a breath.

I looked around. "Where's Rydges?"

"He wasn't with us."

"Nor me."

"Fuck!"

"It was the truck driver."

"Fuck."

"We must have hit him . . . I thought we missed."

"Fuck."

"What'll we do?"

"Go back."

"I need another drink first."

"Me too."

"I'm never going back there."

"No way I'm going back."

"Me neither."

"God, what if he got caught?"

"He's dead if he got caught."

"Dead."

We dawdled, the drama too much for us. Danno went to the toilet—twice. Then we helped ourselves to the Monte Carlos. We waited but he didn't return, and only when there were no more excuses to invent, we plodded out the back and up to the street.

"Fuck."

Far down the road Rydges was moving slowly towards us, blood ruddy on his knees, the top two buttons of his shirt unfastened, or gone, his face smeared with grime and tears.

We sprinted up to him while he continued at his snail's pace. I saw he was limping.

"Man, did he catch you?"

At first it was hard to tell if he nodded or his head simply bobbed with staccato sobs. I put my arm around his shoulders, guiding him back to the house. The others trailed in silence—except for occasional expletives. Beany got him biscuits and drink but he seemed unaware, just moved to the toilet, closed the door. And spewed.

"Fuck."

"I'll take him home," Danno said. I think he may have been crying as well.

Rydges came out of the toilet pale faced and sweating. We stood a distance away, not knowing what to do. And he looked up at us with strange eyes and he spewed again. The splatter must have bounced because I saw some of the spew on my shoes, bits of yellow stuff on my clinkers. Corn, maybe. I never bothered to wipe it.

I remember all this clearly—eight-year-old boys who stumble upon the realization that the world could collapse around them if given the chance. But there was something else to this, a discord to it all. We were guilty but so were others. We just didn't know who was most at fault.

None of us spoke to Rydges about what happened in the bush with him and the blue whale. Danno might have once on the way home, but none of us mentioned it after that. Or even later when it might have helped.

From then on we kept clear of our spot—though Beany said he went back once with his older brother. He said the circle of boulders wasn't there anymore. Maybe some other kids pushed them down. A real truck buster that'd be. Beany would have laughed.

* * *

When I used to get excited as a kid, I couldn't eat—my guts seemed to shrink to the size of a pebble. This was a problem at swimming carnivals, where I could only stomach big white discs of glucose tablets or some orange jelly with drowned wedges of mandarin. My pebble gut always appeared at breakfast before our Christmas jaunt to Luna Park—a fiesta of roller coasters, river caves, ghost trains, and pink fairy floss, which I was able to eat somehow. And it always happened at dinner before cracker night.

"I'm not letting you go before you eat some of your meal."

I pushed some mash, half a sausage, and one Brussels sprout to a clearing on my plate. "What if I eat this?"

My mother moved over to the table and scooped two more sprouts onto the pile. "Deal."

"You know I don't like sprouts. Why don't you cook them with carb-soda like Gran does?"

"Because it destroys the vitamins." My mother was big on vitamins—ahead of her time in that respect. I remember Beany daring me to eat grass once. I picked a bunch and stuffed it down. Better than sprouts, I'd said, and it was.

My father and younger brother had finished their dinner long ago. They now tucked into some rice pudding and tinned peaches, leaving me to play with cold mash and worse. None of the rest of my family ever seemed to suffer from pebble stomachs.

After a few mouthfuls and careful reorganization of the pile into dispersed flatter bits, my mother relented.

"Go on then . . . but don't be too late."

Since I know at least one reader of this yarn—you, dear Juan, my sponsor for want of a better term—will not know what cracker night is, let me clarify. Four hundred years ago, Guy Fawkes was caught with explosives at the Houses of Parliament, which were meant to kill King James 1 of England. In remembrance of his capture, an annual bonfire night in November was celebrated throughout the British Commonwealth. In Australia, the bonfire was usually replaced with fireworks—or crackers as we called them. And in the seventies these crackers were freely available, even to kids. Unsupervised kids. A simpler time.

It was an event of fire spitting wonder, albeit with the inevitable loss of an eye from the odd child here and there. By the end of the seventies, blind kiddies accumulated until an eye count was reached that extinguished the event. It just fizzled away like a wet sparkler. But on this night, in the first half of the seventies, only the big bungers that could demolish a letterbox, a small dog, or tardy fingers were banned. Sparklers, rockets, penny bungers, Roman candles, Catherine wheels, and (my favorite) ball shooters, were all on tonight's menu. The freedom in those days to wander unfettered was joyous. I can't suppose what my parents were thinking to let me out with my mates on cracker night, but they did. And I never questioned their courage.

Dusk was settling into the early evening when I met Rydges on the steps of his front yard. He leapt up, shouldering a hessian sack of crackers, chips, and lollies. He was the best. We strolled up the street towards Beany's place, where the mayhem was to be held. His house faced the long limb of a quiet suburban T-intersection that gave ample space for us to experiment. As we hastened along I saw Heather walking on the other side of the street. Next to her was a tiny old wrinkled Chinese woman—about my height or shorter.

I crossed the road. "Hey, Heather."

"Hi, Tommy." She always spoke softly—like duck-feather down.

"We're off to Beany's to let off some crackers. You wanna come?"

Heather turned to the crinkled woman and spoke in a foreign tongue. I had never heard her speak Mandarin before, but I liked it. It made her more interesting—exotic I guess—although exotic was probably a vaguely-formed notion to a nine-year-old boy.

I smiled at the old woman—the oldies seemed to like that—and she nodded at me with a mirrored grin.

"What did she say?"

"No."

So much for my smiling trick.

But Heather smiled as well, which made it worth it. "I'm taking my grandmother to the bonfire down at the park. She said you can come too, if you like."

I looked around at Rydges who had kept to himself on the opposite side of the street. I think he had already opened a packet of crisps. "I've kinda promised to meet Beany and Danno . . . we saved for ages to buy these crackers."

"That's okay, Tommy."

Before I had turned, the old woman had moved over and patted my head. I looked up at Heather who I could see was embarrassed. She whispered something to the woman—who responded with a cackle and some brief words as she lifted tufts of my hair through her fingers. It was freaking me out a bit.

"Sorry, Tommy. She likes your gold hair. She says it's good luck to touch it."

"Good luck, hey. Maybe she'll let you come to Beany's place if I let her touch it again when I drop you back. Tell her I promise."

Heather spoke to the woman who briefly responded—beaming at me while spitting out her weird cackle.

"What'd she say?"

"No."

This old bird was really something.

As we walked up the street Rydges prodded my ribs. "So you like her, hey?" He paused to juggle his crisp packet and hessian bag, pouring the remaining chip crumbs into his mouth. "Do you love her?"

Rydges could always ask anything without causing a ripple. He never judged, and his awkwardness seemed to buffer any hostility. I felt at ease with him.

"No . . . I love you."

He squawked aloud. "You really are a rat-bag, Tommy. I'll race you to Beany's house." He flung the empty chip packet at my face, but I caught him up within seconds.

The evening was fab. First we took turns lighting the rockets that whistled flames into the sky. I always got a bit nervous lighting rockets, since they could do the most damage if their path strayed, and they always were a bit unpredictable. Sure enough, Beany's dog nearly got skewered with one; missed his skull by an inch. I think it rattled him though, since he didn't resurface for the rest of the evening. The Catherine wheels were the best I've seen—we hammered a nail into the front fence and fastened them there. I think we had half a dozen of these singing spinning wheels, all powered by spurting phosphor light.

The highlight though was the ball-shooting war—Beany and me versus Rydges and Danno. The ball-shooters were the perfect cracker—a long, hand-held tube with a wick at one end and an open mouth at the other. You simply lit the wick and aimed, and a stream of rainbow balls spewed at least fifty feet into the air. We all reckoned whoever invented the ball-shooter deserved a medal. I think Beany and I won the battle, since Rydges was the only one to get hit. I hid behind one of the neighbor's fences and got him from behind. Before he knew it, I lit the fuse and aimed straight into his back. He ran for it but got slammed with all ten balls. I was surprised he managed to yelp at the exact time the light balls struck his back, since he was facing the opposite way and couldn't really see their blaze. I never realized, until many years later, that these balls of light were solid. It's funny how kids can muddle things up but somehow get away with it—though I guess it also explains the impressive number of blind kiddies that were around at the time.

On the way home, I stopped off at the park to see if Heather was still there. The bonfire was ablaze, parents chucking on any flammable refuse they could get their hands to. I couldn't see the point of bonfires. They lacked the pizzazz of crackers, and more importantly, were always under adult supervision. Perhaps it was just an excuse to burn off unwanted stuff each year. They stopped it a few years later when the fire station, which abutted the park, caught ablaze. It wasn't directly lit from the bonfire, but the event really was a smorgasbord for pyromaniacs, and one must have found it too tempting. It's not every day that a fire station gets burnt down. I can just imagine the pyromaniacs' pupils dilate as they saw the larger tower of flames conveniently form just a stone's throw from where they stalked the bonfire. I bet they're still talking about it.

I mingled through the orange-lit faces and recognized some of my classmates who were attached to the limbs of their parents. But I couldn't see Heather, so I kicked on home.

* * *

In the seventies, the Greeks and Italians made up the largest slice of non-English migrants in Sydney. Most were first generation. They owned the fish and chip shops, the fruit and veg stores, the butchers, and the like. Lyrical accents oozed through long and oily work. Wog's work.

A friend of mine in high school always said, if you scratch the surface of an Australian you would find a racist. I'm not too sure if that's still correct, but it certainly was in those days. It must have been hell for them.

Our teachers did try. "I hope you understand, class. We are all the same, no matter what we look or sound like."

Miss Quinter had finished an exhaustive monologue on the dangers of racism—what to do, and particularly, what not to do. It all made sense, of course, but I really couldn't see the point of it being a lesson. I never looked at the few European kids in my class as migrants anyway, since most were born here and lacked the musical drawl of their parents. Anyway, my folks would have killed me if I ever uttered a racist word. I think they would have rather I stole.

The lunch bell clanged our escape. About half of us had lunch delivered from the canteen, the remainder brought from home. My mother's obsession with vitamins meant that I was in the latter camp. On occasion, I managed to swap mine with procured delicacies such as chicken-chip rolls—a Rydges staple. Though today I had corn sandwiches, an un-tradable fare. The mounting summer heat converted my plastic lunch box into a sauna that stewed what started as a barely palatable dish into a mulch of sodden yellow sponge, which I chucked straight into the bin. My healthy lunches kept me skinny all through primary school.

Our year had access to a small field, about the size of two tennis courts, which sprouted next to the main asphalt playground and was off limits to the older years. Grass meant rougher play was tolerated—I think that's why the older kids were held captive on the bitumen. On this day, the whole class was playing British Bulldog. The rules were simple—safe zones were at either end of the field, a volunteer catcher had to tag the girls or tackle the boys, the caught kids accumulated in the center as catchers, until the last one in the safe zone won—after having to run into the waiting arms of usually rough catchers.

Today, Danno had volunteered to be the initial catcher. He was really quick, and eyed me as easy prey—baby antelope meat. I ran straight at him screaming, and a yard before the impending collision, tried a slick side-step but ended up hitting the ground at his feet. I never liked being the first caught—even Rydges ribbed me about it. I think that's what got me worked up.

Now it was Danno and me as the catchers. I noticed a group of girls hadn't run yet—absolutely against the rules. While Danno continued to claw more into the center I sauntered up to the girls. Heather was among them.

"You have to run," I said to the group.

"We have," Lisa Fraschetti said. Her hands were on her hips, her mop of curly red hair ablaze.

"No you haven't."

"Yes we have!"

"No you haven't . . . you dirty wog!"

Well, you could have heard a pin drop. I did suspect that I had gone a bit too far. But in my defense, they were clearly in breach of one of the basic rules of British Bulldog—you cannot camp in the safe zones.

Lisa's cheeks were flushed. "Tom Peters, you are in big trouble!"

I had to think fast. I bolted back to the center and hung around Danno, Beany and Rydges. For the remainder of the lunch break, I never left their sides—stuck to them like glue—they oblivious to my racist rant.

We were the last to enter the class, having soaked our faces with bubbler water outside the toilet block. I moved through the door, never looking sideways, and sat down at my desk next to Heather—cool as a cucumber. The room was eerily silent.

"Tom Peters, could you stand up." Miss Quinter never raised her voice, but I seem to remember this was an exception.

"Miss?"

She waited. So I stood, but kept my gaze straight to the front.

"What did you call Lisa during lunch?"

"Miss?" I turned and saw Lisa who sat with a straight back and a grin that I could have slapped. But I had to keep cool, so I put on my best perplexed look. "I didn't say anything, Miss."

The girls squealed up their protest.

"Silence!" And there was. "Did you call Lisa a wog?"

The whole class gasped in unison. A hanging jury if ever I saw one.

"No I did not!"

I was a very convincing liar as a child. Practice makes perfect, as the saying goes—and I had plenty of practice. Part of being a boy then involved raising it to an art form. But at seventeen, I suddenly stopped lying, and haven't since. Not for any altruistic reasons really, I just found it easier to tell the truth than try to remember the plethora of lies that I championed.

I twisted to look at Beany and gave him my best pleading face. I had to go down fighting. Danno and Rydges spat back in protest to the teacher. They knew I was innocent.

"Silence! David Bean . . . did you hear Tom call Lisa a wog?"

I wished she would stop saying wog. It nearly broke me.

"No way, Miss!" Beany's freckled face glowed with sincerity that comes from telling the truth.

I spun quickly to gauge a reaction from Miss Quinter and could see a glimmer of confusion shining—ever so slightly. Teachers, I think, are well versed in detecting truth or lies from children. I, of course, was an unusually difficult specimen, but she really saw my mates' pleas as genuine. God bless them.

Miss Quinter's gaze floated from my open mouth, down and to my right. I looked at Heather and then quickly back. My throat was dry. I felt sick.

"Heather . . . did you hear Tom call Lisa a wog?" It was spoken very calmly now, almost in a whisper.

"No, Miss."

The class screamed from all directions. I sat down without being asked, I think. I knew I had won. From memory, Beany, Danno, and Rydges managed to out-bellow the protesting girls, but I didn't hear much of it. I zoned out.

And from that second on, and for the rest of my life, I was utterly in love.

* * *

While I'm on the theme of mischief, let me tell you about the police episode. It was late afternoon. The workmen repairing the road in front of our house had gone home, leaving a massive steamroller parked in front of Aunty Barbara's—Aunty out of respect rather than blood. Our local street gang, fostered from houses within a pitching wedge of my place, scrambled over the resting behemoth. That offered much more than the rusted slippery dip in the park up the road. Rust again. My childhood memories seem ochre-stained gray.

Our street was pretty quiet, certainly not a major thoroughfare. Houses lined the peaceful suburban avenue that snaked in a curved incline down to an equally sleepy intersection. I studied the road in repair, sucking in the scent of warm tar from the new asphalt. Dad said when he was a child, he was so poor that he and his mates used tar as a substitute for chewing gum. I picked up a piece of the bitumen and cleaned the dirt off its sticky surface. It looked like shiny liquorice.

I shouted up to the mountain of kids that dangled off the steamroller like baubles on a Christmas tree. "How much if I eat this?"

"Ten cents," Rodney screamed, the opening bidder. He was Aunty Barbara's eldest son, but a year or so younger than me. They lived directly across the road from our place.

Ten cents. Not bad. It would get me a small bag of lollies. "Let's see the dough first."

One of the kids produced a silver coin.

"Let me up in the driver's seat then, and I'll eat it while taking us for a trip down Camarey Avenue."

I lifted myself into the open carriage, looking down the street from on high.

"Go on, eat it," the silver coin kid said.

"Okay, hold your horses. Let me get comfortable first."

I took the shiny liquorice and chewed into its surface. It tasted of grit and dirt and black. How could this be chewing gum? Was my father crazy?

I spat it out onto the lap of Rodney, who roared in delight. "You didn't swallow. So no money for you!"

I picked at bits of gravel that wedged between my front teeth. A cruel defeat if ever there was. To move the chatter away from the gum, I said, "Where are the controls to this baby?"

Hands prodded the controls, pushing buttons at will. The identity of the hands were unclear then, and certainly now. We all had a go.

And then it started—the steamroller that is.

From here I see everything in slow motion. Widescreen. We all jumped off, stepping away from the rolling giant. God, it was impressively big.

About fifty feet away a Mr. Juicy van was parked—the roller's first obstacle. As the eldest kid of the gang, it was my call, so I started the screams. In retrospect quite a heroic act really. Our cries clearly identified us as the perpetrators, but I couldn't let the van be squashed because of a more prudent but less courageous retreat. As our cries escalated to an exquisite panic, the Mr. Juicy deliveryman strolled out of the house. I remember the orange juice bottles in his wire basket that he carried in one hand—I can almost read the labels—but his face is what I remember the most. First he stared at our waving squeals, clearly our words would have been difficult to interpret. I can see his forehead lines pucker in confusion, before he slowly turned to see the behemoth crawling towards his van.

Around this time vampire movies were big at the pictures. Long caterpillar lines of kids with jaffas and minties and choc-tops would wait patiently outside the theatre for the Sunday matinee. I used to go alone—my brother was too young I guess. But once I saw a Count Yorga film for a second time with Rodney. It was his virginal vampire experience, so I thought it best we sit at the front. The movie started real slow, got you nice and cozy, before the first appearance of the vampire from an open closet sucked the heart from your chest. I knew when it was going to happen, so I turned my head away from the screen and studied Rodney's face, whose cheeks were painted with the remnants of a nearly demolished choc-top. When Count Yorga appeared out of the closet, little Rodney's face transformed into a horrified grimace that made Munch's *The Scream* look like the *Mona Lisa*.

This was the face of the Mr. Juicy man.

I have to give him some credit. It's not easy to get your car keys from your pocket while carrying a basket of juice and running in terror, all in one action. This is something a soldier might pull off, or a policeman, but not your average Mr. Juicy man. I think his mistake was not to drop the basket—those bottles would have been worth less than a dollar in those days. But, to his credit, he entered the van, juice basket and all, before the steamroller had struck. I believe the pressure became too intense though, he seemed to fumble to fit the keys to the ignition, which wasn't helped by constantly twisting his neck to gauge the estimated time of impact. In the end, he too had to make a call, and he leaped out of the van, rolling a few times on the grass before crawling to safety. Interestingly, he didn't take the juice basket, somewhat supporting my opening remarks.

The sound of metal heading under steamroller is unique. It starts like chalk screeching on a school board, but as the roller gets a grip, the crunching is softer than you would expect—sort of like crushing dry leaves under foot. We were all silent then, except the Mr. Juicy man, who was whimpering softly, so the sound was exquisitely clear. It took about thirty seconds for the roller to move over the van. I was certain the wheels would get bound by bits of frayed metal, but they didn't. It was like a tank. After its brief taste of destruction, the steamroller moved down the incline of the road in search of other challenges. It was an eerie site—an unmanned steamroller wandering aimlessly down Camarey Avenue. And I thought it began to build up speed.

We were all standing well back, in a sort of a huddle, the Mr. Juicy man and six or so kids. Then Rodney decided to scamper, jumping over his fence and into the side-gate that led to the safety of his backyard. After that, kids flew in all directions, away from the rolling behemoth and the now cursing Mr. Juicy man. I sprinted down the cement drive into my backyard, breathless from terror rather than effort.

Mum was hanging the washing on the Hills Hoist. She stopped when she saw me. "You okay, Tom?"

I took a peg and fastened a dripping sock onto the wire. But I could sense this selfless action had increased her level of suspicion—which was always on high alert—so I jumped on the hoist and swung around, nearly completing a full revolution.

"Go up and do your homework, and leave me in peace."

And so I did.

The police came, of course. So did a television crew, which I didn't expect. It isn't every day that a vagrant steamroller runs amuck in a quiet suburban avenue. The carnage was quite impressive. Eventually, the monster climbed the footpath a hundred yards down the road and became wedged up on the front brick fence of the Climpson's place. The fence was demolished, but the roller was trapped, its wheels turning slowly in midair—like a newborn baby trying to find a teat that simply wasn't there. Mrs. Climpson told the TV reporter that it was lucky her daughter wasn't killed—she was apparently playing alone in the front yard. She was only three, a bit young to be playing unsupervised if you ask me, but I kept this opinion to myself. No other vehicle was completely leveled like the Mr. Juicy van; most cars were parked safely in their drives off the street. There were a few with torn fuselages, but Dad said they were pretty old and full of rust anyway.

Dad said lots of things. He wanted to know how a group of kids could start such a lethal weapon in the first place. The council workman, who was interviewed by the TV, said it was a one in a million chance—we had to know the four-digit code. Dad said maths was never his strongest point, but fluking into a four-digit code didn't sound like a one in a million proposition to him. I think the reporter agreed.

But Dad only started questioning the authorities later. Before that, it was much grimmer. We were all lined up out on the street. Some of our parents were there, but most of the dads had yet to get home from work. The police constable looked unfriendly. My brother also stood in line with us, even though he was watching television at home at the time of the incident. But he didn't want to miss any of the action.

The tall constable wanted to know all about it, why we didn't play in the park instead of the street, why we would want to destroy public property, and how many people, including us, could have been killed? Did we understand what death meant? Some of the kids started to blubber. I must say I was pretty close as well. But I was the oldest, and it wouldn't have been good form.

Then came the question we were dreading. "Who started the steamroller? I want a name."

As the black boot constable wandered along the line, our faces dropped like dominoes, except my brother's—he knew he could escape at any time.

Of course, this called the constable's attention to himself. "Who did it, son?"

"Don't know, Sir."

I looked at my brother in disbelief. What was he doing here?

"We'll stand here all night until I get a name."

The Peterson kid started to whimper, dripping nasal discharge onto his sleeve.

"Or I might take you all down to the Station."

The Station! We never walked anywhere near the Station. Understand, this was the early seventies in Crepundia—the heyday of the Crepundia Sharps, a skinhead group that caused more havoc than those classical music-loving boys of *Clockwork Orange*. Rydges said he had to go there once with his father to report a stolen car and one of the Sharps was in the waiting room. Rydges admitted to me on the quiet he was so scared he farted aloud. The Sharp didn't seem to mind though. The point I'm trying to make is that the constable had found our Achilles heel.

"I think it was Rodney," I said.

"Who's Rodney, then?"

"It's him." The Peterson kid pointed with green goo stuck to his sleeve. His whimpering now eased into a drier snuffle.

"I think it *was* Rodney," my brother said.

I stole a glimpse at my brother, who seemed satisfied being more involved. Helpful if you will.

"It *was* Rodney," others spluttered.

Aunty Barbara moved to her son, who was spitting grief onto the pavement.

"Well, I might just have a few words with Rodney, alone."

"Down the station?" My brother didn't say this in a mean way—more an inquiry. Still, I turned and poked him in the ribs; a whip and stool would have been more appropriate.

"Here will be fine," the constable said, his voice soft now. Rodney's sodden remorse was getting to him, I think.

The sun had fallen out of sight by then, turning the chocolate brick houses silver-gray. We all shuffled away from the crime scene, back into the safety of our orange lounge rooms. My mother was strangely silent, but she had tightly fastened her suspicious facemask that I remember remained on for most of the evening.

And to this day, I wonder whether Rodney really did do it? Or was he just devoid of enough wit to find a swift escape under extreme and present danger—a bit like the Mr. Juicy man?

* * *

I was coming home from Beany's early. His older brother had just turned up with some of his mates. I can't remember how old they were, but they seemed at an age where they could sneak a schooner from the pub without too many questions asked. I didn't fit in with them, that's for sure, so I scampered on home.

Saturday afternoon, rather than Friday, was the beginning of my rest and recreation time. I had club swimming races in the morning, but they were over by lunchtime, so I was a free agent. As I kicked an empty bottle down the street, I thought about stopping in on Rydges or Danno; perhaps Rydges, since his place always had more junk food. As I booted the bottle in a beautiful arc around the street corner, Heather and her grandmother appeared down the path. Heather was carrying a bag full of groceries in both arms; her grandmother pulling a two-wheeled upright shopping stroller that I swear was more than half her size. Fruit and veg sprouted from the open top like a Carmen Miranda headpiece.

I ran on over. "You need a hand?" Old women love that from kids, although in those days I rarely felt the need to obtain that love.

Heather's almond eyes beamed. She nodded without speaking. Soft as.

"Let me take that stroller for you."

The grandmother gave one of her approving cackles and started fingering my hair.

"Sorry, Tommy." Heather spoke in agitated Chinese to the woman, who just grinned and scooped more hair in her palm. The old broad was clearly in a world of her own.

"That's okay," I said. "I know she thinks it's lucky for her, and it doesn't worry me. Let's get this stuff back to your place. Is it far?"

Heather shook her head, her pigtails flapping against her shoulders. And so we moved together along the uneven pavement, the stroller's wheels straining under the load. I did most of the talking, as was our custom, excited at spending some unscheduled time with Heather.

After five minutes we entered a rusted gate that led up to a small white fibro house. The front yard lay bare to the sun, the freshly clipped lawn treeless—no shrubs, or flowers, or anything. Its front porch was also open, devoid of any canopy, the worn concrete slab, like the lawn, uncluttered. A space of bare surfaces, flat colorless planes, a box of a house that sat waiting to be decorated.

I dragged the stroller up the two porch steps. The old woman took the stroller in hand, grinning away, and gave my head a pat for a bit of extra luck. Heather had unlocked the front door and was inside, her grandmother now following behind with the stroller. I thought about tagging along, yet kept at the threshold, peering into the dimly lit corridor. I was about to say my goodbyes from the porch when the old woman came down the corridor and took my arm, motioning with her head for me to enter. Her smile was broad and true and radiated a balmy welcome.

The corridor cut the house into uneven halves. On one side, through two door-less frames, were a small living room and kitchen. I can hardly remember the living room, for I don't think I ever did more than pass it on my way into the heart of the house—the kitchen. What the rest of the house lacked in trimmings, the kitchen made up for it. Atop a bench, mini bamboo baskets towered high, almost touching the low-level ceiling. Pots, pans, and woks glinted from greased surfaces. Rectangular bladed knives climbed on a wall in ascending size, the largest fierce as any medieval sword. Above the sink, a roasted duck with glistening amber skin hung from its neck on a metal hook with dead eyes that scolded—this could be you if you're not careful.

The old woman lifted a large bag of salt onto the bench with a thud. Heather unpacked the vegetables, the flowers of the kitchen. And I found a stool by the small round dining table, watching the room swell.

"Would you like some tea, Tommy? We don't have any soft-drink. Grandmother doesn't like it."

"I'm okay."

The old woman poured a steaming straw-colored liquid into tiny white cups that were stacked at the table's edge. Heather spoke to her gently, I assume telling her that I didn't want any, but she kept on pouring all three to the brim. She lifted the lid that released a sweet perfume, pointed to something floating in the yellow liquid, and cackled something in Chinese while touching her eyes.

"Chrysanthemum tea is good for your eyes, Tommy."

I looked up to see the old woman grinning at me expectantly, so I sipped the tea that scalded my tongue and tasted like grass.

"Nice," I lied.

The old woman cackled and fondled my hair again. Heather responded in tones of anguish that seemed to do something, since the old girl moved back to her kitchen enclosure. Heather came over and sat next to me—just like school.

"You have a neat house," I said.

"Grandmother cooks for the Bamboo Garden sometimes." This was one of the few Chinese restaurants in the area.

"We eat there all the time," I said.

"Do you like Chinese food, Tommy?"

"Yeah. My favorite is beef with black bean sauce and chicken and ham roll."

Heather translated to her grandmother who grinned and muttered a brief response.

"My grandmother likes you."

"Really . . . that's good I guess. Are your folks home?"

She picked up her cup and sipped some tea. "No. They live in China."

I mirrored her actions and sipped at my cup—which gave me some thinking time. The old woman had lifted the duck off its hook and began carving thin slices onto a plate. A nose of roasted meat wafted to the table.

"How come they're in China?"

"They need to work in different cities, hundreds of miles apart. It was too hard to look after me and work and . . ." Her voice trailed off into nothing.

"So it's just you and your grandmother here?"

She nodded, and lifted her head to gaze briefly into my eyes. I lowered mine to the table and sipped more tea. Now that it wasn't scalding, it was vaguely sweet and flowery. I'd had far worse-tasting things in my school lunches.

The old woman carefully positioned a few slices of duck meat and skin, and then added a sliced shallot and a dollop of sweet sauce, wrapped it all up in its pancake blanket, and fed me with her wrinkled fingers. I chewed the mixture, savoring the flavors with closed eyes—flavors too complex for prose to conquer. Only poetry could do it justice. And I'm no poet.

"You like it, Tommy?"

"It's the best," I said with a full mouth and heart.

Heather spoke to the woman who patted my head.

"Grandmother asks if it's better than chicken and ham roll?"

I nodded and the old woman chuckled a reply.

"She says you now know how an Emperor eats."

"Do you eat like this every day?"

"Not Peking Duck . . . you were lucky today. The Bamboo Garden had one left over."

The old woman had prepared another pancake and guided it to my mouth.

"Would you like to stay for dinner?"

"You bet!" It was not a hard decision.

I finished off another four pancakes as fast as they could be made.

"You've got sauce on your cheek, Tommy."

I pawed hurriedly at my face but missed the spot. Heather took a paper napkin from the table, moved her chair over touching mine, and ever so gently wiped my cheek. I felt funny inside. All tingly.

"I should give my folks a call and tell them I'm not home for dinner."

"We don't have a phone, Tommy."

What I had sensed was confirmed—these people were really poor. There was no one I knew that didn't have a phone. And poor was really a stranger to me in those days. School was the great leveler. Everyone had a uniform that cost little to wash by hand. Hair could be cut by a parent if the barber was too expensive – styles were simple enough to be managed at home. Textbooks were given by the school, lunch was sponsored, milk free. We all looked as poor or wealthy as each other. It was only when we moved away from the playing fields of British Bulldog that the poor began to stand out.

"I can run home and let them know. You want to come?"

Heather spoke to her grandmother, who was cutting some greens on the sink. The old woman lifted her gaze to mine and delivered a response that needed no translation.

"Tell her not to worry, Heather," I said. "I'll look after you."

And we left the house together, slamming the old painted door behind us. In the ten minute walk to my place I showed Heather all the sights—the houses of cranky neighbors and vicious dogs, the place where I was dive bombed by a giant flying insect in kindergarten, even the bush Rydges had taken a dump behind. She seemed really interested, especially when I recreated the complete steamroller incident, pointing out the patch of turf where the Mr. Juicy man had fallen, the still-scarred brick fence of the Climpson's place where the behemoth had taken its last breath, and Rodney's house, who had been interrogated by Crepundia's finest.

As we entered my home I felt strangely uneasy. The contrast from Heather's place was palpable—our big television, the polished furniture, the new carpet. I felt ashamed, though I couldn't tell you why.

Dad was sitting on the lounge reading the Saturday papers. He used to love reading the comic section to us—it reminded him of his childhood, I guess. I suppose we all need reminding of that, though you could argue I need less than most. Seeing Heather, he dropped the paper to his lap. I made the appropriate introduction.

"Hello, my dear, welcome to the Peters' castle."

Dad had this thing about the Peters' castle. We, the Peters clan in Scotland that is, did actually have a castle. We had the family coat of arms above the fireplace that had been bricked up long ago. Mum said that the coat of arms wasn't real anyway; it was just made up to please Scottish families who wanted some connection to the old country. Dad saw it different.

"We aren't staying, Dad. I just want to see whether I can eat at Heather's place for dinner."

Mum entered with her apron fastened and beamed at Heather. "I don't think we have met before?" She delivered the words like a show tune.

At this point I should clarify my parents' psyche a bit. They loved all things foreign—food, language, clothing, people. Mum had the recent habit of wearing a Mexican poncho on outings. To this day, I still scratch when I see a poncho. In my preschool years I was often forced to attend in German lederhosen—the full gear, chest flap and all. God knows what outfit I would have been subjected to if school uniforms weren't enforced. So Heather, being the first girl I had ever brought home, with the added bonus of being Chinese, was loved by my parents as if she was their own.

"Who is this pretty girl, Tom?"

My brother, who had been watching a cartoon on the TV, lifted his head to scan the scene.

"Tom's got a girrlyyy friend," he sung.

I wanted him dead. I wanted them all dead.

Once again, Heather came to my rescue. "Your house is beautiful, Tommy."

"Can't stay, Mum. Heather's grandmother is cooking us dinner. I'll be home before dark."

I didn't wait for a response and headed straight back into the corridor and out the wire door. Heather followed and seemed to understand my angst. She was always good like that.

The evening proceeded just as it had begun. I settled in their warm kitchen of woks and steam and ate and grinned and had my hair patted. I learnt some Chinese words that I still know to this day. And, as promised, I skipped on home before the autumn twilight faded into gray.

We all have vivid memories of firsts. The first kiss, the first fight, the first time being drunk, the first time reading Tolstoy. But perhaps my most vivid of firsts, where all of the senses had come together in just one moment, was the first time I had Peking Duck, fed to me by the hand of a wrinkly old Chinese woman who fondled my hair for luck.

* * *

I said the kitchen was the heart of Heather's house. It was the communal meeting place where the three of us ate, chatted, patted hair, played Mahjong. It was where I always entered first, out of respect to the old broad. This was her place, after all, and she was a mother, father, sister, and grandmother all in one for Heather. Anyway, I'd got used to the hair fingering, and she always had something steaming for me to savor. I spent nearly every Saturday afternoon there, stayed for dinner, and crept on home before nightfall.

My memories of Saturday afternoons sing with the chatter of dim sum flavored Mahjong tiles. On my arrival, we would all slump in the kitchen and, depending upon Grandmother's cooking timetable, the three of us would usually play a game. I was a sluggish player—the old woman said they would kill me in China if I played so slowly. Nevertheless, I became reasonably good, always getting an extra hair pat with every win. Grandmother pulled faces when I procrastinated over my hand, which I often did by scoffing some dumplings, making the tiles sticky with soy and dumpling juice. Heather never minded my tardy play. She sometimes played slow just to take the heat off me a bit.

I also became a dab hand with chopsticks, since there wasn't a knife or fork in the house. It was a slow start though. I would recommend sticky rice rather than dim sum for those with chopstick learner's plates. The plop of a dropped dumpling was a constant sound at the table in those early days, soon followed by Grandmother's cackles, then Heather's soft comforting. But, like Mahjong, I soon got the hang of it.

What I was most happy with was my growing grasp of Mandarin. Mahjong tiles helped with the recognition of some characters, and Grandmother decided I needed to learn new words each time I visited. I think she thought I was becoming a good Chinese boy. But I have no doubt, what fast-tracked my skills was Heather's beaming eyes after I successfully crafted a sentence or understood some of Grandmother's spluttering.

"I'm so proud of you, Tommy," she often said. So proud. And nothing ever beat that.

After dumplings and Mahjong, Heather and I would move into her bedroom. If the kitchen was the heart of the house, then Heather's bedroom was the soul. Unlike the exterior fibro and other interior walls, all washed in antiseptic white, her room was painted a brilliant, pillar-box red; glossy, not mat; ceiling and walls. It was mad, and not surprisingly, not of her doing. The Bamboo Garden gave Grandmother the paint after they decided a less vibrant color was needed for their window frames. Apparently, when the landlord saw it he nearly flipped. Heather said he wanted to paint over it but thought it would need six coats of white before all remnants of the blood-soaked walls had vanished. It took a few plates of dim sum and a bowl of congee to calm him down.

The carpet was the same as elsewhere in the house—canary yellow. Heather thought her bedroom was pretty special and called it her tomato-egg room. It had real character, and bright colors were the fad in the seventies—my room at home had a purple bedspread, matching curtains, and an orange wardrobe.

At the opposite wall from the door, under a small window, lay Heather's single bed. It was always perfectly made up, with a fluffy banana-colored bedspread that had a coat like a Labrador needing a brush. Next to the door was a small desk and stool of unpainted pine. I wanted to paint them yellow and red, but we never got around to it. On top of the table was a candle with dribbling wax down its shaft, fastened to a shallow glass ashtray. Her books were always stacked in a neat pile. Her pencil case smelled of school. And on the desk was a small plastic picture frame with a little photo of a smiling Chinese couple, the woman holding a baby that was rugged up in so many layers that its face looked like it was coming out of a cave.

I picked up the picture and saw Heather bite into her lip.

"That's my parents, Tommy. And . . . me."

I touched the glass over the baby's face and felt strange. "You were a cutie."

She stood closer and I felt her shoulder touch mine.

How can such simple contact stay with you forever? What magic is it?

"When did you see them last?" I asked.

"Soon after the photo was taken. I don't remember them. I don't even remember coming here with Grandmother on the boat."

I kept my gaze at the smiling parents. "Do you talk to them on a phone?"

"No, Tommy." It was my turn to bite my lip. I held the photo in my hand and only put it down when Heather's touch moved away. "Do you have any games?"

She shook her head. "Just Mahjong."

"What's in the box?" Resting on the floor was an old, sky-blue chest the size of an Esky.

"Penny, Dotty and Carla."

"No kidding . . . don't they suffocate in there?"

She giggled.

"Can I have a look?"

Heather nodded, moved over to the chest, and kneeling before it, unfastened a little brass clasp. I kneeled next to her on the canary carpet.

"Do you really want to see?"

"You bet."

She lifted the lid. Nested on a bed of cotton wool lay three dolls, their heads elevated on pillows of additional fluffy cotton. She took the first, a Golliwog with a red and white striped dress and matching hair ribbon. It had big red lips and flashing white eyes. Everything else was black.

"This is Penny."

Next to escape was a blonde Barbie with black eyelashes that hung over wide blue eyes. She had pink shorts and a matching sleeveless top with yellow, black, and red checks. Heather twisted her waist and legs into a welcoming pose.

"This is Carla . . . you can bend her legs if you like."

I took the doll and moved her knees into a different stance.

"And this is Dotty. She's my favorite."

Dotty looked older than Heather's grandmother. She had a heavy, shiny pink face with cracks forming a patchwork of wrinkles. Her hair, eyes, and pencil thin brows were painted black. She had little red lips. The rest of her body doesn't matter, she was all head, was Dotty.

I write this with a clear view, like looking at a color photograph, not the usual black and white of my childhood. Of course, you know how I remember the details of the dolls so well, don't you, my dear Juan. You know.

* * *

It is late, so late my street in Havana now rests in deep sleep. Eye flickering REM sleep. I've had a few too many drinks with Billy after his Jazz gig, but mojitos can add clarity. Or so Billy says. The third eye view he calls it, though I suspect you would call it something different. So here we are—words spoken through the vista of my third eye.

I've always known I'm not writing just for you. Whenever I put words to paper of any substantial length—and this surely constitutes that length—I think about publishing. It's an occupational hazard, and I do need to eat, even down here. So, having settled on that, I now have a real dilemma, Juan. A real beauty. While autobiographies are not a favorite genre of mine, I can manage this even in the veil of fiction. Call it a literary challenge.

But it's one thing for you to know why I remember the details of the dolls so well. It's another for my publisher, the public, and for that matter anyone beyond my intimate circle to know. That's a whole fucking different ball game, and one that I'm going to avoid if I can swing it.

* * *

It was a hot afternoon when I saw the blue whale again.

I was taking a short-cut home from Beany's, across the football park and down to the gully where the storm water pipes ran. The blue whale was coming out of the bush at the entrance of the path to our rock-throwing place. I was so close I could see the whale smiling through the curly hairs of his forearm, with a long striped underbelly and a tiny eye that looked at me through red-bleached hairs. He wore navy blue King Gee shorts that rode up high. Big work boots with long tongues. And he was breathing hard, rushing, sweaty pants, with the whale swinging and smiling into the heat.

As we crossed paths the whale looked at me with his tiny eye. But I kept on moving, not changing my stride, my heart racing faster than my legs could keep up with. I kept twisting my head back to see the whale swinging further away, and I only felt safe when I reached the storm water pipes.

I remember sitting down on one of the pipes and resting, even though I wasn't tired.

Rydges came out of the bush-land much more slowly. He dragged his feet like he wasn't sure of the way. Or like he wanted to stay back there in the heat of the bush.

A strange site, him sucking on an ice-cream out there at the edge of the bush. A chocolate Paddle Pop—dripping because the day was hot. Rydges liked chocolate. So did I. Banana too, but chocolate was my favorite. But there were no shops down in the bush.

Just trees and rocks and places to hide.

Rydges didn't see me but I saw him. He even looked down my way but he didn't see me. His eyes weren't frightened, or searching, or seemed wanting in any way. Blank eyes you see at a mother's funeral. With chocolate on his face.

He walked out of the dirt path and lingered a bit at the entrance, then dawdled up the grassy slope away from me—I guess back to his place. And I watched him climb the slope until he became lost in the horizon of the elevated field.

And I remember sitting there a while and panting—but I wasn't tired at all.

* * *

I stare at Rydges in the school photograph. He is amongst the smiling faces, cross-legged out front—he was short so that's why he's seated down there—not on the top row with Danno and Beany and me. But he's smiling like all the others.

Is it a façade, this photograph? A magic trick perhaps? Abracadabra—a flash—and thirty smiling children appear out of nowhere.

Heather is happy. I love those big ribbons of hers, the largest of any of the girls, red, though the photo is in black and white, keeping her pigtails in place. She is happy I'm sure. Danno too. Even Beany.

Why didn't I talk to someone about the blue whale? When it was needed.

Maybe not the first time.

I understood keeping quiet about the first time. We were in the wrong. We could have killed someone with those rocks, the constable would have said. It's what happens to naughty boys like you.

But why not later? Why didn't I talk to Rydges?

I could talk to him about anything. With his fat legs and awkward scurry at the edge of the pack. He would have talked about it, I know he would. His father might have been crazy but I'm sure he would have known what to do.

Because we weren't at fault then. No one could say we were at fault then.

The seated girls look like little angels, with their white collared shirts and gray uniforms and their little hands clasped in their laps. The seated boys as well, with their arms grabbing their knees, with straight backs, shoulders back my little angels, remember good posture.

Abracadabra. A puff of smoke.

And there's Rydges sitting and grinning like the others.

What trickery is this?

What a con.

* * *

In the seventies there were few restaurants in Sydney. And in the suburbs, if they did exist, they were virtually all Chinese. For special treats we went down to the Bamboo Garden, the owner of Heather's red paint. I can't remember whose birthday it was, but the four of us sat one early evening with Dad ordering our old favorites.

"I want honey prawns," bellowed my brother. This sickly sweet fried dish was a favorite of his. It was like getting a second dessert.

The waiter began to remove the chopsticks and replace them with forks and spoons.

"You can leave mine," I said.

My father raised an eyebrow. "It will slow you down, son . . . you know what these lot are like." He waved his eyes at Mum and my brother. "By the time you finish your fried rice, the rest will be gone."

"Let him try, Darren." Mum had warmed to the Asian adventure.

The steaming plates all came at once, unlike in Heather's kitchen, and Dad dished equal portions into each of our bowls. I was particularly hungry that evening, so I picked up my bowl and chopsticks and started into the food with a rush. I never had my pebble stomach at the Bamboo Garden. I remember shoveling the rice and prawn and beef into my mouth like a Chinese sailor coming home after a long day's fishing trip.

When I looked up I saw my open-mouthed family staring at me. They had yet to begin their meal. Even my brother.

"Oh, Darren, look at him. How wonderful!" Mum said. I thought she had a tear in her eye. "Did you learn this at Heather's?"

I nodded while scoffing a honey prawn into my gob.

"I just want to watch him eat." Mum was well and truly in her foreign zone.

I remember not spilling a nibble—I worked those chopsticks like a pro.

At the end of the meal, with the table covered only with the splatter of spilled morsels—you could always tell what we ordered by a careful examination of the tablecloth—my brother started to lick at his bowl.

"You right there, son?" my father asked.

"I'm still hungry."

Dad eyed Mum. "What about another dish?"

"Have you ever had Peking Duck?" I said.

"No, I can't say that I have." He flicked the pages of the menu. "I don't think they have it, son."

"I'm sure they do . . . maybe they call it something else." I looked straight at the Chinese waiter, and said, very calmly, and very carefully, "Nǐ yǒu Běijīng kǎoyā?"

The waiter beamed at me. "Shì de, wǒmen yǒu."

"Great . . . they do Dad!"

Once again I raised my eyes to the family. Dad and my brother just peered at me like I was some object from outer space. My mother was crying. Really. She took her napkin, smeared with soya sauce, and wiped at her face.

"Oh, Darren, did you ever hear such a thing?" And she began to whimper again.

I sat light on my chair, a real fancy pants. Mum kept asking me to say more, testing my skills with the waiter. It was like a lesson at school. Mum would ask me the Chinese word for dog, cat, hello, goodbye—you know, the basics—with the waiter close by to confirm my answers. He seemed to enjoy it more than Mum. My brother even chipped in, asking the ridiculous of course.

"How do you say Eskimo?"

"Don't be an idiot."

"Okay, how do you say astronaut?"

I mention this triumph because it turned out to be one of the most significant of my early life. Not because I learnt Mandarin, or for that matter any language, which was only a fleeting fancy, but because I used it as a bargaining tool to stay overnight at Heather's place on most Saturdays for the rest of my childhood. The happy part of it, that is.

* * *

"Grandmother wants to know your date of birth, Tommy."

We were sitting down at the small kitchen table around chrysanthemum tea and dim sum. It was coming up to Christmas, and the high sun fell down on the little house, baking us without a breather. The kitchen of course was the hottest room, but we never seemed to leave it. We just endured with shining, flushed faces. They had a big box fan cooler, one that had to be filled every half an hour with a bucket of water—it was my job to fill it. It was placed so the cool air drifted onto the table and through the steaming kitchen. Sometimes we opened the small kitchen window that sat above the bench, but the fly screen was tattered, and the summer blowflies that found their way through were the size of beetles.

"February 2nd," I said.

"That's my birthday too!" Heather beamed, and translated to her grandmother.

The old woman got up from the table and moved over to the kitchen bench, wiping down a wok that I'm sure she had cleaned before and mumbling something to herself. Heather spoke to her softly—the old woman replying in the same tepid way.

"What's up with her?"

"She says two rats are not a good match."

My cheeks blushed hot against the rushing air. A ten-year-old boy had no concern about matches—good or bad. But I still felt a strange disquiet at this news. Heather seemed calm though. But then she always did.

The old woman came back over and refilled our cups with the flower tea. She had stopped mumbling to herself, which seemed a good sign, and she started to cackle and fondled my hair; spluttering something back to Heather who also giggled.

"Grandmother says golden rat has golden hair . . . so a special rat."

"Did you have a party for your tenth birthday?"

"You mean eleventh?" she said.

"Wait, you're eleven . . . I'm only ten. That's why you're so tall, Heather."

I remember not caring that we had an age difference. Heather told her grandmother my correct date of birth, and the old woman raised her eyes as if studying an apparition only visible to her. She shuffled out into the lounge room and returned with a paper of Chinese scribbling. Soon, a roaring cackle lifted high in the kitchen. I had never had a good look at her teeth before; I think she mustn't have brushed them much as a kid. A few looked like raisins ready to drop. She moved over and starting pulling at my hair.

"Grandmother says you are a golden ox. Golden ox with golden hair."

The old woman pinched my cheeks with both her hands, lifting up my face so I had a clear view of her sultana mouth.

"Grandmother says golden ox and golden rat are a perfect match." Heather lowered her gaze. The old woman was still chatting away, between a splatter of crowing screeches.

"Grandmother says you can stay overnight if you like."

And so it began.

* * *

I've taken a rest today—a natural gap in the prose of my childhood.

I wander down the Malecón, the sky is blue and cloudless and the breeze falls off the crest of the waves and smiles onto my face. I pass them, couples and more, swinging their legs over the long concrete wall—an idle chatter into the cool blue-scape. I don't speak Spanish well, but the chatter is drifting and lazy. I know this, for the Malecón is not a place for serious talk.

I pass the Nacional sitting up on the rocky ledge carpeted in green on the opposite side of the esplanade, the hotel's façade high and yellow-white against the sky, all symmetrical with sharp rectangles, an imposing remembrance of Havana's lost grandeur. I think of stopping in for a drink in the hotel's open lounge, but the cool keeps me down and I stroll on.

She is different from the others. She faces away from the water, away from the breeze, and she follows me with her eyes as I stroll by. Her skin is black as coal, swinging her legs, long and slight, her white shorts a little loose against her reedy frame. I nod and keep on and she nods back. And her skin glistens in the sun.

I walk on, hugging the seawall, up past the flag poles, more than a hundred as high as six stories it seems from the street, poles that used to flap red, white and blue, waving stars and stripes of a different form but now rise bare without their colored foliage, rusting in the salt air, like a bamboo forest. The guards wander under the sun, around and within the Section, Cuban and American. It's sometimes difficult to tell who is who and it seems unimportant. No one sits in front of the Section, so the seawall lies bare like the poles—this barren stretch of the Malecón a pale yellow scar yet to heal.

I usually don't walk up this far. Normally I'll head back home a block or two inland, down the narrow streets leaned on by worn, two-story neo-colonials, their color bleached and peeling, with dark heads tipping out through broken shutters, clothes drying up on balconies that lean in as well. But today I feel on edge, those hugging streets a bit too much compared to the ease of the open sea. I think all this reminiscing has made me twitchy. So I twist around and head back the same way I came. On my left the sea rushing against the moss-licked rocks and concrete wall that stops it, and to my right the wide road, watched by a hotchpotch of pastel buildings that seem to spend their day trying to keep upright, tilting in different directions, at different heights, in different needs of repair.

She still sits differently from the others, swinging her ebony legs road-ward—away from the water and breeze. She never wears sunglasses—the white of her eyes trace their glance easy within her black face. She grins her buckteeth at me, then moves her red-painted top lip over and closes her mouth, a nervous habit in those with protruding teeth, and kicks her legs that glisten in the sun, patting the concrete next to her. Freeing the space with her hand.

I sit down beside and watch her stick legs swing and glisten and part a bit. And she asks how I've been. And I tell her, fine, which is more or less true. And we sit a while, nothing important said, before heading back down the Malecón together.

* * *

The first time I stayed over at Heather's I was nervous. Petrified, in fact. Even though I was ten, I still wet the bed. Not every night, maybe only once every few weeks, but enough to soak the sheets so there was no dry patch to escape.

In those days there was no treatment for bed-wetting. I remember my parents taking me to a doctor some distance from home—a specialist, I presume. I think they may have thought I was troubled. But the specialist never discovered why, and I got used to it. For the most part my mother did too. She would strip the sheets in the middle of the night—there was a rubber bed pad involved, too—put down new ones, and then I got back into bed and slept as if nothing had happened.

I remember not being able to drink before bedtime. This was a killer, especially in the heat of summer. I used to sneak off to the bathroom and gulp from the tap, but Mum often caught me and chastised me good and proper. My brother never had this problem. I remember him drinking fat glasses of colored drink, with big floating ice-cubes, always in front of me at night, gulping it down with a protracted ahh, moving the cubes in his mouth with his eyes rolling to the back of his head—with me looking on with a mouth like the bottom of a bird cage. I'm sure I can last in the desert longer than most thanks to that childhood training in going without water. But, for the most part, bed-wetting wasn't too much of a drag—except when I slept over. And especially if I stayed in a room with other kids.

Holiday camps were torture. Waking in a little log cabin full of boys, with the whiff of piss floating in the air, and the taunts that rose up and lasted until the bus arrived home. I told my parents I hated these camps but didn't say why. They said I was always smiling when I got off the bus, which was true. It was like coming home after a long stretch fighting the Viet Cong—back to the safety of my little bed where I could piss and not be troubled by it.

Still, that first day I sprinted home and asked Mum whether I could stay over at Heather's. She was delighted of course. I swear we could have announced our engagement and she wouldn't have minded. When I got back, there was a single mattress on the floor next to Heather's bed and a pillow with a satin cover. I can't remember the pattern, just the softness against my cheek. I still sleep on a satin pillow today, my adult teddy bear of sorts.

I changed into my pajamas and lay in the bed with Heather above me on hers. We turned the light off and let the room dim slowly into the night. We talked and talked and I didn't want to sleep and I kept going to the bathroom to empty my piss. Heather never questioned why—and of course I never told her. Girls don't wet the bed as much as boys, do they? Grandmother stuck her head in every so often, cackled a bit, and went back to the kitchen, preparing some dim sum for the Bamboo Garden.

I woke with the sun flush against my face. Heather's window never had a curtain and the morning sun sung out as loud as a rooster in her little tomato-egg room. She lay above on her bed, facing me, sleeping all peaceful, so still I couldn't see her breathe. I felt down between my legs and it was dry and warm and I went back to sleep.

And I loved the world so much I could have cried.

* * *

In the winter, Heather's fibro house was colder than mine. She had a little electric bar heater in her room that glowed orange into the night. I wore heavy flannelette pajamas, so I was a bit scared of the bar heater. My mother always told me stories of people catching on fire in flannelette pajamas, tales so often repeated that I treated my winter pajamas like rags soaked in petrol. I think bar heaters and flannelette pajamas were banned in the eighties—apparently enough young boys did burst into flame to get someone's attention. But in the seventies both were around. Between lost eyes and the burns ward, the life of a child was risky in those days.

It was very cold the first night I crept into Heather's bed. Grandmother wandered the house trying to keep warm, wrapped in a beanie and scarf. She always wore a big white anorak jacket in cold weather—she looked like a Chinese snowman, except it never snowed in Sydney. But the fibro houses couldn't keep their heat, so it might as well have been snowing because it was just as cold.

"Do you want to come in here, Tommy?"

I looked up at Heather, shivering under my thin blanket. "What about Grandmother?"

She smiled. "The bed won't fit the three of us."

Heather's room didn't have a door, which is why the radiator heat never kept us warm—and why I was scared to get into her bed. I didn't know really why I was scared. Sex didn't mean anything to me at ten. I remember sitting with Rydges once at school. One of the popular girls, with long blonde hair that fell straight down to her shoulders, not tied like most of the others, was sitting in the next row in front of us. She had a very short skirt and had her leg stretched out into the walkway between the row of desks.

"Look at those legs," Rydges whispered.

I remember looking at them, the white-pink of her thighs, and not knowing why they should be interesting. I knew what he meant; it had something to do with sex. But to me it was just a leg and could have been my brother's for all I cared. So while I wasn't thinking of sex when Heather asked me to come into her bed, I felt that Grandmother might not feel the same way.

That didn't stop me of course.

At first we lay next to each other not quite touching. We talked about the usual stuff, played with Dotty and Carla for a while, but kept under the covers as much as we could to keep warm. Grandmother walked past in her snowman outfit and stopped dead at the door. She had the hood of the anorak up, which drew a shadow over her face, so I looked into the dark cave of her head, not knowing what face she was pulling. She said something in Mandarin that I couldn't decipher. The words were scratching but not severe.

Heather said something back to her that I understood. "It's very cold, Grandmother."

The old woman stood still in the doorway, her face still shadowed under her hood. I thought it best to keep quiet.

"It's very cold, Grandmother," Heather repeated softly.

She stood for a few seconds more, then turned away and went out of the picture-frame doorway.

We lay down into the warm we created between us and didn't speak for a bit, and I felt all tingly inside. Our chatter started up afresh, hesitant at first, but drew breath into the warm, and we giggled and talked about what seemed to be more important stuff.

And I woke in the morning next to her, dry and happy. And we stayed under the covers with the sun streaming down on our faces. And we kept there, tucked under and warm, until Grandmother called us for breakfast.

* * *

Do you think it strange? A ten-year-old boy staying every Saturday night at a girl's house? Were my parents progressive? Was Heather's grandmother? It was the liberal seventies, of course, and it would have been different if Heather wasn't Chinese. You know—that love of all things foreign that my folks had. And remember, I was just a kid, not like the ten-year-olds in Havana today. And God, they used to let me wander the streets by myself—chucking rocks at ice-cream trucks, slamming firecrackers into Rydges back, starting steam rollers at will. At least they knew I was safe at Heather's.

Was that it? They knew I was safe?

Nah, I don't think so. Safety wasn't such a big deal in those days.

* * *

Dr Pap had an unpronounceable name, a Greek mouthful with lots of papas or ousos or lopols. So we simply called him Dr Pap. His office was on the main road that cut through Bankstown, a walk of nearly an hour from our house, made longer by the gradual incline that never surrendered into a plateau until it reached the top of Berry Road. For a kid it was a drudging walk, and if you weren't feeling sick before you left home, you certainly did when you arrived.

He took out my tonsils when I was younger. I remember the sweet, ether soaked cloth that came over my face, held down by his big furry hands, suffocating me into a stupor. I remember him burning the plantar wart off the sole of my foot, the needle piercing its scream, which to this day remains the most exquisitely painful experience of my life. I was young then, but when I reached an age when I knew that a needle would be introduced to the session, I rebelled. Big time.

My mother liked to tell people the story of getting my first haircut as a kid. She took me down to the barbershop, with the red twisting pole and the big leather chairs and the smell of hair cream—sweet like the ether—and the click of the scissors. It was the scissors I didn't like. They were sharp and looked like they belonged in Dr Pap's office. So I decided not to get my hair cut.

The barber announced in an oily brogue he had never met a child whose hair he could not cut. This was a mistake. It gave me a challenge that I couldn't resist. I hollered and rolled against the chair's leather, with my mother on one side trying to coo me into a calm, and the barber on the other, his blood-red anger rising in his cheeks until his head looked like it could explode.

When I think about it now, it would have been unusual for a child to see this drama reflected in the mirror—on the big screen if you will. To watch this struggle in the barber's mirrored wall would have had an amplifying effect, I'm certain. And it sure took guts to bite a man with scissors. He yelped and threw the scissors down clanging on the floor—and I became the first child whose hair he couldn't cut. I remember my brother grinning in the other chair, sitting like an angel in his booster seat and getting a crew-cut with clippers that looked even more menacing than the scissors. When we got home Dad said they might put a photograph of me on the wall, you know, like the celebrities that have had their haircut in the shop, not that there were any celebrities in Crepundia. Mum said perhaps he could ask the barber when he took me next time, which I remember quieted him down.

The lesson I learnt from the haircut episode was that I could refuse something if there was an extreme need for it. And, after some extreme events at Dr Pap's, I decided when I was about eight to never to allow blood samples to be taken from my arm. I had a run of blood sampling around then. Every time I went to Dr Pap he would order a blood test—I swear he had some kind of a kickback going on. No matter what I presented with, a stomach-ache to bed-wetting to warts on my fingers, he would end the consultation, "I think we should do a blood test."

I really questioned his professional skill from the beginning. But after a series of these ruddy sampling events, I decided enough was enough. And no matter what force was applied from my father—Mum refused to come to a blood test after the barber biting episode—nobody, not Dr Pap, his nurse, or a team of blood sampling professionals, could get blood from me. He would just need to develop a more hands-on approach to diagnosing my ills.

But my resolve to refuse this bloodletting would soon be tested in a way I hadn't anticipated.

* * *

Even as we settled into spring, I remained in Heather's bed. Not at the beginning of the night, since the cold excuse had long lost its appeal with Grandmother, the bar heater now stored away in a cupboard, the evenings warm enough to leave the window open, the balmy spring adrift in the little fibro house. But if I woke in the middle of the night, I would creep on up into her bed, and we squashed in together and slept like mice, all curled up and still.

Grandmother always woke first in the morning. It wasn't unusual for me to open my eyes to her standing in the doorway, shaking her head and cackling something to herself. Heather used to pretend to be asleep when Grandmother appeared. She slept on the side away from the door, directly under the window, so she could hide her head behind mine and wait for her to leave. Once Grandmother had made her appearance and went on with her morning chores, we could relax—and resume our chatter about whatever we had left off the night before.

Sleeping with Heather was like sleeping with myself. It was effortless and never felt weird. We just did it and knew it was right. I never told anyone, even my mates, and neither did Heather. We didn't want to risk spoiling what we had, and I don't think anyone else would have understood. Grandmother said we were like two branches of a tree, and I think that's the best way to describe it.

I only wet the bed once in all our time together. I felt the world falling down and I didn't know what to do and started to cry. Heather woke to my sobbing, and we got out of the bed but she didn't say anything. I remember her silence. I went into the bathroom, took off my wet pajamas and got back into my clothes. And when I came back to the tomato-egg room, she was on my mattress on the floor, the clean dry mattress, and she had left space for me to come in too. Then we went back to sleep together like nothing had happened.

That's what it was like. Two branches of a tree.

* * *

Grandmother had some papers spread out on the kitchen table. She had her Chinese zodiac stuff as well; I recognized these from our rat/ox incident. We had just finished dim sum and I was ready to head off home like usual after Sunday lunch. Heather and Grandmother were talking and I just listened, not understanding much and eating the buns.

"Tommy, Grandmother wants to know what your blood group is."

I shrugged because I didn't know what a blood group was, although I was sure Dr Pap would have the information. I assumed I'd had every test that was available, probably more than once.

They chatted together some more.

"Tommy, Grandmother says can you find out from your parents?"

"Sure, how come?"

"She says it's a new way to test good matches."

"But I thought rats and ox's were real good."

Heather spoke to the old woman who spluttered a curt reply.

"She says a blood group is better."

When I got home I asked Mum straight off.

"Why do you want to know?"

"For a school project." Have I mentioned my lying skills?

Mum would do anything for a school project. She rang Dr Pap the next day and I was told I had never been tested for it—which I found very odd, thinking this was just an excuse for me to have it again and for him to receive another kickback.

I told Heather the bad news the next day at school. Actually, I was a bit relieved anyway, just in case it was the wrong blood group and would make her grandmother upset, after which who knew what would happen. She was capable of anything.

When I arrived next Saturday afternoon, the old woman had her straw hat on and gloves—her going out outfit. And so did Heather. I could see Heather was shifting uncomfortably, but when Grandmother took my arm and pulled me with her back out the front door, I started to get worried.

"Grandmother is taking us to get our blood groups tested."

"You're kidding me." I knew Heather would never kid about a thing like this—she did have a soft, gentle sense of humor, but never around anything harmful, or the need to tear down that my mates relied on. But I just wanted to slow everything down. Denial, I think you call it. "How do we get the test? Can you get it by pissing in a jar?"

Again denial. If there was one thing I could be real confident about—a blood group wasn't tested by pissing.

Heather asked the old woman, who cackled loud and slapped me on the arm.

"I'll take that as a no."

For all the talking I did, I had never told Heather about my fear of blood tests. The bed-wetting was bad enough. I didn't want to add to the list of wimpy stuff about me. But I started to get my pebble-stomach feeling. I thought about making a run for it—and I looked at Heather and she just stared back at me. We were both way out of our depth here.

We dragged on behind the old woman—her pace quickening, I swear, as the incline of the road became steeper. She was like a marathon runner. And when we got to Dr Pap's in what must have been record time, I thought I was going to vomit.

It was all strangely quiet as we approached the door. And I realized, with my fine-tuned experience of visits to the place, that something was odd.

"I think it might be closed, Grandmother," I said.

I pulled at the wire door that held fast. I looked at the sign that gave the opening hours—9am to 12 noon on Saturdays. It must have been nearly three by now. I started banging on the door, knowing there wasn't a soul inside. I turned to look at the old woman and shrugged and kept on banging away. I must say I milked the scene beautifully, but stopped when I got scared that he might actually live in the house, and would appear in his dressing gown and slippers, with a needle as big as a pistol in his hand, ready for action. So I just feigned a sad face at the old woman and moved back out through the gate and away.

The road home dipped down easily in the afternoon spring. The birds chirped up their song and the butterflies flapped and fluttered. And the old woman tried to keep up with us as we glided on down—without a drop of blood lost from our veins. How sweet it all was.

* * *

"What am I going to do?"

Beany, Danno and Rydges stood with me in a huddle. I had decided my problem was serious enough to bring to my mates. We even missed British Bulldog for this meeting.

"Tommy, you hate blood tests," Beany said.

"But do you hate blood tests *more* than you love Heather?" Rydges said.

I looked at him in disgust—I do that face well. But I must admit he did have a point.

"You can't force a kid to have a blood test if he isn't sick," Danno said.

"I'm sure there's a law against it," Beany said.

"You don't know this old broad," I said. "She doesn't care about laws. She just does what she likes."

"My dad says that the Chinese could invade us one day. He says there's a spy working in one of the Chinese restaurants in Crepundia."

Rydges father was crazy, we all knew it. He ran for the local council a few times—we saw his picture on posts skewered in the front lawns around the place—usually on promises to protect suburbia from the Communist threat. He never got elected.

"What about crying?" Rydges said. "Crying works pretty well, sometimes."

"I can't in front of Heather."

"Can't your parents stop it happening?"

"They would love me to have it. Nothing would give them more pleasure than to see me back getting blood tests."

"What does Heather say?"

"She says she has to have it done, but if I don't want to, she would be okay with it."

"She's a nice girl is Heather," Rydges said. He always was the most open-minded of the group.

"But the grandmother will probably kick me out if I don't get it done."

"I think you're fucked, Tommy," Beany said.

"Really fucked," Danno said.

Rydges just nodded.

* * *

The waiting room was full of snotty-nosed kids. We got there early—the three of us—and Heather went with Grandmother up to the receptionist's desk. As they did their check-in, the desk lady kept looking at me through the gap between Heather and Grandmother in a weird kind of way. I guess my reputation preceded me.

We all sat back down and a young kid next to me started barking like a dog—in fact I thought he was a dog until I turned around. His mother gave me a stare, but if you have a barking kid, you have to expect the odd look or two. I tried to guess what diseases the other people had—

the ones who didn't drip with snot that is. Some looked pretty well to me. Probably they were bed-wetters or something like that.

Every so often Dr Pap came in to collect one of his patients, and didn't look at me at all. But I waited, all the while the tension rising up, with my pebble-stomach shrunken down to the size of a pea. I prayed the building might burst into flame or that Dr Pap had to head off for an emergency blood test somewhere. No such luck.

And he called us in—the three of us together.

We sat down in his little white office with shiny sharp equipment in trays and plastic hearts and skeleton bits on shelves, and he looked at me like the receptionist had.

Heather did the talking for Grandmother. "We would like to get our blood groups done."

"You and your grandmother?"

"Tommy and I."

He looked at me even more strangely than before. "Can I ask why?"

She explained, and Grandmother just sat there with her straw hat on her knees. I kept quiet, looking around the room to see if I could see any needles, but I think he stored them away from sight. He kept on looking at me as Heather explained about the Chinese Zodiac stuff. At one point he even smiled. Two customers requesting blood tests in the one appointment must have made his day.

When Heather had finished, he looked over at me again. "I'm surprised to see you here, Tom."

I kept my head down but raised a glance up at him. He seemed to be taking more pleasure in this than was professionally appropriate.

"Very surprised, since the last time you were here I thought we might have to strap you down on the gurney, and I've only had to do this with one other patient in my long and varied career."

When I told Rydges about this later, his father said that Dr Pap may have broken doctor-patient confidentiality when he blurted this out in front of Heather. His father started talking about the Hippocratic oath and other legal stuff. Though Rydges' father was crazy, I think he may have been right on this occasion.

At the time, I just sat there all red and didn't look at anyone.

"I'm happy to do the test for you, Heather. But unfortunately, I cannot do Tom's."

I tried to take in the meaning of these words. It sounded like a reprieve, but that had to be wish fulfillment on my part.

"He needs one of his parents to come with him."

I looked up at Dr Pap, not smiling, just open-mouthed.

"You look like the Governor just rang to stop your execution, my boy."

I believe Dr Pap thought himself a comedian.

"But, perhaps you could explain the situation to your parents, *and only if*—" He said these three words in a higher pitch, then repeated them. "*And only if* they think it is worthwhile, they can come up with you to get the test done."

And he winked at me. And I began to regret wishing he would die in the waiting room.

Heather translated to Grandmother Dr Pap's words, and she became quite animated. You didn't need to know Mandarin to get her drift. But Dr Pap, to give him his due, just sat there and let the words bounce off him.

He gave Heather her blood test and I kept my gaze well away from the procedure. She didn't flinch a bit, I'm sure—the two branches of a tree thing didn't seem to apply when it came to blood tests. And, as we were heading out of the door, Dr Pap said, "If your parents decide for you to have the test, Tom, could you let me know, and I'll be sure to have that day off."

A real comedian was Dr Pap.

* * *

AB positive. That was Heather's blood group. I remember it well of course—it would determine our fate together. Grandmother got her charts out and said I had to be AB negative. There was no other group that matched.

Beany's cousin was a bleeder. Even with the slightest knock it could happen—so bad he couldn't play sport at school. Beany told me he once saw his cousin with a knee the size of a grapefruit after he fell down. So I became a bleeder too. Heather translated my affliction—I could have a blood test if Grandmother wanted, but I might die if I did. Grandmother laughed at this. She lifted my hair up and spluttered something that not even Heather understood—cackled in her farm-town speak, Heather said.

Heather told me some weeks later, when we woke in the morning snuggled down under the blankets, that Grandmother told her that only one in a hundred people are AB negative. Heather said Grandmother thought I didn't need the test, since Golden Ox's and Golden Rats were a perfect match. So miraculously my bleeding disease got better all by itself, thanks to the rarity of AB negative.

* * *

I was a skinny kid and a bit of a late bloomer. I think that explains me looking at the girl's legs with Rydges and not understanding the attraction. But Heather was a year older than me and wasn't late to bloom at all. By the first year of high school, she had lost her pigtails, her hair now straight and long to her shoulders, and developed ample breasts while I looked and felt the same—not even a wisp of armpit hair. When I lay in her bed at night I could feel her breasts under her pajamas. I remember not saying anything, but I was curious, and if she dozed before I did, I would have a bit of a feel. I don't think it was sexual at first, but I'm not too sure.

Eventually she caught me at it. "Tommy, what are you doing?"

I held my breath and didn't answer. Heather just waited for me to reply.

"Sorry," I said.

She lifted my hand and put it back on her chest—and I remember getting that tingly feeling. Then she took it away and we went back to sleep. She did, at least. I think I lay there tempted to have another feel. But I didn't.

From that day, she let me do this on and off. Just brief, and never under her top. Sometimes I fell asleep in her arms, my head lying on her chest. It felt warm and at first a bit strange. But those awkward fumbles were only transient, and in time it became usual for Heather to lie on her back before we slept, with me cuddling into her, listening to the thump of her heart. I seemed to melt into her body—thaw out and soften—the two branches never stronger.

I had become taller than Heather, but in those days it seemed she was becoming a teenager when I just stayed on as a little boy.

* * *

Primary school was a breeze, but high school was another matter. I went to Turpis Boys High—a school of fifteen hundred boys. Heather went to a co-ed school nearby, which meant we saw each other only on weekends. Beany and Danno went to the same school as Heather. Only Rydges came to mine. So I suddenly felt like a weak swimmer in the deep end of a pool, always kicking with my legs just to stay afloat.

The first day, I had my new uniform on—a pale blue shirt and gray shorts, and a blue and gray striped tie. I didn't know what to expect, but I felt neatly dressed and ready to go.

But the school was a zoo.

It was all open to the summer sun, and the cattle of blue and gray grazed uneasily in the heat. The older bulls rutted their horns in and around us, and I stood alone, not of the same kind, and I wanted away.

And that was before the stabbing. A kid in our year stabbed an older boy on the first day. So I came on home and cried and said to Mum I couldn't go back. But she said it was the only school available and I had no other choice.

I'm not going to write much about high school—it makes me scratch. But I sense that doesn't bother you much, does it, Juan? You may even find it important. As a compromise, I'll describe a few events to give you a better feel of my anguish. But then that's it for my high school life, if that's okay by you.

* * *

During the seventies, caning was allowed and our school mastered the technique. It wasn't an uncommon sight for a whole class to be caned at once—boys all lined up outside the classroom waiting for the bamboo rod to strike on an outstretched hand. Usually in those cases only one hit would be given, to keep the physical effort of caning thirty boys from getting out of hand. The maximum sentence was six hits—'six of the best,' it was called. Every male teacher had a cane, some taught with it, waving it in the air to the music of their lesson, like a multitasking baton.

Two teachers are worth a mention in regards to their caning technique. One was Mr. Orangerie, the language master, who was a very short man. When angered he used to spit in a myriad of foreign languages. I swear he could switch from German to French to Italian in one sentence when he exploded.

Now, being short is a disadvantage for the caner—or an advantage for the canee, depending on whose shoes you're in. It's like hitting a golf ball placed back a step. You just don't get that necessary downward thrust you need. Mr. Orangerie solved this by standing on a chair when he caned. And when he was really angry, he would jump off the chair as the rod came down, letting the full force of gravity do its thing. It was quite a sight to see, this little bald man giving a kid a good flying multilingual thrashing. Sometimes he missed his target, and sometimes he would abort in mid swing, because if he struck above the outstretched hand no further punishment could be given. This was the first unwritten law of caning.

The person you didn't want to be caned by was the Physical Education master. I don't remember his name, but he certainly was an athletic man, and unfortunately not short. I remember Rydges being caned by him once. Rydges' lack of sporting prowess made him slack off a bit in PE lessons. One day, he not only forgot his PE uniform, he wasn't participating to the satisfaction of the master.

For those who have not been caned before, there is one basic rule—keep your palm and fingers outstretched and do not move. The natural reflex is to curl your fingers into a fist and move back, which only adds to the drama by making the caner angrier when he misses. Or worse, as happened to Rydges.

He was given 'six of the best' on that day. After about two or three hits, he made the mistake of curling his fingers up. But to his credit, and demise, he didn't move his hand away. I can still hear the sound of the whipping bamboo against his knuckles. He shrunk away and cried, holding his hand tight under his armpit. And when his hand was eventually prised away by the master, his knuckles looked like black grapes. I felt like crying myself.

Eventually the remainder of the sentence was given because of the second unwritten law of caning—that no reduction of the original sentence is given mid-way through the event unless, as previously mentioned, the cane struck accidently at the wrist or forearm. I've witnessed boys who were sobbing wrecks, even consoled by the teacher between hits. I'm sure the teachers would have happily aborted the sentence if they could, but nobody broke the caning laws at my school.

* * *

Karma is a very adult notion, a metaphysical thread entwined in most Asian religions. Yet it's kids that are its greatest practitioners. We just practice it because we know it to be true.

The Principal of Turpis Boys High was a psycho. The rumor was once he was a reasonable man—but one day at a full assembly he announced the death of his wife, and some of the blue and gray livestock responded by laughing. Now, that could make any person turn bad, but the event predated my arrival, so I felt a victim and had little sympathy for the man.

He was tall, thin and hunched over, bald with gray on the side, grim faced, and wizened of spirit. For most of the day he stayed in his office but prowled out occasionally, looking for stray cattle to set right. As his retirement approached, his hatred grew, which peaked at an impromptu full assembly of the junior boys.

We sat crowded on the timber floor of the school hall in open pens, unsure why we were there. Along the walls, evenly spaced, stood the teachers with their bamboo batons in hand. I remember they were the biggest of the bunch, probably selected for the job—and for the sake of their humanity, I pray not volunteers. At the front on the elevated stage stood the Principal.

"The police have just left my office," he said, "and it has come to my attention that yesterday afternoon, boys wearing the school uniform of Turpis High were seen throwing rocks onto Henry Lawson Drive from the nature reserve. This has led to an accident with a woman injured. We don't know who the boys are, but they wore the junior school uniform, and so it is some of you sitting here."

I remember being terrified and sore from sitting on the floor. But most of all I remember being still—my legs, back, head and eyes never moving an inch. For, as the Principal gave his speech, at the slightest movement of any child he would point a wrinkled finger at the accused, who would then stand, move out to the flank of the hall, and be caned. I sat near the back and saw all of this without the need of head movement. I would have preferred to be at the front, when I only had to listen. Maybe twenty boys were caned, maybe more, all guilty of nothing more than an inability to remain motionless on the floor. The acoustics of the hall was pretty good, and the sound of the cane whipping down seemed amplified—the snap as it hit the hand, like a penny bunger going off, but without the smoke. Some of the seated boys would wince as the cane struck skin. But a wince counted as movement for this psycho of a man, and they soon joined the queue and waited their turn to be thrashed.

I can still see the faces of the teachers who did the caning. I don't think they enjoyed it, but they moved efficiently to the task—like brushing their teeth.

* * *

I've just come back from Billy's jazz gig, and we talked about caning over a couple of jugs of mojitos. Billy came to Australia when he was sixteen, one of the ten pound Poms, and did a very short stint in a western suburbs high school that sounded a lot like mine. It's all about *in loco parentis*, he told me—in place of the parent. The school could behave as the parent when they weren't around. He laughed at this, his sweaty mane splashing about. Told me his father would have caned him too, if the bastard had managed to catch him. His old man had been shot in the war, a bullet still in his thigh. Thank God they never bothered to take it out, he said. And he raised his glass to the Nazis.

* * *

Our school rarely supported kids who had different interests. The eccentric were the runts, grazing at the edge of the herd, some grouped in pairs, maybe under a tree if there was one, even if it didn't give shade. Rydges was intelligent, hated sport, and had dorky interests like reading, so his whole school life was a misery. In the end he left the school and never returned. I think he finished his high school certificate at the local TAFE—and good luck to him. But I never saw him again after that.

I remember his visit to the school careers advisor.

"So, son, what do you want to do when you leave school?"

"I want to be an artist, Sir."

The teacher paused in reflection, tossing his well-versed careers knowledge into a formulated plan, something with structure, a foundation to build a future for a student about to move into the heady adult world—away from the family that was Turpis Boys High—and said deadpan, "What's the matter with you, boy? Are you a poof?"

Turpis Boys High—what a fucking zoo it was.

* * *

So, you've asked me to tell you about my childhood. Probably just a standard ploy on your part—the beginning of the conversation, the opening gambit in chess. But I've reread my notes, and I must admit this high school stuff is pretty grim. The bastardization. The fight for survival—Darwinian in all respects, except for the rooting. You must understand though, from the moment I left my purple bedroom to venture out to the great weekday world, my mind was focused solely on one aim—to remain unscathed.

I thought about telling you about the Science teacher who electrocuted us with a car battery as punishment, or made us drink gallons of water—Rydges said we could drown in our own blood doing the water drinking torture, but admitted he preferred it to the cane. That black grape episode really scarred him. But I'm spent with all this *in loco parentis* bullshit. So, one final scene of high school and then I'm done. I must say I wasn't a witness to it—but my brother was.

His maths teacher was scribbling an answer to one of their homework questions up on the board. "Thompkins, is that the same solution as you got?"

The boy looked down into his book. "Sorry, Sir, I didn't do my homework."

The boy was a friend of my brother, so my brother started to object.

"Shut up, Peters, am I talking to you?" The teacher now hovered over Thompkins, whose gaze remained at the table. "You didn't do your homework?"

"I couldn't do it, Sir. My grandfather died last night."

The boy's head kept down. This was no lie and the teacher knew it to be true. Not that it made a difference. "What's the matter, boy, does your grandfather do your homework?"

You see—my school was a hole of a place. Yet I haven't bothered with more detail because I don't think it's enough to explain everything. Well, obviously.

But it certainly adds pieces to the puzzle.

* * *

Swimming was a big part of my life as a kid—but I don't want to mention it much, the mechanics of it that is, other than say it meant waking up at five in the morning, training in freezing cold water, and not having as much time to spend with my mates as I wanted. I was very good at it—and made the State finals for most of the events I entered. Sometimes I won a medal.

The school swimming carnivals were in summer and began only after a few weeks of starting school. In my first race in year 7—50 meters freestyle—I stood on the blocks, looking at the other kids and wondering whether I was up to their speed, even though I had won a silver medal in the same event at the State Championships just weeks before. Starting a new school, especially this school, sucked any confidence right out of you. But I flew off the blocks and did a personal best time—breaking the school record—and accepted the nods of the teachers and older kids. The toughest boy in school, who would later be expelled and wind up in a boys' home, came up and shook my hand. So I tasted the benefits of swimming early in my high school life. God knows how I would have survived without it.

In year 8, swimming gave me my greatest reward. It was at the zone championships, with each of the schools separated along the open tiered platform by a large flapping banner. I was in good form that day, had broken quite a few records, including that of an ex-Olympic medalist—which was announced to the crowd.

When I was on the blocks for one of the events, I noticed Heather sitting in the stand with her school team. Heather never swam, but she told me later she was asked to keep a tally of her school's achievements. I waved furiously just before the starting gun. This happened to be the event that I broke the Olympian's record, and so I won the race by a country mile. When I left the water I waved again. She smiled, waved back, and I saw the kids around her staring at me, then back to her. I didn't care and she seemed not to mind as well.

Heather and I still had our weekend times together. Nothing changed much, except her hair and chest. Grandmother remained crazy and cooked up a storm, my Mandarin improved, which made Mum and Dad happy, and I slept in her little bed in the tomato-egg room. Most of the boys in my year—in fact probably all—didn't have a girlfriend. Thirteen-year-old boys are not at their prime at that age, and the girls, well filled out by then, just weren't interested. Furthermore, in a boys' school there was little opportunity to get one.

Heather's school, being co-ed, was different. I remember Danno telling me he fingered a girl on the school bus in year 7. I doubted the story, but this mystery of having half the school as girls meant my imagination ran to considering the story true. I certainly knew most of my mates didn't have girlfriends, and the ones that did were the coolest in school. Heather hinted to some of her friends she had a boyfriend, but she didn't think they believed her.

Heather didn't like high school much either. She used to tell me bits and pieces during our lazy Sunday morning chatter tucked in bed. She was the only Asian girl in primary school, and nothing changed in high. But young kids weren't racist the way they were in adolescence. Taunting came as easily as breathing, and the slightest imperfection was thrown back in your face. So Heather, even though she was as quiet as a mouse, was called slanty or chink or gook by both the girls and boys. She missed the softness of primary school nearly as much as me and only had a few close friends, all timid like her.

The winners' podium faced the open stand of students at the opposite side of the pool. When I climbed up on the top step, I saw Heather in the crowd and waved at her again. She smiled and waved back. They announced the record, going into great detail of the Olympic accomplishments of the old record holder, and I stood tall and looked at my school team but mainly at her. It was my last event of the day, so I jumped off the podium and felt the eyes of the stadium watching as I moved to Heather's school's section and clambered up into the stadium to where she was seated. It was a strict rule that you kept in your own school zone, but I had the key to the city after breaking that record and could have gone anywhere.

I sat down next to her, kissing her on the cheek. And I felt like I'd really won an Olympic gold medal.

You might find it strange we had never kissed before, even though we shared a bed every weekend for more than two years. I cuddled into her, listened to her heart and her soft chatter, and fell asleep in her arms. I even touched her breasts—through heavy flannelette. But I felt increasingly young next to her, this blossoming teen, and I felt unworthy of anything more than I had.

She blushed and smiled and I kissed her again.

"Shovel face has a boyfriend," a voice came from behind.

I turned and saw a boy whom I'd raced earlier grinning down at her. I stared into him.

"Who the fuck are you?"

"I raced you today. Don't you recognize me . . . gook lover."

"Why would I know an insect like you?"

He flushed up crimson as laughter eased around the crowd. I went to a tough boys' school, and he couldn't match insults with me. So he sunk back down and mumbled something to himself, and I knew he wished he was invisible.

One of the teachers came on up and congratulated me on my swim.

"You coming on over to our school then?" the teacher asked.

This raised a hope I never would have expected. "I'd like that, Sir."

"Where do you live?"

I told him and he nodded.

"That isn't far. It's probably closer to our school than yours."

"It's the boundary, Sir. We are just on the opposite side, I was told."

"Perhaps, if you'd like, I could talk to our principal and see if he would be willing to take you in. How does that sound, Heather?"

She smiled and bit into her lip. And I felt my bare leg slink to touch hers.

"Really, Sir," I said. "You could do that?"

"Where there's a will."

I looked at Heather and she stared at me as if it couldn't be true.

We snuggled together, just like we did in her room, and she showed me her school results, and another slip of paper with my results—neatly penned, with the event and the times and an asterisk if I had broken a record. And I smiled and I kissed her again. Some of the kids came on down and talked to her, and we sat close in the warm afternoon sun and laughed at stuff with the others, some who had never spoken to her before. The school captain came up and said he had heard that I was coming to their school and I looked up at him, with his broad shoulders and good looks, and it all felt unreal.

And as the carnival came to a close, before I headed off back to my school section, I kissed Heather again and told her that I loved her.

And she told me the same.

* * *

In winter, Heather and I often lingered in bed till late in the morning.

"Remember when you lied for me?" I said once.

"I thought Miss Quinter was going to expel you."

"She was pretty angry."

"Lisa didn't talk to me for weeks after that," she said. "Neither did the other girls. I sat down near the bikes at the infants' school and ate my lunch alone. It seemed like forever."

"You should have played with us."

"British Bulldog? I'm no good at sport, Tommy."

"Neither was Rydges. You'd have been better than him."

"I can't throw or kick a ball. Or run fast. I came last at the school races, even in the egg and spoon race."

"Girls are normally good at the egg and spoon."

"Not me, Tommy."

"Anyhow, they talked to you eventually."

"Yes. They came up to me one day—Lisa, Jenny and Sharon. They said I was the only real wog in the group, so it was okay not to tell Miss Quinter about it. Somehow, that made it all right."

"Idiots."

"I know. I didn't want to play with them, but I was really lonely, Tommy. And I'd started to pretend I was sick to stay out of school. But Grandmother knew I was fibbing and said she would make me take her black syrup if I didn't go."

"That black stuff she keeps in the bathroom? It stinks even through the bottle."

"She got it from China. She says two spoons empties your guts out."

"Is that a good thing?" I sidled into the warm of her back. "But you were a real sport, Heather. A real mate."

We liked to play with the dolls and we liked to imagine we were the parents. It seems strange, thinking back on it now, but she didn't have any other toys, and I guess we played this game as a dress rehearsal for times ahead.

"Make sure you come straight home from school," she said to Carla. She bent the Barbie's knees into a walking stance. Carla was our eldest, a blonde teen, lithe but temperamental. "If you don't, I'll tell your father when he gets home from work."

"Where am I working then?"

"At the police station."

"No way."

"Then in the bank. I'm at home with the children, Tommy."

"What about me working at the Bamboo Garden. Grandmother can be the cook and I'll collect the money. It'd be a sweet business."

"Then you'd see Grandmother day *and* night. Are you sure that's a good idea?"

"Maybe not. But I can't see myself working in the bank."

"Then a school teacher?"

"Not High."

"Primary. You'd be good at that, Tommy."

"Maybe."

"And when Penny starts school, I could do nursing."

"My mother did nursing for a bit."

She put Dotty under the bed sheet. "I'll be back to give you your medicine young lady."

"Not the black stuff, nurse?" I could do a good Dotty voice.

"Yes, but I'll add some sugar to it. And I'll give you some ice-cream after."

"I don't like ice-cream."

"Who doesn't like ice-cream?"

"I don't."

"Then, I'll comb your hair and read you a story."

"And what about my reward for getting that needle earlier?"

"Yes, you *were* very brave. Maybe some Peking Duck?"

I took Carla off the pillow and twisted strands of the doll's hair between my fingers, much like Grandmother twisted mine. "Could our children have blonde hair?"

Heather looked at me and smiled. She shouted out the question to Grandmother, who cackled back something that obviously amused her.

"Grandmother said no."

The old woman appeared at the door and stared at me with a scrunched brow. She said in slow Mandarin something I couldn't understand. I shrugged my shoulders and she repeated it even slower.

"You husband now?" Heather whispered the translation.

I looked at the old woman and shook my head. She had the same eyes as the hanging duck I saw on the first day in the house.

Heather lifted herself up and asked how old Grandmother was when she married.

The woman grinned. "Older than you."

I liked listening to Grandmother's stories, Heather translating in a whisper close by, so I could feel the words as a warm breath on my ear. Grandmother was married around sixteen and had never met her husband until a week before the ceremony. Her parents organized the whole thing, and after they were married she moved over to his family home in the next village. He was kind to her but she didn't get along with his mother, who was too loud and quacked like a duck. She said she felt very lonely and cried at night until her husband soothed her with promises that his mother would improve with age. Her husband was older than her and very smart, always quoting Confucius. 'Act with kindness, but do not expect gratitude' was his favorite line. She always told him that Confucius must have had a mother-in-law like hers to come up with a saying like that. She said that, despite her husband's promises, his mother aged like a grape—picked off the vine and left out in the sun.

Her husband worked hard on a small plot of land at the back of their home. They had a daughter, Heather's mother, but she couldn't have more children, even though they wanted. She said that made the grape quack louder, but her husband didn't take a second wife, like the grape had wanted. He said that Grandmother was enough of a wife for two husbands, and not the other way around. Grandmother smiled as she told us this. He was a dragon and she a rat, so a very good match. The grape was a rooster, which Grandmother said explained everything.

She became interested in the Chinese zodiac because of the love and hate in her family, which she saw could only come from the heavens. She studied the charts kept by an old man said to be a hundred and five who lived in the same village. He taught her everything he knew, happy that he had found someone to continue the science he had long practiced. When she was around twenty he died and she became the village astrologer—which she offered usually free of service, to the displeasure of the grape. But she grew fat because she was invited to every wedding, which she had invariably approved—and she laughed as she told us this.

Grandmother's husband died before the grape did. He got a bad cough and became hot and died in her arms. Heather's mum was only eight when it happened. So the three women lived alone and worked the land with the help of the villagers—whom she had advised with kindness. For this reason they never went without, even when the drought made the soil crumble like a baked dog turd. She shook her head as she told us this.

I liked to watch Grandmother's eyes as she told her stories. They danced around as she saw the things she was talking about. Sometimes I looked behind expecting to see someone there.

At the end of this story I remember chirping up at her. "Grandmother, if you're a rat and I'm an ox, then we're a good match too!"

The old woman laughed.

"Like my husband said. Finally you have arrived, golden ox—my second husband."

And she walked away cackling into the kitchen.

* * *

How old am I at this point? I'm wearing shorts so it must be summer. In the winter we wore long gray pants. My shirt is pale blue, like the sky, so I'm at high school. Perhaps I'm in year 8, with little hair down there, a skinny, blonde kid with eyes like those at a mother's funeral.

This morning, I woke sweating and scared. The same last night. I woke in my childhood, though the shouts of Havana spill through my window. It's raining and the breeze off the Malecón smells of the ocean, not that hot-dry smell of the bush-land of my childhood.

Strange, but the sound of the cars is just the same. Maybe that's the problem. My wax earplugs soften the Malecón traffic to a purr—a whoosh—hidden from where I lay in my bed.

On a mattress of dry leaves.

With the purr of the traffic below.

Looking up at the blue through the trees.

And the heat of the day.

Dear Juan, my skin is still scratched from the bush-land of my childhood. Make of it what you will.

* * *

It was the last weekend of the winter school holidays, and I had spent two weeks with my family on a driving trip down to Victoria, swinging back up through the Snowy Mountains. The snow time was fun, but the drive a real chore, with Dad's tape of the great bagpipe tunes of the Scottish Highlands testing the patience of us all. It was Saturday afternoon when we arrived home, and so I raced on over to Heather's.

It had started to rain, with a wind gusting up that slanted the wet into my face the whole way over. By the time I arrived it was pelting down, and I used my knapsack as a feeble shelter against the downpour, keeping it there as I strode up onto the open front porch and banged on the door. The wire door was locked, which usually meant they weren't in, but I went around the side and peeked through Heather's window, and then to the backyard, finding the kitchen door also closed. The rain kept on coming—there was no shelter around this box of a house—so I took the spare key from under the mat and went inside.

The house seemed strange to me, but I couldn't tell why. It was cold as ice, and I went first into Heather's bedroom and sat wet in front of the bar heater. The tomato-egg room lit only by the orange element, and I sat listening to the sound of the rain hitting the window, waiting for them to come on home. It was an odd feeling shivering in this room of fire colors, listening to the gray outside, waiting for the front door to open. I saw Heather's old chest on the floor and thought about playing with her dolls for a bit.

But when I opened the chest they were gone. And I realized, virtually at the same time, that the strangeness of the house that hit me when I first entered was the lack of smell, the Chinese kitchen smell, that usually lingered in every nook of the house.

I waited there hours but they didn't return. And when it was dark, and I became hungry, I walked back home.

I went back the next day. But the house was still empty. I sat on the step and waited until it got dark before heading off home again.

I went back the next night and nothing had changed.

And I went back the following weekend—and then the next—but the little box of a house sat empty as before.

And I kept on going, until I saw the "For Lease" sign on the front fence, about a month later. After that, I never went back.

* * *

Mum went to the real-estate agent and they said that Heather and Grandmother had left without letting them know. They even left the furniture and all of Grandmother's kitchen stuff in the house. I went with Mum to Heather's school, and they said she never returned after the holiday break. Mum said perhaps the police should be notified and they said they would do this, and I think they did.

While I was there, the sports master recognized me and came on over. He shook my hand and Mum's too—which made her proud—and he asked whether I was still interested in transferring over to their school.

But I told him no.

Transcript May 3rd 2010

Interview with Tom Peters by Juan Carlos Rebelde

JCR: Before we start I just need to have it on record that you don't mind me taping our conversation? It keeps our typists in work.

TP: No problem, Juan.

JCR: And you're welcome to have a copy. In fact, let me make a note to my secretary [Long pause] Done. You'll get a copy every time I do.

TP: As you like.

JCR: I read your manuscript last night. Twice, in fact.

TP: I hope you liked it.

JCR: Very much. If you don't mind, I thought we'd start off by discussing it this morning. Just to clarify some things in my mind. I've made some notes on the manuscript, in pencil, I hope that's okay?

TP: Clarify away.

JCR: Your story of your childhood stops in year 8 of school.

TP: Yes.

JCR: How old were you?

TP: Thirteen I think.

JCR: That's quite young to be finished with childhood. You don't have anything else you would like to add, after that age?

TP: Nothing of relevance.

JCR: School kept on about the same?

TP: Same old same old.

JCR: You went well at school?

TP: Enough to get into Arts at Uni.

JCR: Liberal Arts yes? I wished I'd done Arts. Maybe one day. I've taken some courses in the evenings at the University of Havana, English literature was the last. But too much Chaucer for me.

TP: I would've thought 20th century Russian would be more the style of Havana Uni.

JCR: Now, now, comrade. We let you in, didn't we?

TP: My books are hardly an opiate for the masses.

JCR: Let's not bring Marx into our discussion. It's too boring. Typist, don't type that bit please. [Short Pause] I bet she will though. [Short Pause] Now let me look at my notes [unintelligible mumble] Yes. Beany was your best friend?

TP: In primary school. I lost track of him soon after going to high school.

JCR: Interesting, because from what I read, I felt you were closer to Rydges.

TP: [Medium pause] Possibly.

JCR: More connected somehow. He was the one whom you could talk to about anything.

TP: I guess.

JCR: Yes, that makes sense to me. [Long Pause]. This little task I set you, is this your first autobiographical piece of writing?

TP: It's the only one I've written in first person. Like most writers, I add bits of my past, filtered through the eyes of other characters.

JCR: I read this novel of yours, written some years back. *The Hanging Dog*?

TP: Did you like it?

JCR: Yes, a strange story. It was not autobiographical at all, I would think.

TP: No, I think not. Nothing much in that story ever happened to me in real life.

JCR: Is it more difficult to write pure fantasy like in *The Hanging Dog*, as a writer I mean, or was it easier to write my task.

TP: This was easier. Much easier. No imagination involved, just some editing down to pick the story out of the chaos.

JCR: Yes, that was my guess too. Because you write what you have seen. A much quicker process. The dialogue was made up though?

TP: In a lot of cases. I didn't have a tape recording of my life, as you seem to like. But some of it I remember pretty well, and the rest conveys the sentiment of what happened.

JCR: A literary device, yes? But the descriptions of the surroundings seem to read as you really remembered them.

TP: Yes, which is why the writing is easier.

JCR: Like the colors you describe. I've made a list. [Medium pause] The chalkboard was?

TP: Green.

JCR: The Perkins paste tub was?

TP: Pink.

JCR: The jelly at the swimming carnival was?

TP: Orange. Flavor and color.

JCR: What was the color of your school uniform in primary school?

TP: [Medium Pause] I can't remember. High school yes, but not primary.

JCR: Yes exactly. You call them gray and white in the manuscript. From the black and white photograph you have kept, any color would be shades of that. And you describe your high school uniform very precisely, even the colors of the tie. Our high school memories are always more vivid. [Medium pause] What was the color of the Valiant that you threw the rocks at?

TP: [Medium pause] I can't remember.

JCR: Yes. And you didn't give it a color in the manuscript. But the things you remember the color of, you describe them as such. The red hair of Lisa and Beany, the jelly, the chalkboard. And what you didn't remember is left in shades of gray or without description. Mainly without description. I'm impressed with the consistency of this.

TP: Glad I could please.

JCR: What was the color of the ice-cream truck?

TP: [Medium pause] Red.

JCR: Yes, red striped. It is interesting you remember this so well. It was a truck that you threw the large rock at but missed.

TP: [No audible response]

JCR: Your literary style is often colorful though. In *The Hanging Dog*, you describe lots of things with color. I made some notes [unintelligible mumble]. What is the color of the chef's picture frame? Or the [pause] plaster wall of the library? Or the [pause] fisherman's boat?

TP: [No audible response].

JCR: Bear with me Tom, this interest in literature is not just a fancy of mine.

TP: [Long pause]. I can't remember.

JCR: Yes, exactly. Because you've made them all up. Pure fiction.

TP: I guess. That makes sense.

JCR: But in this manuscript, besides Heather's dolls—which we both know the reason for the detailed color memory—the colors are as they really were.

TP: As you say.

JCR: Like the red ice-cream truck.

TP: Red stripes.

JCR: Like the blue whale tattoo. All blue.

TP: All blue.

JCR: Even the small eye.

TP: Even the small eye.

JCR: [Long pause]. And the color of the hair of his arm you said was red.

TP: [No audible response].

JCR: And his shorts, King Gee according to my notes, were?

TP: Dark blue.

JCR: Yes. Navy blue you wrote. These are very detailed color memories.

TP: [No audible response].

JCR: I even think you could draw the tattoo. It seemed like that to me at least. Reading between the lines, that is. Do writers like us doing that?

TP: [No audible response].

JCR: So what I'm saying, there are only two explanations for such a detailed description. Either they really were as you have written, or you can describe them the same way you describe Heather's dolls. Would you agree?

TP: [Short pause] Yes.

JCR: And I have no reason to believe, unless you have been hiding something from me, that it's the same reason as the dolls.

TP: Yes.

JCR: So the detail of the ice-cream truck and its driver, the blue whale tattoo, is real.

TP: Must be.

JCR: I must say, a very vivid memory.

TP: Yes.

JCR: And what was the color of the drink you and the boys had after escaping from the blue whale?

TP: [No audible response].

JCR: Let me turn the page to make sure I wrote it correctly? [Medium pause]. Yes, here it is.

TP: [No audible response].

JCR: Tom?

TP: [Medium pause]. I can't remember the color.

JCR: But you wrote it was yellow. Let me read it. [Short pause] 'I entered the backyard to find them sprawled on the lawn, holding cups of yellow drink.'

TP: [No audible response].

JCR: An odd color for a drink. It must have been lemon [Short pause] or pineapple.

TP: [No audible response].

JCR: So you don't remember the color of the drink. This is strange to me, Tom. It's the only inconsistency in your color writing. [Long pause]. But I think it makes sense, doesn't it? [Medium pause] It's the same reason you can't remember the colors of the fisherman's boat or the library wall or the picture frame in *The Hanging Dog*. This passage is pure fiction.

TP: [No audible response].

JCR: That section was a bit differently written too. The prose more rich, as you would write in the third person, like in *The Hanging Dog*. And there was a lot of swearing, yes? Everyone kept saying fuck. How old were you then, nine? That's a lot of swearing for boys of nine. Not angry swearing I thought, more of despair. [Medium pause] The blue whale is true of course, no doubt about that. Such a vivid color memory. But I think the escape you made the first time, and seeing Rydges coming back down the road crying, then later him coming out of the bushes with the blue whale following, I don't think that really ever happened. To Rydges, that is.

TP: [No audible response].

[Long pause]

JCR: You were Rydges in those scenes, yes?

TP: [No audible response].

[Long pause]

JCR: I'm sorry, Tom. I know this is upsetting. [Long pause] I think we should take a break for a bit. Perhaps meet in the afternoon. Unless you're okay to continue?

TP: [No audible response].

[Long pause]

END OF TAPE RECORDING.

Tell Me About Your Time In Cuba

I had come to Cuba from Salvador Bahia, where I'd spent some months writing a collection of short stories based in the Pelourinho. My agent was against it but I did it anyway.

The Pelo is like Havana in many ways—a pastel of old colonials that rise and fall in a high mound overlooking the blue of the ocean. The color is vivid, some vistas as painted on a large canvas backdrop from an opera, and the color bleeds and peels like Havana, the bright façades hiding the detritus—and there is much need of repair. The faces around are black too. And they smile and laugh and shuffle their feet in the same musical way.

I stayed in the heart of the Pelo in the Casa Amarelindo, its entrance opening onto a cobblestone path that dropped steeply to one of those canvas vistas in a long square further down. My room was on the bay side, and I wrote on the balcony or in the palm-filled bar that opened to the sky by a winding iron staircase. I had two caipirinhas for lunch every day and I wandered in the cooler late afternoons in search of stories, which were never far away. I was being a good boy at the time, so my life there was rather solitary but still pleasant and productive enough.

I left Bahia and Brazil after Fat Tuesday. I had watched the Carnaval as popcorn on the vast lawn leading up to the lighthouse at Forte de Santo Antônio da Barra. After a while I went to a party my friend had organized, which stood high opposite, all protected and safe and clean, and I watched the trio elétrico snail past into the evening. I watched, sipping Red Bull and vodka, the swarming blocos packed behind tightly manned ropes, as thick as arms, dancing a trail behind the great speakers and the lit up bands on top—leather clad with shiny bronzed bikinis at their sides—the samba moving the bloco as a great wave of hands; and the popcorn kept outside on the street, waving their arms, and their hips low and writhing, sweating skin all black as the night. And I watched the cream helmets of the police who moved like caterpillars with their truncheons black like the skin of the street, and the white eyes against the black that widened and flurried away from the helmets' path, and the percussion and the bass that shook the ground as the trios passed.

And I watched a group of youths run at the base of the stand until the truncheons, the same color as their skin, met them, belting down on their skulls and backs and legs, their arms twisted back to protect their heads, with bruises forming proud welts on their flesh. I watched this up high and protected, with the other faces all white as ivory, with ruby-red lipstick bright against the white, with their eyes that looked over the fat sticks that fell down on the boys—their white gaze floating above and over as if it wasn't happening—which I guess it wasn't—all safe and clean and high above it all. And the loneliness of it got to me.

And so I left Salvador the next day.

And went cold turkey, as was my plan.

It is a withdrawal without the catarrh, the watermelon pupils, the gut cramps. No spewing in a bucket soiled with the mud of my ass, dear Juan. This cold turkey is served up on a plate, thinly sliced at first, then in big chunks of white meat and skin and cranberry sauce.

I left my yellow-scored treasure in the waste bin of my room, not flushing it as I normally would—watching it swirl around a bit, to dissolve with the scum at the bottom of the bowl.

Though it can't do much harm, can it, if the maid happens to find it?

This yellow-scored treasure of mine can't do much harm.

Can it, Juan?

* * *

"I'm here to farm," I said for the first time, just to hear how it sounded on my lips.

"Farm good in Cuba?" she asked.

"For me . . . the best."

She chewed at the straw in her mojito—her second that I knew of, the first gulped down without the need for it. She looked up at me, with her downy-fine moustache rippling as she chewed.

"Farm tobacco?"

"Cassava."

"What cassava?"

"Manioc. You get tapioca from it."

"Ah mandioca, sí." She slurped some more of her glass and smiled up at me again. "I like mandioca. I cook good mandioca."

The air of the bar was wet and heavy, which leaked through the timber bars from the pedestrian Obispo Street, all sundrenched and bustling. The chatter spilled in and out and covered us like a big warm overcoat.

"Yanela make you mandioca, sí?"

I smiled and pointed to the ring on her finger. "You make for him?"

She shook her head. "Husband gone."

"Gone where?"

"To hell." She grinned at me and sucked more of her mojito. "Where farm in Havana?"

"Close by, but I haven't started yet."

"You farm Australia?"

"No, never."

"You crazy, sí?"

"Sí."

She flashed her white teeth into a grin. "Yanela make good mandioca for crazy farmer." She looked around at the others as they moved over to the corner of the bar. "Where you stay?"

"Hotel Nacional."

"Oh . . . lot of money."

"Enough. I'm just there until I find a place."

"Casa better. I look for you, sí?"

"Your house?"

"No. We just meet." She laughed and her moustache laughed too.

"I didn't mean . . ."

"You sweet boy."

"Boy . . . I haven't been a boy for thirty years."

"Experience better, sí?"

She chewed her straw and watched the women in the band, like her all dressed in black, who were waiting to play.

"My casa little. Mother, Yanela, and Benita."

"Benita is your daughter?"

"Cat." She slurped up her drink and drifted off the stool. "No rest for us. Guantanamera, Guantanamera. I hit you if you ask play Guantanamera."

Light flung through on the women in a loud haze—on bongo drums and guitars and a big double bass that nearly touched the low ceiling. She picked up the maracas and chattered into the huddle and they started to play a salsa. I looked around and watched the clutter of the bar and their smiles and their swinging heads in the heat. Their dancing shoulders. Their dancing eyes.

The floor was filled with tables of gringos, gray haired and young, fat cigars and Minoltas. I turned to the barman and signaled for another drink and I realized my head was moving like all the others. The white grimy tiles glimmered behind and the barman swung his flask in time to the music.

Outside, the sun shone bright on the street, and the color poured in on us. Through the timber bars, Old Havana slowed and listened with their black faces; smiled and nodded; some twisted their hips and skipped. An old man, toothless and gaunt, held a little girl and twirled her to the beat and she laughed and pushed him away. He took his dance down and out of sight and more came and looked in through the bars. The bongos sung up the salsa and the girls all danced in their black garb and grinned out into the mall and the inside clutter of tourists and locals and all.

She moved so nice. Her skin dark chocolate. Her hair black and permed flat. As she swung her hips the silver bangles on her wrists jingled with the maracas. She smiled at me, and my head swam with the mojitos and the heat of the song. And the music flooded the bar and continued to rush out onto the street—music that was penned some time ago, but surely meant only to be played in this little sundrenched bar on Obispo Street.

* * *

The Hotel Nacional was expensive, but it felt like a safe rock to live on when I first arrived in Havana. Cuba is not for the faint hearted, as you well know, Juan. It can throw up fences in your path when it wants, some with slats just wide enough to squeeze through, others so high you shrug and go back the way you came.

When I first arrived, my passport was taken at the airport. I knew my visa and papers were all okay, so I went with the flow, but I always get nervous whenever my passport is out of sight. I was taken with a small herd of other foreigners to a long table and asked to open my bags. A meticulous check if ever there was—a message more than anything.

Of course, as you know, they did have something to worry about with me. But they had no way of finding that out at the time.

After I arrived and settled in the Nacional, I took a cab into Old Havana. I had walked only a block before a woman approached me. She was young and pretty and spoke lyrical English. I knew that whatever she offered I'd be better off without. But I took the scam, an expensive drink in the bar where some of the Buena Vista Social Club were supposed to play, I can see you smiling at this Juan, with an espresso close by. These scams come flying in all directions in Havana, and one is bound to smack you in the face eventually.

But then back in Obispo I met Billy.

The mojito woman and her group had just played a session and were passing the hat around. They didn't bother with Billy. His gray mane shone with sweat, his face flushed with the red and blue lines of the often parched. A bulbous nose to match.

"I'm not an alcoholic in the true sense of the word." He grinned and dropped his sweaty forehead down and touched mine. The sticky heat clung to Billy like a wet mop. "But, Tom, what's better than a drink? Tell me, sage. Tell me this and I'll stop drinking this instant."

"Amour?"

"Oh, the L word. How dare you bring that vile utterance into the sanctity of this establishment." He crossed himself. "What the fuck has love got me. This is what I love the most." He lifted his glass in the air. "No doubt about it . . . this is the great darling of my life. My doctor says I've the liver the size of a newborn calf. I told him if I succumb I'll donate it to science, but the old bastard said it would be better going to a delicatessen. It would make the best fucking pâté in Havana!" When he laughed sweat splashed onto the table like early rain. "But I love it, Tom. The taste of it. The floating never care of it. It raises me off my seat . . . this piss weak little stool we're sitting on. I'm levitating, my good man." He swigged his rum or scotch or something of that color. "You see, I'm not an alcoholic because it just isn't harmful to me. It has to be harmful doesn't it? I mean . . . a day-to-day harm. I can live with the big liver. The nasty end. Vomit up blood, or get the shakes. Fall on people even if I haven't touched a drop. But the journey, Tom. If it ain't harming the journey, then bring it on!" He gulped down the dregs. "Am I a fool, Tom? No bullshit now . . . I kneel before you, sage. Am I a fucking fool?"

I was in no position to argue. "Sounds like a plan, Billy."

He beamed. "I knew you would understand. From the first moment we met, I knew you would get it. Let's drink to it then." He turned to the barman. "José, what the fuck is holding you up?"

The barman wiped a glass and raised an eyebrow just enough to register Billy's request.

"It's just math, Tom. The balance sheet of life. You add up the good hours and subtract the bad. Whoever has the highest number wins!" Billy's grin left no doubt as to the magnitude of his score.

"I like the music here," I said. "These girls are good."

"They're all right."

"That's an impressive scar you have there." The bottom button of his shirt was unfastened showing a ragged keloid across his midsection.

"The bastard nearly killed me. It was my fault though. He took my wallet, which was okay. But then he wanted my watch. And I didn't want to give it to him. My own stupid fault." He gulped at his tan drink. "They caught him on the same day, just up the road. He answered the door with the fucking watch on. I felt sorry for the poor bugger."

Yanela had finished passing the hat around. Some of the other players were sitting with customers at little round tables. A pair of men with fat cigars lent back on their chairs in front of us.

Billy lowered his head to mine, his wet nose brushing against my cheek. "These bloody Italians and their cigars. And they want only one thing." He sat up straight in his stool and turned to the barman, pointing his head in the direction of the cigars. "Tourists really piss me off, José."

The barman smiled.

Billy took out his wallet and showed me a picture of a young boy whose face was the color of his drink. "My son. I saw him yesterday. What a card he is. His mum, not so much." He shone a wide grin at me. "But he keeps me young, this little lad of mine. Fancy that, I'm sixty-six." He emptied his glass. "Yet there's other ways to keep young at heart."

"You've lived here a while then?"

"On and off for fifteen years. But I'm out of here if the bloody Americans ever come back. As soon as they land, I'm off."

Yanela came over again with her hat and shoved it in Billy's face. She pulled a face at him, her fine moustache rippling on her lip.

"For me, darling?" he said.

"You love us, you say, but never money?"

"Is there a better customer than I? You comprender?"

"I comprender. I comprender everything about you." She smiled at me and looked back at Billy. "You farmer friend give good money."

"How much?"

She showed him my five CUC note in the hat.

"Jesus, Tom, pace yourself. These girls will take your bloody bank account if you give them a chance."

She waggled the hat. "I have a problem home."

"That's not *my* problem." Billy's face colored up. "Who do you think I am, Father fucking Christmas?"

Yanela stared at him and then at me. I wasn't sure what to say so I kept quiet. In time, I've got used to the wounded silences that often lingered around Billy's angst.

"You play tonight?" she asked at last.

"Tomorrow," Billy said.

"Where?"

"La Zorra."

"You play music?" I asked him.

She looked at me and nodded her head. "He play good."

"You come and see me?" he asked her.

She pulled a stool over and sat in a triangle with us. "I might." She looked at me. "You come too?"

I liked her downy moustache. I liked that she didn't hide it. And so I said I'd come.

We had another round of drinks. The mojitos were weak, which was probably for the best. I looked over through the open timber bars that separated the inside from the street. I had noticed two teenage girls who had hovered outside for a while, I thought just listening to the music. But they had remained after the session was over and kept on looking over at us.

"Billy, do you know those girls?"

He turned and grimaced in their direction. "Just ignore them."

Yanela twisted a glance and smiled back at me. Billy sat in his stool uneasily, and sipped his drink.

The teens had a conference in the street, before the taller girl came into the bar and over to us. Her hair was curled and painted with golden streaks. Her sandstone colored face brushed with pink rouge. Her eyes lined with blue. She looked about fifteen, if that—and if she wanted the part of Lolita, it was hers for the taking.

Billy looked up at the girl who stood shy in front of him. "I . . . am . . . with . . . my . . . friend. Comprender?" Billy had lived in Cuba for fifteen years, but I soon realized had never learnt a word of Spanish. Except for 'comprender.'

The girl smiled at me.

"This . . . is . . . a . . . bar. You . . . underage. Comprender?"

She kept smiling at me and I held my breath a moment. I wasn't certain the others saw her smile the same way. Billy didn't seem to raise an eyebrow, even though she kept that Lolita look of hers, always pointed in my direction.

I breathed up a sigh and broke the spell—the booze-lit bar now painted a shade lighter.

The girl stood still a second or so with a frown, then twisted around and, tall narrow legs bending like stilts, went back into the hurry of the street. I watched the two in conference again, but it was only brief, and they soon moved away, arm-in-arm, and out of sight. Yanela stared at both of us and looked like she was going to say something insightful. But she sat quiet with her hat full of coins and said nothing.

A silver haze cast onto the players as we drifted easily into the afternoon. Of white rum and lime and mint and salsa. We watched the tourists come and go and we didn't have a care in the world. Yanela's maracas shook the salsa up and I watched her all smiling and tired. Cuba has a tired feel about it—a long sweaty tired that picks up after a siesta, then drifts tired into the night. And wakes tired.

Later, as dusk brewed, I saw Billy nodding his head to the street—deep and pendulous—like an actor at a curtain call. Soon the blond-streaked Lolita came into the bar and over to us. She didn't look tired at all.

She said something to him that I couldn't understand. I wasn't sure what it was because of the music or the language or the mojitos. Behind, her friend slinked at the bar's entrance—her black hair styled tight to her head, seeming almost painted on.

Billy gave a nod and said something in a whisper that I didn't catch. I watched the maracas dance a salsa as she skipped off to her girlfriend—and take her arm back into the street.

"Who are they?" I asked.

"My girlfriends." He shrugged his shoulders and shone up a grin. "What can I do? They want to fuck me."

* * *

The next night I caught a taxi to Billy's jazz gig at the Fox and the Crow—a low-lit basement in the Vedado. I got there before the first set, at half eleven.

When I arrived, Yanela greeted me at the door with a fumbling kiss. She looked nice and had fresh eyes, even though she had played for most of the day back on Obispo. I paid the twenty CUC cover for both of us, not cheap for Havana, and she took my arm into the dim downstairs and I felt light on my feet.

Billy had kept us a table at the front of the stage and seemed pleased to see us. He introduced us to the band, all leaning easy around their instruments like good jazz musicians always do.

Billy gestured across the room. "Isaac, come and meet a friend of mine."

A man with a goatee came over.

"This, Tom, is the guy who runs the joint . . . and pays me, though not a fucking lot."

"Big crowd tonight," the goatee said.

"They smell talent, Isaac,"

He pointed to our table. "Only the best for Billy's friends. You're welcome here any time. First drink's on the house."

"Dos mojitos," Yanela said.

"I'll say this for you maraca girl," Billy said. "You're consistent."

The session started and Billy's voice was like crushed velvet. It surprised me—I don't know why. Perhaps I was expecting a revisit of the fake Buena Vista Social Club. But I was relieved he was the real deal. We sat with the saxophone and trumpet, the percussion and keyboard, and drank slowly into the night, Billy grinning at us while he played—so we felt like the whole set was for just for us.

> *My baby don't care for shows*
> *My baby don't care for clothes*
> *My baby just cares for me.*

Billy's voice was the color of the night.

> *My baby don't care for . . . cars and races . . .*
> *My baby don't care for . . . high-tone places . . .*

I soaked it in, unwound, my head settling in its familiar, friendly, safe place.

"He good, sí."

"Very. Have you and the chicas played here?"

"No. This número uno." Yanela's smile tasted like syrup.

"I like your band just as much."

"You sweet, farm boy." She reached over and held my hand.

"Maybe Billy can organize you to play here?"

She shook her head. "No Guantanamera here."

> *My baby just cares for*
> *Just says his prayers for*
> *My baby just cares for me.*

At the break Billy came and sat with us, his gray mop sweat-stuck to his face, his eyes—performers' eyes—shone with the need to be nowhere other than on stage. More goatees and berets came up and said hello, and Isaac shouted us all another round of drinks.

"You Australian?" Isaac asked.

"I have no fixed address really."

"You have . . . how do you say . . . itchy feet."

"Sometimes so much they bleed."

Isaac grinned. "We get a lot of itchy feet coming to Cuba." He motioned to the waiter who brought the drinks to our table. "Where you go next?"

"He farm," Yanela said.

"Itchy feet yes . . . but not many farmers." He waved to a table behind us. "You make sure we see you some more." He drifted away into the low-lit haze.

And I wondered whether I would be able to come here again, further down the road. Whether I could dust myself off, scrape the grit from under my nails, and find my way back for a bit.

And I wondered whether I'd be welcome.

* * *

At the end of the evening I walked with Yanela, arm-in-arm, down the quiet streets of the Vedado, sparsely lit from the odd balcony door. We chatted about Billy's jazz, his talent, and how she wished she could write music like him as well as play it.

I told her she was talented and she kissed me. I liked the touch of her downy lip and my light feet kept on as we walked down the gray-coffee side streets.

When we reached her casa she asked me inside. I kissed her again and told her she was beautiful, but I couldn't come up.

It took only five minutes to walk back home.

* * *

Obispo Street is a narrow pedestrian way of bent old colonials, which runs down a shallow slope for eight hundred meters or so to the Plaza de Armas, then just a short skip to the neck of the bay. Every city in Latin America has something akin to Calle Obispo—a place to amble, a meeting of eyes and smiles and handshakes that spill into bars, and music and little eateries and trinkets for tourists, with carts of flowers and sellers of scams and the hustle of it all. The journey down Obispo can take ten minutes or an afternoon.

When I first arrived in Havana I was drawn to the street. I wanted to stroll unnamed, where I could taste the city full on, or dodge around it if I felt the need. I thought about finding a little casa on the street to board, so I could drop out into the bustle when I needed an escape from my solitude. But I was worried about the noise at night, so I looked off track a bit, where dogs lazed in the sun and linen dried on little worn balconies, and no one sold flowers or cigars or anything, out in the open at least.

I needed a safe place as well, of course, before I learned to till the earth. A place of transition—a Dantean Purgatory in Old Havana.

I moved into the open green of the Plaza de Armas and sat on a marble bench under the shade of a vast tree. It was midday but the park kept the heat at bay. I had just browsed the second hand booksellers that lined the edge of the trees. Most of their wares were in Spanish, weathered tomes of Che Guevara and Revolución, a nice memento for a son if I'd ever had one. I found some Hemingway paperbacks in English and bought a novel he wrote only a hundred meters away, back on Obispo. I opened the book under the shade of the leaves.

No man is an Iland, intire of it selfe...

She sat down next to me and started kicking her thin black legs up and down in the shade. She smiled and stretched her legs out straight—with delicate, snow-white sneakers and socks only a half an inch above their lips. And her little white shorts. All white against the black.

She smiled at me again. A big bucktoothed smile, and I wondered about her teeth.

And therefore never send to know for whom the bell tolls; it tolls for thee.

I gazed ahead at the marble statue that stood high above the foliage. He had a thick bowtie and a long white coat, and he stood at ease with one hand in his pocket, looking straight at me. There was no wind blowing, and the red, white and blue flag drooped in the still air, up and to the right of the man.

She kicked her legs again within the invisible pool of the shade.

I put Hemmingway on my knee and sat quiet for a while.

"It beautiful day," she said. Her voice was husky.

I kept my gaze at her stick legs that waded in the shallow gray. "Yes, beautiful."

"It good book?"

"The best."

She made little splashes with her legs. "It too nice a day to be outside."

I smiled.

"Sí, señor. It too nice to be in park, too nice to be at beach, too nice to be—"

"—anywhere out in this glorious day."

"Sí, you understand." She wrapped her top lip over her buckteeth, yet managed a grin.

"What about the art museum?"

"Señor, it far too nice day to be in museo."

"How about lunch in a good restaurant?"

"Better, but no long lunch." She smiled. "It too nice day."

"It looks like we're running out of places."

"No worry, señor. I find us a place."

And I wondered about her teeth again, and all that went with it.

* * *

I looked down all sweaty over her as she lay on her back with her head turned away. So she could imagine I wasn't there? Or imagine I was someone else?

I understood this well.

I was drawn to her by this.

Her name was Rosie and she had a big horizontal scar on her stomach down low where her female parts were found. It was a thick-bubbled cord, the color of a bruised pear, and I played my finger over it. She told me about the bad job the doctor had done. How, after the birth, they took everything out they could find. She shook her head and read my Cuban *Lonely Planet* as I traced my finger over the bumps of the scar.

After we met in the park I took her for lunch at a tourist café that lay open across from the water. This was my first meal outside of the Nacional. I gave her a menu and she looked over it tentatively. I ordered fish and congri, and she had fried chicken and moros. When the food came though, she picked the thick batter off the meat and ate only a mouthful. Perhaps she had eaten just before we met, although I didn't think so. I had two mojitos and she had a juice. She was as skinny as a rake and I thought I understood why.

The food came to the table quickly and we didn't have a chance to say much. In fact, I can't remember what we talked about at all. The mojitos were strong, and a wind blew off the bay, and I felt surprisingly good.

The waiter had found a place for us—just next to the café where an old woman smiled and waited outside for us to come. She told me how much, and I gave her the money up front. The old woman made a clucking sound, pinched my cheek, and took us inside and up the stairs of the casa. The walls were freshly painted sky-blue, the ceiling white with ornate cornices of tiny painted fruit. Cherries and grapes with green leaves. She showed us the pristine tiled bathroom, with the wash facilities of just a hose and bucket, then took us up to the bedroom—a little hamlet of a room—with a crimson cupboard painted with flowers, and a double bed with a floral spread to match and pillows as white and soft as cotton wool.

As I lay with Rosie she showed me on a map where she was from—Holguín—a long day's bus travel away. I wondered where she stayed in Havana but I didn't ask her. I wondered whether her child was in Holguín, and about the rest of her family, but I didn't ask that either.

I had never been with an African woman before. African descent of course—her family tree would trace back to the West African slave trade, either directly or over the ninety mile Windward Passage from Haiti, or a bit farther across the Caribbean Sea from Jamaica.

She found a way to please me, and I paid her very well.

When we were leaving, the old woman was waiting for us outside the casa—cooling in a breeze that drifted from the bay. She shone a wide grin and took my arm back inside showing me the downstairs lounge, which was as cozy as the hamlet upstairs. She couldn't speak English, but Rosie told me that the room was available. So I moved in the next day and the old woman became my second mother.

* * *

The old woman's name was Estelle, and she was waiting for me outside the sky-blue casa the following morning as if she had never moved. This was her little patch of turf, just outside the front door of the house, which sat as a small freestanding box, two stories with white timber shutters—all alone amongst the taller colonials on either side, with bars on their doors and windows, and large balconies that tipped toward the bay.

Estelle lifted her arms and clicked her tongue against her palate—the way she greeted her neighbors who passed by on the foreshore and invariably stopped to chat with the breeze and the heat and the water out front. Her face was the color of karri pine, a rich orange-brown from these long hours spent smiling out at the sun.

After a week or so I bought her a hat and a fold-up canvas chair. She kissed me and seemed pleased, but whenever I returned home, the hat would be sitting on the chair and she would be standing next to it like she was waiting for a bus. Sometime she would keep a pitcher of iced limewater on the chair, which she poured into plastic cups and shared with the passersby, clicking her palate in welcome.

As my Spanish improved, I learned Estelle's husband had died ten years before. I'm not sure from what. Her son lived in Miami and wanted her to live with him, but she never stayed for long. She had photographs of her grandchildren on every bench top in the house, and she made lacquered boxes, with seashells embossed on their tops, to give to them each time they visited. After a month, I told her if they came I could move back into a hotel, and she kissed me and shook her head. And later in the night she knocked on my door and gave me one of the boxes, too.

We ate together on most evenings. I would write my childhood memories into the dusk, with a plate of fried empanadas sitting next to my laptop, which I grazed on before dinner. Virtually every night, congri was brought to the table in a big copper pot. It was made fresh daily with salted pork. Usually we would have a salad, and sometimes an extra meat dish or fish. On Fridays we'd have lobster.

We sat together at the table in the lounge room, always laid out with a white cotton-laced tablecloth. I would have my pocket Spanish dictionary on hand, and we would talk in broken dialect that took its time lazy into the meal, and she would tell me about the people she had chatted with during the day. I could feel the story collection beginning to build, though writing it would have to wait until my work with you was done, Juan.

My bedroom window opened out into the front of the house, and I had a view of the water from my writing desk. When any friend of Estelle's had something more interesting to say, she would lead them down toward the edge of the road and wave up at me. This gesture was in the guise of an introduction, but its purpose was so I could put a face to the story she would tell me over the evening congri. A gossip over rice and black beans.

There was Señora Echemendía, whose son was said to be in jail for smuggling computers into Cuba. Estelle laughed at this and said Javier wouldn't know where to get an electric shaver. He was really in jail for . . . she took my dictionary and shuffled the pages clucking her tongue as the pages flapped. In time she frowned and shook her head—she couldn't find the word—so she got up from the table and went outside. A few minutes later she brought the waiter in from the open café a few doors away.

"Marijuana," he said. He looked at me like Miss Quinter giving the answer to a geography question.

Estelle made her clicking sound, pinched his cheek, and he went back out into the night.

"No computadora." She chuckled.

A regular visitor in the sun was a gray haired man, always well dressed in a waistcoat and bowtie. His face was usually hidden away by a panama that tilted over his forehead—and from my window up high, it kept his identity a mystery. Estelle had never taken him to the edge of the road, which I thought strange for such a regular acquaintance. He looked to me like he'd have a few stories to tell. I broached the subject of the man as we sat with espressos on the table. Estelle made espressos like the Italians, boiling water up through the ground beans in a little silver pot.

"Ah, Señor Pupo." She smiled, reached over the table, and gave my face a soft slap. "Él me ama."

I didn't need my dictionary for that. "He loves you?"

"Sí, he love me."

Señor Pupo was an old lover of Estelle's, before she met her husband—just after the revolution. I asked her whether he was a widower like her.

"No. Su esposa está viva." His wife is alive. "Muy muy vivo." Very, very, alive.

She shook her head and told me how, before her husband died, the four of them used to play dice together in an old club in the Vedado. She told me how he always asks to come inside the house—to use the toilet or get a drink or come in from the heat. Sometimes he pretends to be ill. She told me that even if he collapsed on the street and had a fit, he would never be allowed to enter the casa.

I asked her whether she had a boyfriend, and she said she had no time for them anymore,

"Ese tiempo ha pasado." That time has passed.

* * *

It was late afternoon and I sat at my desk, having just wrapped up the tale of the fireworks, I believe. From the corner of my eye I saw Estelle waving at me from the edge of the road. On her other arm clung a gray haired woman who had a suitcase in her hand. I waved back, and the gray woman nodded her head, and they moved back toward the front of the casa and out my sight.

When I came down the stairs a couple of hours later, they were both sitting at the table. Estelle rarely drank, but there was a bottle of Havana Club and Tukola on the table and a couple of tall glasses half full. Estelle stood up and staggered over to give me a kiss. She dragged me to the table and poured a hefty mix of three-parts rum, one-part cola, and plopped a cut lime into the glass.

The gray woman looked like she was less used to alcohol than Estelle, and she lurched on her seat like it was a mechanical bull. As I approached the table she made to stand, but I quickly placed my hand on her shoulder to avoid the fractured hip that would surely follow.

"No tenemos el hielo." We have no ice, Estelle said. They had used it all up. "Es Señora Pupo."

Ah.

Señora Pupo hiccupped after her introduction. Estelle's ex-lover's wife was indeed very much alive.

I looked through to her bedroom and saw the gray woman's opened suitcase on the bed, with a few items laid out on the spread. I suspected the bottle of Havana Club had interrupted the unpacking. Señora Pupo hiccupped again.

Estelle gulped at her glass, then swiftly leapt into a passionate slurry of Spanish—of which I understood little. When we needed to communicate in a more sophisticated way, I used the Spanish translator on my laptop, which I quickly set up on the dining table. The program had an audio translator as well, but the rum-slurred words of my storytellers seemed well beyond the capability of the speech recognition software. So I sat comfortably with my glass of Cuba Libre and watched the tale slowly unfold by the one-finger typing of two old women who were as pissed as newts.

Señora Pupo had left Señor Pupo—for good. She had been cleaning out the attic with the aim of renting the room, when she came upon a bound lump of letters, still in their envelopes, with the postage stamps ranging over a decade. They were all addressed to Estelle, and all marked to return to the same sending address—to Señor Pupo—at the club where he still played dice twice a week with a group of old men in the Vedado. Most of the letters were unopened.

They were, of course, immediately opened and read by Señora Pupo. They described Señor Pupo's undying, yet unrequited, love for Estelle. Some were just a few sentences, the shortest 'te quiero,' I love you, while others went on for pages. Señora Pupo had read these in the attic while her husband was playing dice. By the time he returned, she was packed and gone. And when he did arrive home, he would find the letters all neatly placed, one after the other, in a trail that started at the front door, and snaked into their bedroom, ending at a photograph of Señor and Señora Pupo on their wedding day—but with Señor Pupo's head cut off at his shoulders.

Señora Pupo gave up a staccato of hiccups and looked like she might fall off the chair again. I saw a vision of her standing behind a Zimmer frame with one leg shorter than the other. Both women looked up at me with their eyes full of rum and fervor. I had finished my drink but longed for another.

"Él es un cerdo." They both said this as one. "Él es un cerdo . . . Él es un cerdo." He is a . . . something.

Estelle typed it in with her index finger stiff as a pencil. Señora Pupo tried to help as well.

I read the screen and nodded. "He is a pig." What other response could I give?

Estelle said that Señora Pupo would be staying with us until they found a way of removing Señor Pupo from his lodgings. I offered to move out for a while, but the gray woman hiccupped a loud protest. Estelle said they would both sleep together in her bed. They were little and would have plenty of room.

She laughed and typed in another message.

"We always slept together as children. But my sister snores."

* * *

"They'll cut poor Pupo's balls off," Billy said.

"Where will he go?"

"Nowhere. This is Cuba. You can't just sell up and move into a condo. I tell you, he'll die in that house with his balls stuffed deep down his throat. Ask our friend about it."

The girls had finished their session on Obispo, and Yanela sat with us at the corner of the bar in a triangle.

"What's home like now, Maraca girl. With your ex . . . *Amour*?" Billy raised his eyebrows at me as he said the L word.

"Good . . . when *he* not there."

"When *is* he there?"

"Every two day. Some more, some less."

"Cozy."

"He sleep on floor in front of TV. Not my room. He go, when other girl husband go."

"Cuban musical chairs."

"My mother hate him."

"Of course she does, my dear. Of course she does. What does Shakespeare say . . . hell has no furor . . . ?"

"Hell hath no fury like a woman scorned," I said.

"Well said, Tom. You know Shakespeare, maraca girl? Shakespeare? Comprender?"

"It's Congreve, actually."

"Really, Tom? Anyway . . . truer words have never been spoken."

Yanela chewed at her straw—her fine, furry moustache all a ripple. She was beautiful when she chewed her straw.

Billy said, "Why do you wear that wedding ring, my dear?"

She shrugged. "It still fit."

"What about you, Tom, any old rings or skeletons?"

"I'm sure not as many as you, Billy."

"That goes without saying, and I have some years on you. But you're not a youngster . . . well-travelled for the second half of your forties I'd guess."

"A reasonable guess."

"So you've had time to collect the odd skeleton or two."

Yanela stopped chewing. "What is skeleton?"

"Some dark and nasty past, my dear."

They both looked at me. For a moment, I wondered what they might be seeing.

"Doesn't everyone have them?" I said.

"Everyone not you."

"I've . . . some."

"What number?"

"Really, only one."

"Is skeleton alive?"

"Yes, indeed."

Billy emptied his glass. "Who's up for another round?"

"I'm going slow."

"Come on, Tom."

"I not slow."

"You're never slow my little maraca girl."

"I not you girl. I terminado school. Comprender?"

"I think you've had enough juice for tonight. You're starting to get cheeky."

"Buy drink for us."

"You girls would take the shirt from my back given half a chance. Comprender?"

"Don't want shirt, want Mojito."

We smiled as one, sharing rum-drenched breaths in the keep of our little triangle. Sunlit beams of cigar haze and laughter cut across us.

"My two girls pinched my fucking watch the other day," Billy said. "I looked for it everywhere before I realized it was gone."

"It seems that watch of yours has been passed all over Havana, Billy."

"It's a fake Rolex, but I've become quite smitten with it."

"Did you get it back?"

"I haven't seen them since. But I will, or it's terminado for them."

I tilted my head to a table away from us. "Are those Americans over there?"

"Sí. They give big money. Muy generoso."

"They don't look like government workers. I thought it was illegal for Americans to come here?"

Billy shrugged. "The boys come from Mexico after spring break. The Cubans don't seem to mind."

"Muy muy generoso."

"They might be muy fucking generoso, but once they're allowed in by the busload, I'm fucking out of here."

"There's lots of Canadians around," I said.

"They're all right."

"Canada muy generoso."

"Listen maraca girl, there are more important things to a person than being muy generoso."

"¿qué?"

"What do you mean, what? A spirit of the soul. Someone who is honest to their art. Comprender?"

"No."

"You fucking monkey."

This sounded even worse than calling someone a wog and Miss Quinter's face flashed before me. "Jesus, Billy."

"Well, I get so fucking frustrated with this mind-set."

Yanela sucked up the dregs of the glass through her mangled straw.

"What do you want to drink then?" Billy said to her.

"Mojito."

"José, three Mojitos. And make them strong this time. Sí?"

José said sí, and Yanela smiled at the American boys through a window of our triangle.

"Tom," Billy said, "I'm going to get you that appointment at UNEAC."

"What UNEAC?" Yanela said.

"Union of . . . writers . . . artists . . . of Cuba. I'm a member. It's how I've been allowed to stay here for so long with you and José. We want to keep Tom here too, sí?"

"Sí, sí. Mandioca farmer allow UNEAC?"

"He's a writer. Our very own Hemmingway."

"Hardly, Billy. I'm no Hemmingway."

"Well, give it time, and more mojitos."

"You two loco."

Billy held our hands. "My dear, we three are perhaps the last island of beauty in the world."

"I know that line," I said. "But who said it?"

"Uncle Monty."

"Monty you uncle?"

"Oh how I yearn to see Norman again, with his red hair, and his book of poetry stained with the butter drips from crumpets." Billy erupted in a blush of crimson-faced laughter.

"You two real fucking loco!" Yanela chewed into her straw. Have I mentioned, she was beautiful when she did this.

* * *

So I had two mothers now.

Whenever I came home during daylight, Estelle would be standing outside next to her sister, who sat low on the canvas chair with the straw hat tied tight under her chin.

There had been no news of Señor Pupo since his first and only visit, a day after the Exodus. I thought he was brave. Foolhardy, but brave. It's what began to win me over to him.

His arrival was announced by a panama hat that sailed into the sky at the level of my window. Panama hats must have some kind of aerodynamic uplift from their brims, because this one kept floating like a bird of prey before it eventually landed with a skip on the road. Apparently, Estelle was responsible for its flight. I watched as Señor Pupo slinked away from the shouting women, chasing the hat through the cars, and managing to catch up to it without being struck down.

"Jugar en el tráfico," the women screamed. Play in the traffic. I heard their demonic laughter rise up below my window. At that minute, I made a vow never to cross them.

Señor Pupo was a handsome man—this the first time I saw him without the panama shading his face. Like Señora Pupo he was all gray, with a full head of hair long over his neck, and his eyes lit up below a thick gray brow. His upper lip was adorned with a handlebar moustache, and he reminded me of the marble statue in the Plaza de Armas. To his credit, he brushed his hat off, neatly placed it at the habitual tilt over his face, and moved back towards the casa—only to take a delicate sidestep away down the street when the sisters shrilled something that could have diverted a charging bull from its path.

He never came back after that. Not physically at least. For Señor Pupo was a man of letters and so addressed his pleas, as was his custom, in writing. However, the letters were returned, as was also the custom, unopened.

And, unbeknown to my mothers, I started to develop empathy for the man. This compassion may have been unfounded, but he grew up large in my mind—the heroic romantic—the flawed Latino with a huge heart and little else.

So I found out where the dice room was in the Vedado where I could meet my hero—Señor Pupo.

* * *

My mothers and I sat together around a copper pot of congri and a plate of deep fried chicken. A thin veil of oregano gently covered the table.

They had spent the afternoon carting Señora Pupo's most treasured possessions back to the casa. Cardboard boxes, stacked haphazardly, cluttered the lounge room. Señor Pupo had been home the entire time, watching the women go about their business without raising an objection. He was only allowed to speak when spoken to, which was apparently rare. Señora Pupo said he looked like a puppy on a lead. Estelle thought a dead fish. I tried to imagine something in between but failed.

The black jacket still hung over the back of the lounge chair. Señora Pupo had presented it to me when they first came back. Estelle looked eagerly over her shoulder.

"Muy fino." Very fine.

I agreed. The velour was worn at the elbows, but the pink silk lining was intact without a trace of repair. Señora Pupo preened some lint off the jacket with a clothes brush.

"Muy muy fino." She beckoned me to put it on, Estelle beaming over her shoulder.

The jacket fit perfectly.

"Hombre muy guapo." My mothers turned me around to display all the angles. "Muy guapo . . . muy guapo." Very handsome.

The jacket, of course, was Señor Pupo's favorite. They told me he knew they had taken it, and that he was happy about it.

"He smiled when I packed it into the box", Estelle told me on my laptop translator. I tried to imagine a dead fish smiling and, again, failed.

They turned me slowly around like a mannequin. And as I twirled, a strange feeling came over me, like my upper body was wrapped in Señor Pupo's skin—my empathy welling up within the warmth of the velour—as if he had found a way of being transported to the sky-blue casa—through the jacket, with me as his shaman.

They wanted me to have it, but I refused. This strange second skin feeling keeping on well into the debate. So I took the jacket off and placed it where it now sat—Señor Pupo resting easily on the lounge with us all. And I wondered whether he could smell the fried chicken and oregano from the chair.

* * *

The dice club in the Vedado was in the basement beneath a ballet school. As I arrived, a troupe of young girls in black leotards strutted out of the entrance like little black herons.

When I entered the club it was not as I imagined. It was a stark space, not larger than a big living room, with a couple of framed old photographs of Che and Fidel, and a tiny bar stocked with some bottles of Havana Club. There were six or so round card-tables with worn green felt, some tilting at an angle, like the players, all in a haze of cigar smoke. From above, the ceiling drummed with the sound of pirouettes.

I lost faith in what I was doing there.

I looked around and saw a panama hat on a timber stand in the corner of the room. Señor Pupo was sitting with two other men rolling dice in a cup. He found my gaze, raised an eyebrow, and leaned his head in the direction of the empty chair. I sat down and the men greeted me with a nod.

I wasn't sure what I should say.

"¿Juegas Cubilete?" Señor Pupo said. His handlebar moustache was even larger close up.

I told him slowly that my Spanish was poor, and I didn't know how to play Cubilete.

"That is not true. Your Spanish is excellent," he smiled. "But it gives me a chance to practice my English."

"You don't sound like you need any practice."

"One always needs practice."

I stared at my hero in his paisley bowtie, speaking with the precision of an Oxford don.

"Cubilete is like poker with dice. Five dice, with only five of a kind giving you points. A child can learn in minutes. But I warn you, we play for high stakes." He pointed over to the bar. "The winner of each round pays for the drinks."

"The winner pays?"

"Sí. On our table, there are never losers."

He introduced himself formally as Antonio Luis Pupo, but I could call him Tony. His friends were Héctor and Pedro. They could speak some English, but he would translate as necessary.

So I learned to play Cubilete with three old Cuban men. And was always a winner.

* * *

I played twice a week, Mondays and Thursdays, starting soon after lunch and finishing late in the afternoon but always before nightfall.

Señor Pupo was a retired English teacher. Héctor and Pedro had taught at the same school—Héctor science and Pedro history. Héctor rarely spoke, his mouth busy with a cigar rather than words. Pedro, in contrast, had much to say, and was always interested in my gringo opinion of his world-view.

"Russia too cold for comunismo."

"My friend believes that communism can only thrive in a warm climate," Señor Pupo said.

"China, Laos, Corea del Norte, Vietnam, and Cuba."

"Isn't North Korea cold?"

"Sí. Corea del Norte cold . . . and loco. El comunismo terminará."

"My friend is expecting the end of communism in North Korea at any time. A winter revolution."

Pedro flashed his rum-bruised teeth at me. "What you think?"

"I like your theory."

"It's always best to like Pedro's theories."

Héctor nodded his head and sucked deep into his cigar.

Pedro rolled the cup of dice—his third and final chance, but failed to score.

"Pedro, you haven't won a round in seven years."

"Sí. I no luck." He grinned. "But I thirsty."

Héctor nodded his head and spat out a cloud of smoke over the half-filled glasses. Héctor seemed an extension of the card-table—his arms growing out like thick roots from the moss-green surface. He was the scorekeeper, and in time, I noticed how the ten-point rounds always ended just after Héctor's glass became empty. We drank the Havana Club neat—a custom that took time to adopt. But the communal sipping of the cheap rum kept us in sync, in both heart and mind.

"You world traveler?" Pedro asked at one point.

"Yes, I guess."

"I never gone from Cuba."

"This must be hard for a history teacher."

"The Education department had organized a trip to Russia," Señor Pupo said. "He was to go, but it was cancelled when the wall fell in 89."

Pedro nodded. "Sí. In winter!"

"They were strange and difficult times here," Señor Pupo said. "No petrol from the Soviets. Cars stranded in the streets, left where they ran dry, like fallen soldiers. Some pulled by horses to their homes."

"Sí. Horse car . . . un viaje muy tranquilo." A very smooth ride. Pedro grinned.

"But no petrol meant no tractors and trucks. And that meant no food."

"Sí, Sí. Héctor era un hombre flaco." Héctor was a thin man then. "Un hombre hermoso." A beautiful man. Pedro leant over and gave him a kiss on the forehead.

Héctor nodded his head and drew more into his cigar.

"Pedro, where would you go now if you had the chance?"

"Moscow y St Petersburg."

"And you, Tony."

"I was born in Havana and have lived in the Vedado all my life. Only in two houses. That of my youth, and that of my marriage. At my age, I have everything here I want. It is impossible for me to leave, even for a second."

"Antonio está loco," Pedro said.

"Yes, I might be mad. That is true."

Héctor nodded.

The ballerinas drummed down from the ceiling above us—we their invisible audience. The gentle thud of youth an elixir of sorts.

"I go soon," Pedro said. "Mi aniversario."

Héctor lifted his gaze from the dice to Señor Pupo. A silence drifted into the smoky haze. The table of men had never talked of his homespun tragedy directly, but it hung about the table like Banquo's ghost.

"Then you should go home soon, my friend," Señor Pupo said.

I looked at him. In the weeks of playing the dice, I had never revealed my identity to him, never told him about his second skin in the lounge. I played and drank and soaked in the warm fog and was content. I didn't know why I was here, but it rewarded me like no other place.

Pedro stole a glance at Héctor and leant back in his chair. "I marry for fifty four year. So thirty minute more, no hay problema." He took up the cup of dice. "My roll first . . . I feel luck this time."

* * *

I love the isolation of Cuba—an island untouched by its surroundings whether it wants to be or not. You are never battered by the outside, here. I stopped watching the news on TV, reading newspapers, or listening to radio many years ago. It's one of the reasons I like to travel to foreign-speaking places. In Cuba, all my news is local, told to me by the person sitting opposite, by someone with a connection to the events, a connection that I can appreciate and value myself. I prefer Pedro or Billy's worldview to that of the radio station. And I feel much better for it.

No man is an Iland, intire of it selfe. Perhaps this is so, but I'm willing to give it a damn good try—as you well know, my dear Juan.

* * *

"You no UNEAC?"

"I no UNEAC."

"Because mandioca farmer?" Yanela said.

"No. Because I don't write in Español."

It was the weekend, and Obispo sung up an easy stroll down the way. Tourists and locals alike, playing in the Sunday heat.

The band members' families had come in and out of the bar throughout the afternoon—like a church social—their men hovering large around the seated tourists, holding little curly black-haired babes with mini-plaits tied with ribbons the color of the street, dropping them down into the salsa playground, watching them scurry around the tables full of cheer, then lifting them back up into the high safety of their arms, dancing in their arms, as their mothers swayed their smiles back at them, and played up the music.

"How long you stay?"

"My tourist visa lasts two months," I said. "But I will try for a business visa."

"Mandioca farmer?"

"Something like that."

"You *not* mandioca farmer."

"I will be. When the time is right."

Yanela looked at me hard. "When that? When you start farm?"

"I'm not sure. Maybe soon. It's hard to be certain."

Billy waved at us through the bars and came over. Out in the street, I watched his two girls, the tall blonde-streaked and the small black-haired, gliding arm-in-arm down the slope of the pedestrian path and out of site. Sometimes I thought these nymphets weren't real, just nameless apparitions with immaculate hairstyles. I made a mental note to check whether they had feet at their next showing.

Billy brought his bonhomie into the sunlight. "My friends, how is this fine day treating you?"

"I see you found your watch," I said.

He slid the fake Rolex against his wrist. "Yes, my chicas found it when they were cleaning. It was under the bed."

"What amazing good fortune."

"Yes." He grinned. "They are amazing."

Yanela gestured to me. "He not UNEAC."

Billy pulled over a stool and we sat in our triangle formation. "Don't fret, maraca girl. In the labyrinth of Cuba, there are always avenues to explore. Comprender?"

"No."

"I . . . will . . . fix . . . it. Jesus, I just spent a morning with this. I can't escape."

"Speak Español."

"I only speak the Queen's English, my dear," he said with an aristocratic lilt.

"You not Queen. Buy me mojito."

"Well done! You've broken your record. I've been here for no more than twenty fucking seconds before you asked me to buy you a mojito." He waved at José. "But you will have to earn your drink this time, maraca girl." He winked at me.

"I give music . . . you give mojito. Good deal."

"I swear, if I cut you, you'd bleed mojito," Billy said.

I imagined her dark chocolate arm oozing lime juice.

A man came over and tapped Yanela on the shoulder. He was tall and sculptured and looked like he'd come straight off the page of an advert for Havana Club. She turned to him and they talked together, rough-edged talk like an arm wrestle, though she never left her stool.

I saw the bongo player looking over at him, and then the guitar players and the bassist. The talk went on for a minute or so, ending when Yanela handed him a key. It seemed like he had won the bout, and he walked out and gave a nod to the players and some nodded back.

"Cuban musical chairs," Billy said in a low voice.

Yanela faced us again.

"Is that your husband?" I said.

"No."

Billy nodded his head at me.

"We divorce."

José came over with a tray of drinks.

"Cheer up, I bought you a mojito while you were in conference," Billy said. "But you'll have to play for me." He took one of the two Tukolas and sipped it. "This has no rum."

"That would be mine," I said. "Sunday is a rest day."

"In the name of the Father and the Son, and the Holy Spirit. Amen." He crossed himself.

Yanela shook her head and gave up a hint of a smile.

"I used to be a choir boy, back in Camden Town," Billy said.

"You still boy."

"Youth is wasted on the young, my dear. Congreve, Tom?"

"Shaw, actually."

A man came over to us and was introduced by Billy as his movie man. He took out a stack of DVDs from a bag, some with photocopied covers, some just in clear plastic sleeves. Billy studied each carefully and bought three or four.

"My chicas love Russell Crowe." He waved *Master and Commander* at us. "They're not bad quality. I'll lend you some."

A few chords from the double bass called Yanela and the others to their instruments, and as the music started, the street slowed to peer through the bars. A haze of sunshine slanted across the room, lighting up the black clad girls out front—guitars, bongos, and double bass now caressed like their children, who watched on the floor just at their feet.

Billy winked at me, dropped off his stool, and chatted something in a whisper to a table of camera-clad tourists.

Yanela addressed the audience. "We sing for you. I hope you like. Any request?"

"Guantanamera," the camera table shouted up. "Play Guantanamera!"

And Yanela poked her tongue out at Billy, who laughed and seconded the request.

* * *

Héctor poured the rum into our glasses. He had won the entire round in the first play—with five Aces.

"With such a win," Señor Pupo said, "we pour double shots."

"Sí. Llene el vaso," Pedro said. Fill my glass.

There had been four short rounds, and we were feeling the heat of the rum as one. We rarely got drunk—the drawn-out contest kept the alcohol low in our blood. The other tables grinned over to us, and a couple asked Héctor to join them so they could also share our fortune.

Pedro reached over and touched Héctor's shoulder. "He stay. Esta es nuestra familia." He shone a grin at me. "Tom, Havana is good, hey . . . when Héctor play Cubilete. No dig sand tonight."

"No dig sand," I said.

We had talked much about what I thought of Cuba. Pedro was most interested, but the others seemed curious as well. I think they didn't really understand why I was here, and I wasn't entirely sure I could explain.

"I have no interest in politics in Cuba, or anywhere else," I had told them when we first met. They liked this. "I'm not sure I know what I think of Cuba, or rather I'm not sure I've been here long enough to know."

"We don't expect you to understand our country as we do," Señor Pupo had said. "But how you see it comes only from your eyes."

"Let me tell you a story. It's not my own, but from Japan, by a writer called Kōbō Abe."

Señor Pupo translated to the table as I told it, one sentence at a time.

"There was a poor village that was built amongst vast sand dunes. The sand was the wrong type to be used for building materials, for agriculture, for anything. But the natural current of the dunes, with the wind always driving in the same direction, rained the sand over the village without rest. Sand became a layer of the villagers' skin—it was in the water, the food, between their toes, and stuck on their lashes. They slept with it. They ate it. They made love with it."

Héctor sucked on his cigar and said, "Amor duro." Hard love.

"At the far edge of this village, just below the largest dune, a woman lived in a little timber house. Her husband and child had been killed when the dune had collapsed on them—they had drowned in sand—so she now lived alone. Her job was to remove the sand from the base of this great dune, which fell down at her doorstep. The sand was easiest to shovel at night, and so she slept during the day and dug in the darkness, usually till dawn. By keeping her house from being swallowed by the sand, she protected the next house, and so the ones after that.

To me, Cuba is like the sand woman's house."

The little herons danced above the ceiling as we played lazily into the afternoon.

In between a round of the dice, Señor Pupo asked me why the sand woman didn't move to another village. I said I didn't really know—but I thought he would have a better idea than me.

He took a swig of rum but didn't respond.

* * *

Usually my mothers alternated weekly in cooking the evening meal. Señora Pupo's speciality was Boliche, and we ate it most nights of her weeks. She said the secret was the extra paprika and garlic, and not to hold back on the orange juice. She also said it was Señor Pupo's favorite.

Señor Pupo's jacket had never left the lounge chair, and whenever the Boliche was served, I made an exception and wore it. My mothers thought this was odd—they never said anything, but I could see it in their eyes. Over the years I've become fine-tuned in detecting the odd stare or two, as you could well imagine, Juan.

On this evening, they began to quiz me on whether I had a wife or girlfriend back home. At first, this topic of conversation caused me no concern. The great bonus of my mothers' poor English is that I can control the conversation, like Señora Pupo adjusting the spices in the Boliche. This frustrated Estelle, who responded with animated Spanish that my translator couldn't handle. Perhaps there should be an 'Excited Latino' option on the speech recognition program.

"¿De dónde viene tu novia a vivir?"

"¿Dedónde viene tunovia avivir?"

Eventually all of the words joined in one cacophonous plea.

"¿Dedóndevienetunoviaavivir?!"

Even if she managed to get the translator to decipher the phrase, she had no way of confirming this because she couldn't read the English translation. This lead to her one finger typing, which slowed the interrogation so much she often gave up.

However, on this evening, she was stubbornly persistent.

"¿de . . . dónde . . . viene . . . tu novia . . . a vivir?" Where does your girlfriend live?

I shrugged.

When she threatened to get Alex, the waiter at the tourist café next door, I knew I was beaten and had to respond.

"I'm not sure where she lives," I said slowly.

Estelle spat out, "Increíble! Él debe estar casado!" He must be married.

"No," I said.

"Does she know where you are?"

"Yes."

"Does she write to you?"

"No."

"Do you love her?"

"Oh, yes."

"Sí . . . no . . . sí . . . no. No estamos en los tribunals!" We are not in court.

Señora Pupo slapped more Boliche on my plate, giving me a respite. She could read my worry face more easily than Estelle. Señora Pupo was the quiet sister, who mulled over an issue before responding. She was the female Héctor of my blue-casa family.

I brushed some lint from my jacket. The Señora stood from the table and came back from her bedroom with the clothes brush. She twisted my shoulders to face her and stroked the charcoal velour like an animal preening its child; her eyes welling as she did this.

I felt a shifting of my skin, like slow moving lava without the heat. Señor Pupo was inside of me again, seeping through from the jacket. I reached to tilt the invisible Panama down over my forehead. Adjust my bowtie. And I wondered what my hero would be thinking now, sitting at the table of paprika and garlic and gentle preening—and I felt disappointed that I had absolutely no idea.

"You love her, sí." Señora Pupo bent over and gave me a hug. "Sí, you love her."

And I realized Señora Pupo was hugging her husband and not me.

The Boliche tasted different. I could detect the lime and oregano distinct amongst the flavors, the chorizo strong against the delicate beef, the cumin as well.

Señora Pupo watched me eat and gently sobbed. And we quietly finished the pot-roast without speaking another word.

* * *

Señor Pupo began appearing at the card club unshaven. Pedro made a joke of it, but looked troubled. I often forget to shave, so it meant little to me.

"He shave two time a day."

"He have big balls," Héctor said.

"Bull's balls."

Señor Pupo smiled and threw the dice. "Why not shave?" Pedro asked him.

"Why should I?"

"Because that you."

"Maybe I'm not me anymore." He rolled the last dice but struck out with four kings.

I said, "Why don't we go out for a drink later tonight? I know a good place in calle Obispo."

"Sí, Sí," Pedro said.

Héctor nodded.

Señor Pupo did not look up. "I am busy tonight."

"What busy?"

"Shaving."

"It has a great chica band," I said.

"Chica chica, sí."

"Not tonight my friends."

I wanted to understand my hero's pain but I didn't feel worthy of it. I was too new to the family. But I felt I needed to know, more for myself.

We played slow into the late afternoon. The haze of cigar smoke, the sweet smell of rum, the tapping of little angels' feet tumbling down and over us. After the play I walked with him to his casa. The Hotel Nacional sat high in the background. The early evening was orange-red.

"I like the outside bar at the Nacional," I said.

"I have never been."

"Then it would be a pleasure to take you there."

"I am not dressed for the place."

"Neither am I."

We made a detour to Señor Pupo's home, where I waited for him to change. He returned, shaven and dapper, in a cream linen jacket and pants, and his paisley bow tie. He asked me whether I needed to change, but of course that was impossible. So I made an excuse that the distance was too far.

The Bar Galeria at the Nacional sits along an arched colonnade held by marble columns, all looking out onto a palm-filled lawn, with little white benches, and a fountain in the center. Grand lounges keep you low to the terracotta, and the breeze from the Straits of Florida comes up to meet you. Time passes very easily there.

"This is a beautiful place," he said.

We ordered a bottle of wine and he seemed happy. I was excited to be with him, one on one, without any distraction from the dice. A trio wandered the colonnade playing a bossa nova. And I sat and waited for the alcohol to ease itself into the chat. To open and reveal whatever it might.

"I am lost, Tom."

"I know, Tony."

"It is my fault, but I am lost."

He told me about my mothers, beginning with Estelle.

"She is like a rose with big thorns. I have bled, sí, I have bled. But I cannot stop from being scratched. I have never stopped loving her. From the very first day."

He told me that he married Señora Pupo to be close to Estelle.

"This love is selfish, I know. We all lived together for a time, after we married. Just the three of us. This was the time of great change in Cuba, the best time, sí, the best time of my life. But my rose left us when she married. I understood of course. He was a fine man, Romario. He loved her very much. How could he not? But he died too young and left her without love."

"So you returned?"

"Everyone must find love where it is found, Tom." He looked at me and held his stare a moment. "I wrote to her, when Romario died. She needed to know she was loved. I kept writing and will keep on . . . until the end. It doesn't matter if she will not open the letters, as long as she knows she is loved."

"And Señora Pupo?"

I watched his hand shake with a fine tremor. "When we first married it didn't seem real. I was with Estelle and my wife, we were young, there was revolution, there was something strange in the feel of life that I cannot explain."

"Did Señora Pupo know that you loved her sister?"

"Sí, I think so. But I was always faithful to her . . . in the flesh, you understand? When Estelle married it was a difficult time for us. My wife was not at fault, only my selfishness. But we got through this and I grew to love her very much. She is so different from my rose; she doesn't have the spikes, just the petals."

"So you love them both?"

"Sí. I love both. And now I have lost them both."

I thought about confessing where I lived, but decided against it. For no good reason really.

* * *

I walked along the Malecón. The waves rushed against the seawall, splashing the salt spray up onto the path. When I arrived home to the sky-blue casa, I was dank with the smell of the ocean.

Estelle was sitting at the table. My laptop translator sat next to her like a member of the family.

"Why did you stop seeing Señor Pupo in the time before you were married?" I asked her.

Señora Pupo was asleep in the bedroom. Estelle put her finger to her mouth, but typed in her response without an objection. It was as if she was waiting for me to return home with the question.

It was not the answer I expected. "Él era muy serio con su amor." He was too serious with his love.

* * *

The Malecón was black. I could hear the waves crash against the rocks, rush against the seawall, but I couldn't see them. I couldn't see anything. Except . . . further down I saw someone sitting on the wall, a yellow lamp-lit blur, so I walked on in the dark toward the light. Cars hurried down the road, but I couldn't see them either. Everything was just black—the Malecón like a mine shaft with warm sea spray air, black rushing waves and Dodges, and the lamp-lit blur further down, that slowly got bigger as I followed its glow to the end.

I got there and Rosie was sitting under the lamp looking ahead, swinging her legs at the road, and I said hello but she didn't seem to hear me, didn't look at me either, she just stared straight ahead and kept swinging her legs and didn't say hi or anything. So I kept walking—I didn't stop at all, just kept on going to the next yellow lamp-lit blur down the way. I thought it wasn't far, only fifty meters or so, but I kept on going for minutes and the blur stayed small and yellow and the waves crashed and the cars rushed on but I couldn't see anything it was just too black. I walked for an hour, more than an hour, watching the yellow blur slowly get brighter and form into shape, a two-headed shape, no, two separate shapes sitting on the wall. I moved quicker and the lamp lit them up—their hair sculptured and streaked—and they didn't look straight ahead at all, they looked at me, smiling straight at me, and the wall they were sitting on kept moving away, like a moving walkway at an airport, so I started to jog to keep up, with the sound of the waves and the cars and my breath all rushing, and they kept smiling at me as they slowly drifted further down into the black shaft of the Malecón.

It must have been twenty minutes before I caught them up. They grinned at me, salacious, arousing, and the closer one, the slightly taller of the two, the more Lolita of the two, started to lift her dress up from below her knees, lifting it slowly as if she wanted to hitch a ride, using an old fashioned showing of her leg, and I ran faster to her, and she smiled and she lifted the dress up higher still, and her lamp-lit skin came into view more and more and I realized she wasn't trying to get a ride at all, she was showing me something on her thigh, and so I ran to get a closer look, sprinting now to keep up with the wall and the girl, and I saw it on her moon white thigh, saw it smile, with its little blue eye, and its blue tail and fins, and his large closed mouth with blue lines along his belly and his eye that tore deep into me. And I cried, but they kept on smiling at me, and so I kept on too—until the crying woke me up.

Like it always does.

* * *

It was noon. Calle Obispo was crowded and sun drenched. I had wandered from the Plaza de Armas, up the full length of the street, and had turned back with the aim of landing at the chica bar. It was my midday routine. Routines were becoming more important to me the further I travelled into Purgatory.

The way was thick with tourists and the high sun glared against the concrete surfaces and the light played its tricks amongst the crowd and the open doorways. The two Lolitas turned, their blonde-streaked hair perfectly sculptured as always, smiled at me, and moved down the street. Their heads at least, since their bodies were lost in the swarm, keeping ahead about four persons deep, staying at that distance even as I slowed my pace.

I was being pulled on a leash. Drawn rather than dragged.

It was hot in the sun and my pulse thumped.

I decided to sit a while in an open tourist café half way down the way. The place was crowded, like the street, but there was a spare chair, and I sat at a table with some women and my pulse eased off a bit.

I ordered a Tukola and kept looking out onto the street, but the girls didn't reappear. I was annoyed with myself for forgetting my sunglasses and made a mental note to keep them with me in the future, if only so I could avoid eye contact, if the need arose. The table women were from a cruise ship, and we talked about the boat and how much weight they had put on. They asked me where they should go shopping, and I told them Cuba is wonderful for many things, but shopping was probably not high on the list—unless they liked cigars or rum. After fifteen minutes I paid the bill for us all, and went back down Obispo, hoping to find my way clear.

After half a block, the Lolitas turned their heads and smiled at me again. They kept in front at the same distance as before and stayed like that, the taller turning her head more, a wanton beam, and my pulse thumped and I felt short of air.

I stopped in the middle of the sidewalk and bent down to try to catch my breath. The crowd was all legs around me, I like a boulder in a rushing stream. When I lifted myself up the teens were waiting for me. I fell down again into the rushing legs, held my breath until the meat of my lungs burned, a tightness in my chest, then floated back to the surface sucking in air. At their mercy. So we continued down the street, with me on their leash, and their turned hairdo smiles with my pulse racing all the way.

A dog on a leash, this is the best way to describe it.

I walk with them as far as they wish to take me.

I have no control over it.

When I stopped they stopped, the leash slackening, allowing a feigned stare through store windows at nothing in particular, or to let me piss against a lamppost.

And when finally the leash was unclasped, I escaped into the bar— away from the sun and the lust.

Yanela came up and gave me a kiss. I waved to José and the girls— Billy wasn't there. I waved at people I didn't even know.

My heart was still moving at a hefty pace, the air thin and hot. I tried to keep my gaze from the street, focusing on José shaking cocktails, a waiter counting the change, the colors of the bottles, the names on the labels, anything to keep from looking out.

In time, I settled down into the mojito-flavored salsa, the guitars and maracas and her downy-lipped grin—my noon routine with the chica band, the familiar warmth of it all. But every so often my fight to stay focused failed, and I peeked through the bars and onto the street.

They should be at school. Perhaps they played hooky? They looked like the type of girls who would do that—although I had never spoken a word to them.

Billy came in later, sweating with the day.

"Billy, is it a holiday?"

"Not that I know of, though every day is a holiday for me."

"So, it's a school day?"

He nodded.

"Those girls of yours, your . . . girlfriends . . . they go to school don't they?"

"Sí. They are very studious."

"Is school finished yet?"

"In another hour." He motioned to José for a drink.

I looked outside but now there was no sight of them.

"Tom, you're not trying to make a move . . . you know, on a man's true love?"

"Loves." I kept my gaze down at the table. "And no, Billy. You don't have to worry about that."

"You see, I'm very attached to them."

My eyes stayed low. "Like your Rolex."

"Tom, you don't approve?"

I lifted my chin and saw he wasn't annoyed—as far as I could tell. "I never judge, Billy. Believe me, I'm in no position to."

He nodded. "Of course, some may disapprove. Or *many* may be a more accurate word."

I looked at him though he kept his eyes away.

"And when my sister came and visited I kept my little Rolex lovers in the closet, so to speak."

"I understand."

"Really?"

"I certainly understand why you kept them in the closet."

He swung a gaze around the bar. "Dirty old man . . . it's such a nasty label, don't you think."

My heart galloped. "Very nasty."

For the first time in a while he looked at me, but with a strange face. "Tom, are you all right"?

"A good question, Billy. I suppose it depends on definitions."

Is it my eyes, I wonder? Is it my eyes that give me away?

"It's my skeleton in the closet, Billy." I slurred the words. "Or maybe it's the mojitos."

"José hasn't made a strong mojito since Fidel wore short pants."

"Then it's probably my skeleton."

He looked jumpy. "Look, I understand if you—"

"Billy, trust me. As I said before, I'm the last to judge . . . for I'm simply in no position to."

"Well, let's drink to that." He stared, sweat laden, at me. "For it's my understanding, Tom . . . and please correct me if I'm wrong, for this is very important, very important indeed. It is my understanding that it's your turn to buy the drinks."

* * *

"Potato?"

"Sí, papa."

"Before you say mandioca."

"I start with potato, and later mandioca."

"I like papa . . . I cook you good papa."

"It's a deal."

"When you start."

"Two weeks."

"You visa."

"It's all organized . . . it's all good."

"UNEAC?"

"No. Mi padrino . . . my Sponsor."

"El agricultor."

"Sí. The farm organized it all."

"How long?"

"Six months."

"Bueno."

"Muy muy bueno."

She took my hand, held it tenderly. "Baby's hand . . . not farm hand."

"They've only been used for writing."

"And hold mojito."

"Tukola."

"Why mojito no more?"

"I take a rest for a while."

"Be strong for papa farm?"

"Sí."

"You loco papa farmer."

"Muy loco."

"You write?"

"Every day. Like eating."

"Escribir y cultivar."

"Sí. Write and farm, write and farm. This is my life now in Cuba."

"Una buena vida."

"Sí. A wonderful life."

* * *

We don't speak much, Rosie and I.

Afterwards, I like to lie in her arms in the sweaty heat; play with her purple scar, which she doesn't seem to mind. She always makes time after, no rushing off, even on a Friday or Saturday night. Rosie is good like that.

I like the imperfection of her scar, the humanity of it. Her teeth. Her sagging breasts lined with stretch marks; a relic from breast-feeding, or maybe she was fat once, hard as that is to imagine. Maybe that's why she only picks at her food when I take her for a meal. But I don't think so. Her stick legs have never been plump, I'm sure of it. She has a lithe physique that will always be hers. Even when she tires of her trade and can sit lazy in the evenings, back home or somewhere quiet, away from the hurry of Havana, sitting lazy with a light rug to keep her stick legs warm, until she falls asleep with a book on her lap or the television droning or something like that.

"What you think about?" she said.

"I like your scar."

She slapped my hand. "I give it to you." She laughed. "Look, you have scar on knee now."

"Yes, it's not as pretty as yours though."

"When you get?"

"I was a kid."

"Fall off bike?"

"Nope." I ran my finger over the livid knolls of her wound. "My mother wouldn't let me ride a bike. She was scared I would break something."

"She maybe right. She nice, you mother?"

"The best." I moved my hand down to the old scar on my leg. "I scraped my knee in the bush. Got dirt in it. 'You'll get tetanus if I don't get you up to doctor Pap this second,' my mother said. I had to get a needle—doctor Pap liked giving needles. My mother had some phobia about getting tetanus. Whenever I had a scrape she would get the Dettol out. 'Keep still, Tom, it's supposed to sting. If it doesn't you'll get tetanus . . . and then you'll know it.'"

"I not understand."

"Tetanus." I lifted my head from Rosie's stomach and grimaced in mock torment. "Mum said my jaw would lock and I would scream and eventually stop breathing. My mother always had a dramatic reason for her remedies." I rested my head back on the soft pillow of Rosie's flesh. "Anyway, she would say to me, 'What are you doing in that bush, there are snakes down there, and if you get bitten by a brown, you have about an hour to get to doctor Pap's for a needle or you'll start to bleed in your internal organs. And then you'll know it.'"

Rosie played with my hair, and the heat of the room sat over us, and I closed my eyes. "If I ever came home scratching at my skin she always asked me whether it was from a snake or a spider, what color it was, as if I didn't know what a red-back or funnel-web looked like. 'Yes, mum, now you mention it, I was bitten by a five-centimeter black funnel-web . . . if you hadn't asked me I wouldn't have remembered. We better get going and get me a needle right away.'"

"We have no bad spider or snake in Cuba. You safe here."

I kept on my safe pillow of scarified flesh. Warmer than satin. Softer.

"You have dogs. Billy told me someone got rabies last year in Havana."

"Boy."

"And he died."

"Sí."

"But it must be so rare. What's the chance of it? One in a million."

"My daughter want dog."

"Or one in ten million."

"But I no let her."

"Thank God there's no rabies in Australia. My mother would've had kittens every time she heard a bark."

"I like cat."

"Every kid had a dog."

"But daughter not like."

"Dad said they protected us."

"Maybe I get her little dog. More like cat."

"When we played in the yard. Especially when we were left alone."

"Maybe."

I drifted to sleep, and when I woke in the evening Rosie wasn't there. I had become used to this stealth of hers—a phantom that faded in and out of my life, like the salsa, rum, a cup of dice. And other things.

I checked my wallet and it was untouched, which made me smile. And I thought about where she might be. Maybe business was brisk after five, a rush hour of a different sort—a quick one before heading back home.

So I made a plan to head off, before dinner with my mothers, and look for her down by the Malecón or the Plaza de Armas or Parque Central. And if I didn't find her I'd go for a wander after dinner, and into the night, until I did.

* * *

I could not see them from my bedroom window. Even if I stood, my desk that sits below the frame prevented me getting enough of an angle to see them talking. But my window was open, to chill the afternoon heat that always rose to my room, so while I couldn't see them, I could hear them clearly. And I realized my Spanish was improving, because I understood most of what was said.

"She is sleeping," Estelle said.

I heard footsteps shuffle in the kitchen and wondered whether they could hear them as well.

"We don't mind waiting," Pedro said.

"She will sleep for hours. She has taken a tranquilizante."

I heard the tranquilizer step into the downstairs bedroom.

"Or we can come back, Señora," Héctor said. "When she wakes."

"We are her amigos, Señora," Pedro said.

"And I am her sister. Talk to me if you have something to say."

"Señora be razonable," Pedro said.

"This is my casa and in my casa I'm always reasonable."

Pedro said something that I didn't catch, but from the tone I knew it wasn't complimentary.

"We are worried about Antonio," Héctor said. "He looks bad."

"I thought you were my sister's friends?"

"Flaco." Thin, maybe.

"Then tell him to eat." Her voice rose up. "Or feed him yourselves!"

Pedro ranted up something indecipherable, but mujer imposible, impossible woman, fit into it more than once.

Héctor said, "Señora, could you tell her we came to see her. We want to talk . . . a su conveniencia."

Estelle said something in her excited Latino brogue, and I heard her heavy footsteps enter the casa.

I stood from my chair and thought about revealing myself—shouting out a greeting through the open window, or running downstairs and hugging them both. Asking them in for coffee. An empanada. Sitting them all down together, my mothers and amigos Cubilete, over coffee and empanadas. Or even better, around a jug of Cuba Libres.

But you see, I'm too much of a coward, Juan.

Of which you are probably aware.

And I watched Pedro and Héctor walk across the avenue arm-in-arm, following the road back to the Vedado from where they came.

* * *

We were sitting in our triangle formation in the late evening. The Guantanamera girls were done for the night as the bassist passed the hat around one final time. The tables all merry. The girls pleased but spent.

He appeared at the entrance, with a loud Hawaiian shirt and a beaming grin that flashed a full set of teeth at me. "Tom, welcome to Havana!"

I waited for Billy and Yanela to turn before I motioned him over.

"Surf's up," Billy said, looking at the shirt.

He came on over and wrapped his arms around me. "Surprised?"

"Flabbergasted."

"Can you imagine . . . me in Cuba! The allure!" His accent was thick with Brooklyn. *The allu-were!*

"How did you get here?"

"Those two broads at your home, they were so charming, they even gave me a plate of rice and beans. Look at this place. Pinch me, Tom. Is it real?"

"I meant the country?"

"I was in Cancun at a conference. Working hard for my buddies." He patted my shoulder. "So I thought I'd come and see how it's all going, smoke a cigar or two, and see if I can prize something from that laptop of yours."

"And the allure."

"And the allu-were!" He scanned the bar with a giant arc of his neck.

"It's good to see you, Hymie." I introduced him to the table. "This man is a friend of mine. And also, unfortunately for him, my agent."

"Hyman David." He shook Billy and Yanela's hands. "Hyman is spelt with an 'a' not an 'e'. It means life . . . so there's some connection with the anatomical homophone." He grinned as he always did following his signature introduction.

I pulled over a chair and we sat in a clumsy square.

"You're American," I said.

"Born on the fourth of July. Give or take a couple of months."

"Is it legal for you to be here?"

"I'm visiting my client, who happens to be Australian. Can I help it if he decides to write a novel in Havana? It's a perfect alibi."

"I think plea might be a more appropriate word. Where're you staying?"

"With you."

"That's not funny."

"Hotel Ambo Mundo."

"You pronounce the 's'."

"Ambos Mundos . . . no wonder the cabby looked at me strange."

"I bet you asked to stay in Hemmingway's room."

"I slipped them a fifty, but no dice. He said he would show me his room tomorrow. His typewriter and everything."

"That costs only two CUCs."

"So I'll visit it twenty five times. I'll make it a pilgrimage. Speaking of which, can a brother find a synagogue around here."

"I can't say I know."

"Then buy me a beer."

Hymie was born an orthodox Jew—frum from birth—and would die an orthodox Jew—with the orthodox bit surgically removed. His words, not mine. We were the same age, and I felt comfortable around him, though he was a bit excessive for most people. By the look on Billy's face, he was about to be added to the list. Yanela looked entertained though.

"Do they have a Sam Adams here?"

"This is Cuba, Hymie."

"Try a Cristal," Billy said deadpan.

"Four Cristals," Hymie said.

"Three and a Tukola," I said.

"Sorry . . . Tukola for the lady."

"The Tukola's for me."

He reached over and felt my forehead and gave me one of his drawn out stares. "Have you a fever or something?"

"Or something," I said. "I'll tell you later."

"He becoming farmer," Yanela said. "Get strong."

"Farmer?"

"Potato."

"A potato farmer?"

"Sí."

He gave me another long glare. "Is this for a new book?"

"Again, later."

Hymie looked at Yanela. "He wouldn't know the correct end of a shovel."

"That would be the bit to hit you on the back of the head with."

"He's lived in an apartment for as long as I've known him. Twenty years. I've never seen him grow anything."

"I grew a beard once."

"Not a herb."

"And sideburns."

Yanela grinned even though she couldn't have followed the banter. Hymie had this effect on some women, but it was always difficult to predict with whom.

"I've read those Brazilian stories of yours by the way."

"And?"

"Can you turn them into a novel."

"What do you think?"

"All right, they're a bit disconnected to string together, and they cover your usual range of styles. But short stories are a real tough sell at the moment."

"They always were."

"I could sell it as a novel in two seconds."

"Then take a minute."

Hymie looked at Yanela. "Don't ever work with animals or writers. Promise me this."

She smiled again.

"Do you have coffee in this place?" Hymie said.

"What is cawfee?" Yanela said.

"Coffee," I said.

"Our Cuban friends aren't used to American accents," Billy said. "Cuba has magnificent coffee . . . perhaps in contrast to your abode."

I wasn't sure whether Hymie noticed Billy's edge, but he wouldn't care if he had. It takes a lot more to shake Hyman David than a shot of anti-American sentiment.

"I'll get you a cup back home," I said.

"No, don't worry. I'm too excited as it is."

"The allure?"

"The allu-were!" He looked at Billy. "So tell me comrade, where can I get me a nice fat cigar?"

* * *

"I still don't know why you're here."

"I told you, I was so near and I have always wanted to visit Cuba. And I haven't seen you for almost a year."

We sat slouched in the late morning quiet of the Ambos Mundos Hotel. A lobby of dark chocolate timber. The smell of cawfee in the air.

"Have you seen his room yet?" I said.

"Papa's?"

I nodded.

"Yep. Take that Erector Set of an elevator up to room 511. Tell him I sent you. He still owes me twenty-three visits." Hymie waved to the barman and ordered another cup. "This is good."

"Better than Starbucks."

"And a hell of a lot cheaper." He stared long at me again. "What are you writing then?"

"Actually, it's an autobiographical piece."

"A novel?"

"Perhaps. It's still forming."

He looked a little askance. He knew my story. "An autobiography. You surprise me."

"I'll change the names of course—when it's done."

He raised his brow at me. "To protect the guilty."

"Guilty is not quite the right word."

"Maybe not, but can you think of a better one?"

I shrugged.

"I hope this novel of yours is nearly finished."

"I'm afraid not. Still very much a work in progress."

He stared longer this time, even when the barman brought the espresso over. "Then I gather a long delay is expected, with your farming plans and everything." He sipped at his cup. "Were you planning on telling me?"

"Your surprise visit beat me to it."

Hymie gave up a sigh.

We sat silent for a while. I listened to the high ceiling fan click with each rotation.

Hymie twisted his head to take in the scene. "I like this place. Might stay on a while."

"That's not necessary." I kept my glance down at the table. "But appreciated as always."

"I'll talk to my secretary, move things around a bit. The break will do me good."

I kept my stare on the espresso cup.

"Papa never had a literary agent you know," Hymie said. "Like a lot of people in the business, I've fantasized what it would've been like to look after his writing. And him. He had a reputation of being a difficult bastard."

"But not as difficult as some, hey."

"No. Not as difficult as some."

The fan clicked in the quiet like a slow clock.

"Reality," I said.

"Reality?"

"I'll change the names to protect reality."

"So why does reality need protecting?"

I lifted my gaze to him. "Only lies need constant nurturing to keep them alive."

"Well, Tom, I don't know what the fuck that means. But if you need protection from the truth, feel free."

* * *

The close proximity to Hemingway's room had an immediate effect on Hymie. I had left him alone for a few hours, and when I returned he told me how he had made the pilgrimage again and already started writing.

"I won't tell you what it's about, but I have this great agent who just can't wait to sell it."

Hymie has actually published three books, all under different pseudonyms. His first, and biggest seller was a cookbook—*Kosher Curries: Spice up your life according to Leviticus.* He had travelled the Levant for a month collecting the spices and recipes. The book's back cover had a photograph of him, his face pixilated, being detained by US customs for not declaring the spices, which were hidden in his dirty laundry. According to Hymie, when they opened it, the bag rose off the table with the reek of a curried jock strap.

His second book, less successful, was a crime novella, *The Hasidic Detective.* The protagonist's tormented ruminations on whether to capture the killer on Shabbat met with some controversy at the time. His last book, another novel, was published two years ago. Hymie describes the sales as exceeding his expectations, if it had been a collection of botanical poetry.

The remarkable thing about Hymie's publishing record is, not only does he publish with a pseudonym, but he is represented by a pseudonym. A living, breathing pseudonym. Hymie believes it's unprofessional for agents to peddle their own manuscripts—he is proud of this stance, taking the literary high moral ground. But his morality is fluid enough to allow him to represent himself by creating a real pseudonym. "Chaim Pollak," the author of *The Hasidic Detective*, was really David Klein, a small-goods importer from Brooklyn and best man at Hymie's wedding. Hymie represented "Chaim" at all stages, from writing the book to taking part in phone interviews, only producing Klien to sign the contract at Random House, attend the launch party, book signings, and occasional face-to-face interviews. Hymie, of course, never left Klein's side during all of these 'sightings,' as he likes to call them. Hymie said such intense representation was what a bright new novelist like Chaim Pollak deserved. Random House was impressed.

Only occasionally did the living pseudonym stuff up, usually during an unsolicited interview, with Hymie not present. When the author of *Kosher Curries*, Shmuel Halevi—aka Aaron Bergman, Hymie's dry cleaner—was cornered by a journalist for the ingredients of Haifa Pigeon—one of the books signature dishes—he fabricated the entire recipe. This included a chef's pearl—*roast the bird until both wings lift from the carcass*. Unfortunately it was published. Fortunately in *The Jewish Week*. Hymie had Shmuel over for dinner and served up the revised spicy bird. Apparently, it wasn't too bad, but they never managed to finish it. Hymie said his sales went down after that.

"So, are you going to represent yourself?" I said.

"No. I am going to represent Tiphanie Spade."

"A woman this time?"

"I have many female clients."

"None with balls."

"She's one heck of a gal."

"Tiphanie Spade. Sounds goy?"

"No, she is Jewish. It's her pseudonym. This book needs a non-denominational touch. A separation of the Church and State-of-mind." He turned to me. "And it could only be told by a woman with a sensitive pen. A Brontë. Charlotte, not Emily." He slapped my thigh. "But enough. You know writers don't like talking about works in progress."

It was Tuesday, and so I took Hymie to the Cubilete game. The cigar haze against green felt. Fidel and Che and rum that stung the throat. The allu-were of it all.

My friends had never spoken so intimately with an American before, and certainly not one like Hymie. He wore his Yankees' cap, the N on Y a beacon on his head that shouted up—I'm all red, white and blue; bring it on if you dare.

When he sat at the table, Pedro's mouth opened but failed to produce a sound. I suspect he had too many geopolitical theories to sort through in his head. Héctor put the flask of dice down and mulled over his cigar with a grin. And even my unshaven hero seemed buoyed by our foreign invader.

"Comrades!" Hymie shrilled in thick Brooklyn.

Heads turned from the satellite tables and there was a silence for a second.

"La tierra de El Duque! Orlando Hernández!" He pointed to his Yankees' cap. "We are practically related."

Héctor laughed, and cigar spit sprayed over the table. "Hernández good. But we have better player in Cuba."

The game paused as they argued about the merits of Cuban baseball, an enthusiastic dialogue drawn out by Hymie's schoolboy Spanish. When Hymie was told that the Yankees' Mariano Rivera was born in Havana and not Panama, indeed Héctor was his Science teacher for a couple of years, Hymie finally conceded the superiority of Cuban baseball, and stood to introduce himself with his signature overture.

"Señor Vagina," Héctor sang out to the room. Stained-toothed laughter shone up in the haze. "But in Habana we name you Señor fabricante de la arena."

Hymie looked to me.

I shrugged and Señor Pupo winked at me. "Mr. Sand Maker."

The gentle thud of little black herons timbered down on us in time to an old recording of Swan Lake. The sound of rolling dice and entrechats spilled into the low-lit space. And I felt safe as always.

Pedro took longer than I had thought to play out his first hand. But he was excited and I waited eagerly to see how he would begin.

"Amamos a América," he said. We love America.

We all stared at him.

Pedro rolled the dice again. "Amamos a América mucho." He drew three kings from the table. "We love America because we have good place to send our criminals."

We all laughed.

"Soviet is cold country—"

The table protested as one and Héctor grabbed Pedro and kissed him. But my friends saluted Hymie with a rare extra glass of Havana Club, and we settled down into the afternoon as if he had just returned back to his family after a long jail sentence.

"Las victorias imperialistas!" Pedro shouted as Hymie won his first game. "Double drink for imperialistas brother."

"You let me win."

"No, Señor fabricante de la arena. Americano always win."

Hymie puffed on his cigar—he had apparently found a supply.

"A Partagás cigar," Señor Pupo said. "These are very special."

"I bought a box from a taxi driver who took me from the airport." Hymie gave one of his long stares to Señor Pupo. "And another from a kid who told me he was Castro's grandchild."

Señor Pupo grinned. "Ah, little Arturo."

"Both boxes turned out to be little better than rope with a colorful band. No, these babies I saw rolled with my own eyes in the factory in the center of town."

"We Cubans can't afford such a brand."

Héctor nodded his head.

Hymie looked over to me uneasily.

"Americano always win," Pedro said, in a tone where sarcasm, if present, was well hidden. "But not win Bahía de Cochinos."

"Cochinos?" Hymie said.

"Pig." He sipped at his rum. "But win after, sí."

My friends nodded their heads.

Hymie kept on edge in his seat. A rare event. He looked like he was waiting for a tooth extraction.

"But I really can't take them back home with me," he said slowly. "US customs are like bulldogs. So perhaps, if I'm invited back to play, we could have a few rounds with cigars instead of rum as the prize."

"Sí, sí."

"I should have bought them with me." He looked over at me. "I left them at Estelle's."

"Estelle?" Pedro said.

"His landlady."

The table sat quiet for a while. Estelle was a common name in Havana, but I felt suddenly trapped. Dry in the mouth.

Pedro sipped on his rum. "What her appelido? Nombre familia." Family name.

I gazed over to my hero, who seemed disinterested with the interrogation. "I'm not sure."

Pedro shook the flask like a maraca, drawing out the silence. The dice scuttled on the felt and a cheer rose up. Five queens.

Five queens a majestic distraction, as was the rum that followed.

We played through the afternoon and Hymie won a second round, promising to return with cigars as the bounty.

After the game we walked with Señor Pupo—a fragile figure by now, with the gaunt face of the homeless. Which of course he was. I had become eager for some private time with him, to sort out some uncertainties I was developing. Hymie's visit made this difficult. But this statue of a man held the answers—I was certain of it.

When we parted at the street corner leading to his casa, he turned to me. "Espinosa Begueri. Her full name is Estelle Espinosa Begueri."

Then he walked away.

* * *

"Why do you think we'll fuck it up, Billy?" Hymie said.

"You Americans have no subtlety."

"Castro is subtle?"

"You're an American . . . the subtlety of the culture is beyond you. Yanela, help me, my little maraca girl. Do you want to see busloads of Americans coming here?"

"Sí."

"Forget about the tips. If you could get the same money from the Canadians, would you want them to be here?"

"I like Señor Hymie."

"I like him too, but that is not the point. Do you want to see Taco Bell and Rancho a-fucking-migos down on calle Obispo?" He turned away from our table and shouted up. "José, do you want your son to stitch Nike shoes to ship home to some fat kid in downtown USA?"

"My son isn't fat," Hymie said. "More cute chubby."

"In the US of A it's cool to have money, Hymie. Your art is money. Your God is fucking money. Tom, help me out."

I held up my hands. "I'm just a spectator."

"Look, Hymie. You know I love you. How could I not with that shirt? Jesus, what is that color?"

"Moroccan sunset."

"Not even the Beach Boys would be seen in a thing like that, and that cigar of yours, the size of a dog's cock . . . if you had a dimple under that lip of yours I could desex your chin . . . and that baseball hat . . . you are beautiful, you really are. But I don't want to meet more than one of you at a time. You're best as a solo act."

Hymie removed the dog cock from his mouth. "Aren't you a jazz musician, Billy? Noo Awlenz, Billy Boy, Noo Awlenzzz."

Billy scraped his hands through his long gray mane.

"Satchmohhh, Billy Boy."

"Okay, okay. We make an exception for musicians."

"And writers," I said. "It's what they do best."

"I know," Hymie said. "I've been visiting the shrine."

Billy was bloody but not bowed. "Okay, we let these in, but only these. Happy?"

Yanela sucked on the straw of her mojito and grinned. "Señor Hymie, you know Tom long time." She lifted her finger and pointed to her ring.

"Married? Tom? What is it about this place? Those old women you hang out with asked me the same question . . . although they couldn't understand my answer. No, Tom has been many things, but married is not one of them."

"Chica?"

He sucked on his cigar. "Women can't stand the sight of him."

"I serio." But she didn't look serious with the grin on her face.

"I set him up once, with my sister."

"I'm trying to forget."

"Not as much as she is." Hymie played with his wedding ring. "Yanela, you have my blessing to marry him."

"He no like Yanela."

"That's not true," I said quickly. "And Hymie, I thank you again for your constant bungling attempts at marrying me off."

"It's nothing, really."

"Nothing, now that your sister has found a much more suitable suitor."

"I don't like him. He's orthodox."

"But please, while you're in Cuba . . ."

The debate hushed up when one of the Lolitas came, manicured, to the table, her twin leaning sultry against the open doorway. I looked up at them through the streaming sun that lit down from behind, their faces veiled in the play of light. It seemed like I was in a Caravaggio painting, and wondered which of the two Marys was Magdalene.

She didn't look at me, but I didn't move an inch. I looked down and saw she had feet.

"Yes, my dear?" Billy said to her.

Dear? Dad used to call my grandmother, "dear". *Sit down near the fire, dear. What a wonderful new hat you have on, dear. I love the flowers and fruit.*

"You are going to get me into trouble . . . gran problema, dear. Comprender?"

Hymie stood. Of course he did. "Hola, mi bella . . ." and sung up his signature introduction.

The teen shook his hand, with eyes that hid their meaning from me.

Yanela said, "¿Has terminado tu tarea?" Have you finished your homework?

She nodded. Billy pulled a face but he hadn't made the translation. Yanela took charge in her oily Spanish brogue. I'll translate her taunts.

"Does Billy help you with your homework?"

She shook her head.

"What is he good for then?"

"Listen, Maraca girl, don't you understand gran problema!" This from Billy.

"Has he written a song for you?"

She nodded.

"Billy, sing us her song!"

I sat as stoic as a journalist at Billy's trial. Hymie caught some of the meaning and bore a grin as loud as his shirt. Billy didn't understand a word.

"Bring your friend over as well. Is she scared to come inside?"

She turned and motioned her head for the shampooed twin to join us.

"Jesus . . . you no comprender? Gran fucking problema!"

Yanela turned to the barman. "Can the girls come in and visit their family?"

"What family?" José said.

"Billy is their grandfather."

"This is too fucking much, go! I . . . see . . . you . . . later."

"Don't be mean, Grandfather," Yanela said.

I watched Lolita blush and I felt for her. I wanted to sit her down, them down, just the three of us, over a glass of Tukola, some mixed nuts, pretzels maybe, but I wasn't really sure how best to broach it. I like your hair, who does it, how long does it take, the streaks must take hours, are they natural curls, the perm lasts how many days, weeks, do you take turns to fuck him, or do you fuck him at the same time, or do you do other things not even he would admit to?

I started to find it difficult to breathe. Sweat poured down my forehead.

She turned away from us and back to her twin, whose face I couldn't read because of the dancing light. They said something to each other that I wanted to hear, but couldn't. I just followed them with my eyes as they took their corona-lit bodies back into the street.

And I wanted to get up and follow them further, to put on my leash once again, but didn't have the courage.

* * *

The screaming started in the late afternoon.

I had been writing at my desk and saw them out of my window—jostling for position on the path outside the casa. Señora Pupo stood hunched at one apex of the triangle, her hat fastened tight, the wide brims flapping with the breeze, her arms down by her side like in school detention—although I doubt she had ever been. Señor Pupo stood at another point, one hand on his panama hat, the other lifting like a conductor that rose or fell with the tumult. Estelle completed the triangle, with both hands raised, flapping mad hands, claws. And they stayed in this triangle throughout the entire performance, on the wide path with the bay behind, kept always apart by some invisible force that none of them understood.

The Spanish was far too fast for me to follow, spat within the noise of the street, but they told me about it after. I can write the scene now, see it clearly as it happened—a play with three characters on a barren stage without props, the stage lights streaming down on each of them, the rest poorly lit, superfluous.

Señor Pupo opens with a plea, he loves the Señora, he wants her to come home, he is sorry, he is flawed, he knows this, they know this, but he wants her to come home. His hand reaches out as he says it, his fingers, palm soft curves, ready to make contact.

The Señora keeps her eyes down, arms flop, she wants to speak but she can't, she is fastened to the stage. She could sit if she wants, she could play the scene out on her little outdoor chair, for she never moves. She has practiced what she wants to say, but the words don't seem right now, and she can't muster the authority to speak from her heart. It's not pride that stops her; it's a lack of strength she has never before needed.

Estelle gives her time to speak. The audience waits too. Estelle is the younger sister but much stronger, in will, resilience, and pure spite, when she wants—she knows this to be a fault, but her strength and spite go hand-in-hand, and she needs her strength, with the loneliness and all.

But the Señora doesn't speak.

So it's Estelle's turn, she has waited long enough, and the lights dim on the others. Estelle doesn't protest about the bond between sisters, forged in time and never broken, or the duplicity of the years of letter writing, the relentless deception, the breathtaking disloyalty. It's the selfishness she focuses on—the selfishness of it all. She raises her claws as she says it—a man who is not satisfied with one love—such a great love so he says, a love that brings him to his knees, even now he kneels as she speaks—is not a man worth knowing. They are harsh, these words. She feels the spite rise acid in her mouth—a man not worth knowing—who is he to crave two loves, what god does he see himself as, needing two loves when she has been left loveless in the flesh for so long. This is the essence of the case. How dare he crave more love when she has been left with none?

The triangle keeps still. The stage lights adjust to give all an equal presence. The audience seems satisfied. It all makes sense. They wait for a response to rise up from someone, a retort harnessed by love or spite or something known only to the players.

Traffic whishes by in the background. The barren stage is slowly illuminated—players and set lit up as one.

So we wait.

But they have had their say, and nothing more is said.

* * *

In the evening I ate Señora Pupo's Boliche with the velvet jacket on. The spices danced on my palate, the beef fell apart with the lightest touch, the rice and the juices.

My skin felt like molten syrup, cigar and rum flavored.

I ate like a madman—wolfed more than savored. This meal was meant for my hero. I wanted to feed him through his grief. Fatten him up.

I saw them looking strange at me, Estelle and the Señora, fine-tuned as I am to these strange looks. But I kept on with the stew, piling it on my plate. A feast served for two.

Afterwards, I sat, heavy bellied. Satiated. I kept the jacket on while my mothers fussed around me. The new skin felt good this time. I had two espressos. I wouldn't be sleeping.

It's the morning after that I'm writing this—your assigned task coming to a close, dear Juan. After the Boliche I went up to my room, sat at my desk, and wrote about the Lolitas and the turmoil on the pavement. My mothers went out and wouldn't return until late. My door was wide open. The night in front lit up yellow from the road; red taillights of Cadillacs and Plymoths and Dodges, their white torches flashing through the rain, reflected jagged off the shining street.

I saw her before she spoke, my window a mirror streaked with beads of rain. She smiled at me in front of the erratic lit night. A face in the street.

"Hello, Tommy."

I kept my stare at the reflection, worried the face would disappear if I turned around, or blinked.

"Did you miss me, Tommy?"

Heather's almond eyes grinned back at me from the window.

I held my breath, then gave up a sigh, bending around to face her in the flesh.

She came as she always did—and I grinned at her and said, "You really took your time."

Transcript June 9th 2010

Interview with Tom Peters by Juan Carlos Rebelde

JCR: You are happy for me to record our conversation again.

TP: Do I really have a choice? This is Cuba. You are the Comandante. [Short pause] I didn't have a choice with that little sample that was taken today.

JCR: Sample?

TP: The blood.

JCR: Oh, yes, that sample. Well, in such a place as this, accidents can happen. It pays to be prepared.

TP: Dib dib dib.

JCR: But, I have the tape-recorder in front of you. If you say no, I will respect your choice.

TP: Yes, I must say you usually do respect choice. That's why I'm here.

JCR: And there are no hidden devices, that I know of at least. [Short pause] Don't type that last sentence. [Short pause] She will, of course.

TP: Look, record as much as you like. I give you my indefinite consent.

JCR: I appreciate that. Thank you for the updated manuscript.

TP: I enjoyed writing it. And there is the happy ending.

JCR: I'm glad. I feel like your Cuban agent.

TP: Hymie might be out of a job then.

JCR: [Laughter] I wouldn't dare try to replace him.

TP: He won't be too relieved about that.

JCR: Agents get good money?

TP: When they get authors who sell. Hymie is mainly a literary agent though. Non-fiction makes more money these days.

JCR: Unless you have Harry Potter as a client.

TP: True. One of those is all you need.

JCR: He is your closest friend?

TP: Hymie, I guess so.

JCR: You seem to make friends easily. In the short time in Havana, the attachments you've made, they seem strong to me.

TP: Strong, but fragile of course.

JCR: What makes you say that?

TP: [No audible response]

JCR: Tell me about the prostitute in Havana. Rosie.

TP: [Short Pause] No question about colors this time? I crammed for this.

JCR: I don't think you needed to. This was an accurate account, I'm sure. [Long pause]. The prostitute?

TP: What is there to say?

JCR: You said she pleased you. What type of sex do you have?

TP: [Laughter] I won't ask you why that's important.

JCR: No. The answer would be too long.

TP: It's did have.

JCR: You won't be seeing her again?

TP: No. I'm always faithful when Heather is here.

JCR: You think she will stay long?

TP: I like to think forever. [Medium Pause] But I always do.

JCR: It would be a bit impractical if she did.

TP: No more than any other aspect of my life.

JCR: We might have to agree to disagree on that.

TP: Let's do that.

[Long Pause]

JCR: But we have been through that many times. So let's push ahead to Rosie the prostitute. Is that her real name?

TP: Yes.

JCR: Fitting. [Medium pause] What type of sex did you have?

TP: You name it.

JCR: That surprises me.

TP: Jesus.

JCR: Do you want me to make a list?

TP: Are you serious? [Long pause] Oral sex. Intercourse. Vaginal.

JCR: Oral sex, you received or gave or both?

TP: Jesus. [Medium pause] Received.

JCR: She sucked you. Any other oral sex?

TP: I bet your typist is amused right now. [Medium pause] She just sucked me off. Happy?

JCR: Positions with intercourse?

TP: I stood on my head.

JCR: [No audible response]

TP: I think you've been reading too much Freud. Stick to literary fiction.

JCR: [Medium pause] Okay, Tom, let's compromise. Are you willing to answer a single question with a simple yes or no? And then we move on. But the truth, or there is no point in asking.

TP: If it will get you off the topic, yes.

JCR: I think you had other sexual activities that you haven't told me about. Have you?

TP: [Medium pause] Yes.

JCR: Thank you. [Long pause] You've made close friends in your short stay.

TP: I like the Cuban people.

JCR: Billy is hardly Cuban. He is one of our typical Havana émigrés. I must admit more colorful than most, but otherwise typical. Their most important attribute, the common thread for them all, is that they can escape if need be. This gives them a better opportunity to relax, with less desire to climb those fences you talk about. Or shovel away the sand.

TP: Would you like to interview him? I bet his sex positions will keep your typist a lot more amused than mine. You may even learn something.

JCR: No, you are much more interesting, Tom. [Long pause] You are remarkably relaxed. [Medium pause] It is quite remarkable.

TP: [No audible response]

JCR: Señor Pupo. He isn't like a father figure.

TP: Not Freud again.

JCR: No, he isn't a father figure at all. He is the quintessential tragic hero.

TP: I stand corrected. Maybe you should stay away from literary fiction, as well.

JCR: You haven't had your one-on-one meeting with him yet? To ask him the questions [unintelligible mumble] Yes, here it is. To sort out uncertainties that you are developing.

TP: No, I haven't found the right time.

JCR: Do I need to ask you what those uncertainties are?

TP: I have lots of uncertainties at the moment.

JCR: Of course.

TP: I promise I will let you know when they arise. Or are solved.

JCR: Okay, another compromise. This is good. And I think I know how we can achieve this, more formally. [Short pause] Have you told your mothers about the farm?

TP: Not yet.

JCR: Difficult, yes?

TP: Yes.

JCR: Who knows about it?

TP: Everything?

JCR: Yes.

TP: Just Hymie.

JCR: And Heather.

TP: That goes without saying.

JCR: You don't think you should let others know?

TP: No.

JCR: Have you seen your accommodation? Does it meet your needs?

TP: At the farm? Yes, thank you. My needs are simple. Quiet. A desk to write. And a bed that fits two.

JCR: You are funny. [Short pause] And you are remarkably relaxed.

TP: [No response]

JCR: I'll say uniquely relaxed, in my experience.

TP: [No response]

JCR: Tom, I want you to keep a diary. Every day. I don't care what form it takes. But it must be daily. [Short pause] Reasonable?

TP: I'm a writer. Diaries are our bread and butter. Like taking a crap.

JCR: It may not be as easy as you think.

TP: I like a challenge.

JCR: That's clear. [Long Pause] I'll get you a copy of this interview. Did you get the others?

TP: As promised.

JCR: Any questions then?

TP: What's your typist's name?

JCR: Remarkably relaxed. [Medium pause] Oh, you didn't give me that description you promised about the first time you found Heather.

TP: Right. I've finished that some time ago. I'll drop it in.

JCR: Good. I look forward to reading your diary. Could you hand it to my secretary each day?

TP: That's a bit painful.

JCR: Humor me.

TP: Can I send her an email instead?

JCR: I prefer you to hand it to her in the morning, before you farm.

TP: I'll be starting early.

JCR: If she isn't here just slip it under the door. It won't take much of your time.

[Long pause]

TP: You know something, this diary might be longer than you're expecting.

END OF TAPE RECORDING.

Tell Me About The First Time You Found Her

> *Pilgrimages to the Ganges, the Gaya and the Godawari are merely worldly affairs* – Guru Granth Sahib Ji, 1195

"I never seen her," she said.

"She would be older than that now." I kept the photograph on the table as the waiter brought over the tea. The ceramic top rattled when he dropped it on the bench, lifting jasmine into the space.

"How old?"

"My age. Twenty-five. Actually, twenty-six."

She shook her head.

"Recognize anyone else?"

She studied the photograph and shook her head again.

"What about that handsome guy?"

"That you?"

"Well done."

"Your hair darker now." She smiled up at me. "And you all look same to us."

I poured the tea with a smile. "I could distinguish her from you . . . from anyone here . . . in an instant. From fifty meters."

"She look from North, not Yunnan. Beijing girl, I think."

"What about the old lady? Also Beijing?"

"Can't tell. But farmer. Too much sun."

"You can tell all of this from the Polaroid?"

"Zhen Ying number one guide."

I tucked the photograph back into my pocket. "I've been told she looks like a Yunnan girl."

"Who told?"

"Someone in Beijing . . . or Suzhou."

"Suzhou girl most beautiful. Beijing round face."

"And Yunnan girls?"

"Smartest." She grinned. "She from Yunnan?"

"I don't know, that's my problem."

The restaurant hugged us all, candle lit, the slate gray and crimson outside barely creeping through the open doorway.

"I take you to show tonight. Very old music . . . oldest in China. You will like." She sipped her tea. "You not eat much. You like food?"

"It's very good."

"I like Sichuan best. Spicy. Lijiang food spicy, but Sichuan more."

"I had it last year, or the year before. In Chengdu."

"You been so many places. Mr. Tom is egg . . . white on outside, yellow in."

I laughed. "No, not me. There are too many people here and too many rules for my liking." An old couple came in and glanced over at our table. "And too many stares."

"We don't get tourists. Too far come. Westerner go Shanghai, Beijing, Yangtze cruise. Not Lijiang. Egg man special . . . so looked at like panda."

"Maybe that explains it. But I'm not so sure."

She smiled. "You funny boy, Mr. Tom. But you smart . . . you hire best guide in Lijiang."

After tea, I walked alone in the light rain of the dank afternoon. The cobblestone path curled its uneven course, red lanterns lit, the wet silver light reflecting from the trail like alligator hide. The unfriendly timber houses that leaned over the path on both sides joined like gouts of clotted blood. The faces that leant out were unfriendly too.

Always staring.

China was a country that could stare without blinking.

I slipped again. These old shoes of mine, having lost their tread some time ago, kept my gait unsteady. In the adjacent doorway, an old woman seemed to show concern in the intonation of her response, and I smiled and took out my photograph and showed her the question neatly penned in Chinese on a separate sheet.

She studied it carefully. She shook her head. And I nodded and kept on my deliberate way.

The alley gradually widened into what might be called a street, with a canal of olive water thin on one side. A cherry blossom hung pink near its edge, and a wisp of light strained through it like fairy floss. Nearby, a bridge, no longer than four strides, joined a lantern-lit shop to the path. Lijiang felt unfriendly, but it held its beauty like a polished vintage car.

The shopkeeper popped out, holding an elderly umbrella. "You umbrella?" He swung it like a golf club.

"I like to be wet."

He looked at me but didn't understand. I crossed the bridge and held out the photograph and the page that went with it. He looked hard and went into his shop, and my heart stopped for a second or more. When he returned, looking over his black rim glasses, he shook his head and I moved on without buying his merchandise.

The rain, though never strong, kept on. My coat was made for a Manhattan winter, but I was wet and cold and when my feet started to ache I followed the path up to my inn that overlooked the town, a mosaic of chocolate-gray tiled roofs, curved up at the ends, a patchwork so tightly crammed that it hid any life below.

And I slept a bit, before being woken by the innkeeper who announced my guide had arrived. It took me a moment to remember. Old Chinese music.

* * *

The Naxi orchestra sat in three layers, their ancient instruments—reed, string and percussion—screeching like the primeval birds that were painted on the walls behind. The high notes of the women, also screeching, jarred the senses, and it seemed we had all been taken some place where the mythical birds and humans came to entertain for a brief moment as one.

Afterwards, we sat in the same unfriendly restaurant, though it had started to grow on me. You see, Juan, I was a creature of habit even in those early days.

My guide asked, "What you write about?"

"A talking dog."

She brought the bowl to her chin and scoffed rice into her mouth. "Dog talk in Australia?"

"This one does, but only to me."

"I read some books by Western. No talking animal."

"Really? No Richard Adams? George Orwell?"

"Never hear of them."

"This dog has much to say."

She looked at me strange.

"He is the judge and jury of all dogs. There are no laws except for his word."

"Like old days China."

"Something like that. Except if he sentences them to death . . . he has to do the killing himself."

"In old China, Emperor watch . . . but no blood on hand."

I poured the tea. "Decisions become more complex when you have to do the killing."

The waiter came over and tried to remove some of the yet empty plates but was brushed away by my companion.

"There is little blood spilled in my story," I said. "He takes them to a park where some stairs fall steeply down on one side to the road below. The stairs are lined by a fence of iron bars, and there is one bar missing, just at the top, and a little ledge that ends above a sheer drop."

"They push off?"

"Not exactly. You know how dogs get their heads caught through the bars of fences? He makes them push their heads through these bars, and no matter how big they are, even the bulldogs, they can always seem to manage it. And when they're stuck, he bites their leg and they jump off the ledge."

"He hang them?"

"He hangs them."

She kept on with her rice for a bit. "You make lot money writing?"

"None as yet, though I am beginning to publish."

"How you eat?"

"I live simply."

"Still need money to live . . . even in Lijiang."

"I came into some money when I was younger."

"Dead ancestor?"

"Dead ancestor."

She kept on with her rice. "You think ancestor happy you write with money?"

"I think so."

She pushed her plate away and waved at the unfriendly waiter. "I like dog story. But China only read Chinese. I translate when finished. Deal?"

I laughed. "We'll see."

"Why you wear sunglasses in dark room?"

"It makes me feel more comfortable."

"You funny, Mr. Tom."

I yawned. "Mr. Tom is tired. It's been a long day. Tomorrow I want to go to the police station. I'll need you to interpret."

"We go Jade Dragon shan after?"

"No, Zhen Ying. Tomorrow, after police, I write."

"Okay. Day after tomorrow."

"We'll see."

She stood and waved again at the waiter. "Husband and child waiting for dinner at home. I work day. I work night. We both need rest. I pick you up at ten. Okay?"

And I said okay.

I rarely wandered anywhere in China at night. There was no point—the faces veiled by darkness, my photograph anonymous. But Lijiang had become somewhat of an exception. The rain had stopped, but the cobblestones were still slippery as I climbed the zigzag path to the inn.

The town in the evening was even more beautiful than in daylight. The red lanterns hung down like strings of plump pearls, their light transforming the timber houses with fresh blood, the alligator path and trunk and leaves all the same vermillion shade, the shadows painted as with a brush, and the thin strip of canal reflecting all this back to view.

So I wandered the labyrinthine alleys even though I was spent—a random journey, yet always rising with the slope of the land.

It wasn't from fifty meters that I saw her. It was probably half that. Front on. She was above me on the path ahead. She stood as if I wasn't there. The alleyway was dim and the shadows cut across her, so I couldn't be sure. The play of the light. I remember that first feeling of tingly panic. My lungs eating the soup of the air. Eating not breathing.

It wasn't just the ponytails twisted the same way, her almond eyes.

Her dimples.

It was something else I couldn't identify in the shadows of the ally.

But she was young. No older than eight or nine.

She left the path and entered somewhere, and when I got up to the spot the doors were closed on both possible entrances.

I knocked on the first and waited.

From where I stood, the lane was empty, though it curved sharply just yards ahead, the sound of a doorway slamming, some mutterings, all out of sight.

I knocked again, resting my ear against the timber but heard nothing. I stepped back a pace to see if any sign came from the second floor—though it seemed dark and lifeless.

So I knocked on the next door and pressed my ear to the timber. A sound maybe in the back.

I did the math as I waited. Eight from twenty-six makes eighteen. Grandmother was married when she was young. It was the Chinese way. It all made sense.

The air seemed to thin out a bit and my panic settled.

Then the door opened.

A man older than me, mid thirties maybe, shirtless, round bellied, stood at the doorway.

"Is there a little girl living here?" I measured her height with my outstretched arm. My hands made to twist faux ponytails against my ears.

He just stood and stared at my pantomime. I'm not sure he understood.

But if he was the husband, she was the wife. I pulled out the photograph and the translated description. 'Have you seen this girl before? She was fourteen here and now would be twenty-six. She may be called Heather. Have you seen this old lady before? She is her grandmother.'

He took the paper into the light of the hallway and seemed to study it for longer than the others. He turned the photograph over. He turned the page over. He was careful with his examination.

But he shook his head.

I looked over his shoulder but couldn't see any movement. The end of the hall seemed to open up into a kitchen space, the smells hauntingly familiar. I stepped in and he looked at me strange but didn't stand in my way. I went further down the hall, not rushing so as not to alarm him. A steady stroll, though my heart was racing—just popping in for a chat, old chum. I entered the end room. A single bowl of half eaten noodles sat on a little table. And when I turned, the round-bellied man hadn't left his position at the doorway—though he kept his stare intent. He seemed frightened more than anything, as the egg man was invading his home.

So I left him to finish his meal.

***

"How you know she daughter?"

"I just know."

"It dark here at night."

"The lanterns were close by, I'm sure it was her."

The sky was clear, and the morning light threw silver onto the cobblestones every time we changed direction.

"Don't walk fast."

"It's just down here a bit."

It was the quieter edge of town, away from the shops. Some of the houses seemed unoccupied, ragged at the edges.

"We are here." I bent down and picked up the pen I had wedged under the step of the noodle man's house. The door was open and my guide shouted some greeting from the entrance. Dear Juan, I must tell you that I was embarrassed every time I listened to Mandarin without understanding a word. I had travelled throughout the country many times, but never managed to recapture the skill learnt as a child through warm whispers and a taste of dim sum.

The round-bellied man came down the hall. I took a step back and let my guide take over. We had discussed what was to be said, and I trusted her accuracy and saw the effort she made. I knew she thought I was crazy, with this strange pilgrimage of mine, but she was rooting for me.

"He say no girl live here. His wife visiting sister with son. She back tomorrow. Next door owner away too. One week. They older, one son but not child, and not live here."

"How old is this man's wife?"

She translated my question and the man stared at me a second before answering. Thirty-two. He was thirty-eight. She had asked the latter for me. She could sense I didn't trust him.

They talked some more. There was no girl of the description in any of the houses around us.

So she took me to the closest school, and then one further on. And for the next week I sat outside both, switching back and forth in the morning and afternoon, but the little girl never appeared.

* * *

"I worry about you."

"Did you talk to the noodle man's wife?"

"Yes. I follow her to market. Show her photograph. She know my mother. Cut hair."

"And?"

"She know nothing." She lifted her hand to the waiter. "You not shave."

"I not shave."

The waiter came over.

"You want same omelet?"

I nodded and she ordered for me.

"Why you not write dog story?"

"I can't concentrate."

"And you not eat. You like stick."

"I've always been thin."

"No. You lost weight just time you in Lijiang."

"I'm in a café, aren't I?"

"But I always eat what left over. I have two lunch, two dinner. I get fat. My husband complain." She bent over and whispered, "I think he jealous." She sat upright and laughed. "But I tell him you crazy Western in love with needle in sea."

I removed my sunglasses and rubbed my eyes.

"You not sleep?"

"I not sleep."

She shook her head. "You stop fishing for needle. I set you up with . . ." She paused and threw one of her faces at me. "Husband must work . . . Chinese girl won't be with . . ." She shook her head. "You not work. If my husband stop work I stop . . . being wife."

"Did you order rice?"

"One bowl. What animal you born?"

"Ox."

She pulled another face. "Western ox not same as Chinese ox. My brother ox. You not my brother."

"Actually, I'm a golden ox."

She laughed. "You not eat, you be golden chopstick."

After dinner I took a stroll around the noodle man's house. I couldn't call it wandering anymore; it was too deliberate, each street traversed in full, making sure I covered every inch of the town.

Have you seen a girl who looks like her though younger? About eight years old. The script of my page now expanded by two sentences.

Have you seen a girl? What about your friend? Has he seen her?

I kept to the lit side of the streets. No hiding in the shadows.

And then, in a quiet little alley, I saw her. Twenty meters away. Her back to me.

What was it about her that I knew it was her?

Her walk? Something else?

"Hello," I shouted.

She turned her head a bit but kept walking.

I quickened my stride.

She turned up the street where I first found her.

"Hello, stop a second," I shouted louder.

She turned and I saw it was the same girl. She didn't seem afraid but twisted around and kept on walking. The door was open and she turned into the noodle man's house. Just ten meters away.

I started to panic. The air thickened.

The door was open. There was noise in the kitchen. Voices. Laughter.

I went down the hallway. The noodle man was sitting at the table. And a woman was sitting with her back to me, with long black hair to her shoulders. Ink black.

And the little girl sat on a chair near the man. Jesus.

She stared at me. Jesus.

What was it about her? Jesus.

The man looked up at me. I could see he was scared. He said something loud but I didn't understand.

What was it?

And the little girl smiled.

And the woman started to turn in slow motion.

And I saw what it was. What I couldn't identify until now.

The gray school-dress. Jesus.

The leather clinkers. Jesus.

And the little girl just sat there smiling and the man shouted something again and the woman kept turning her head slow like the second hand of a clock—tick-tock, tick-tock—until she bent fully around to look straight up to me.

Jesus.

And in the chaos of it all, with their wide-eyed stares and the air full of soup and the little room not blood-red like the streets but vivid white, casting no shadows, with no play of light—I heard the words that brought my journey to an end.

"Tommy, you found me."

* * *

Asia is exotic, and so was China in those days. The smell of the land, people, refuse—a hotpot of powdered horn, scorpion, the stars—ox and rat—bubbling away, slowly to be sipped with nothing discarded.

This was the setting of our first meeting, Juan. And I accepted it just like any of the Saturday overnight stays of my youth. I accepted it all.

We left the noodle man's house immediately, together. I didn't wait for the worried faces barking commands I couldn't understand, hands raised, pointing, I didn't wait a second.

"Come with me, Heather."

And she did.

We scampered, like we did at school, scuffing leather against bitumen, now cobblestones, turning in and out of the vermillion-lit streets, jogging like we were late for class.

"You found me, Tommy." She kept saying it and I grinned at her and we ran together on the playgrounds of our childhood.

When I reached the inn, I didn't bother to acknowledge anyone, we just hopped up the stairs together. I had the key in my pocket, I didn't care what they thought, if I was breaking any rules with my visitor, I didn't care.

And when we sat on the bed together, I stared and stared.

"You are thin, Tommy."

"So I've been told. 'Chopstick' was the word used."

"And your hair is darker."

"No more swimming to keep it blonde."

"I liked your swimming. Did you know I wanted to swim with you, but Grandmother wouldn't let me?"

"You never told me that. I don't even know if you can swim. That's crazy, hey? All those years spent in a pool and I don't know whether you can even swim."

"Crazy."

"Jesus, Heather."

When she smiled at me I felt at one with the world, a part of every morsel, the space in between.

"Is Grandmother here?"

"She's gone, Tommy."

"Shit." I closed my eyes. "I miss her so much."

I opened my eyes and she sat there cross-legged on the bed, and her dimples were just the same. Everything was just the same.

"What have you been doing, Tommy. All this time?"

"Looking for you."

"Not since we left?"

"Not straight away. I waited for you to come back. I waited and waited."

"I'm sorry, Tommy. I had no choice."

I kept my unblinking stare.

"What about school?" she said.

"It ended when you left."

"Oh, Tommy."

"You can't imagine, Heather, what I went through in those years after you left. You can't begin . . . to imagine."

I remember every detail of this meeting, dear Juan. I remember crying at that second. Tears came in the gap of begin, in the precise break of the syllables. Heather sat in front of me, square on, and I remember every detail, the chair, the walls, the table, the colors, yes Juan, no fiction here. I remember everything as if it's happening before me now.

"It's your turn, Heather. Just talk to me so I know you are real."

"You are funny, Tommy."

"Talk to me."

"Should I tell you about when we went? Grandmother and me in the night?"

"Yes, talk to me."

"She woke me up when I was fast asleep. She said they had come. They couldn't wait. Don't get upset, Tommy."

I wiped my face. "Just talk, Heather, please."

"We had a fight. She didn't want me to take my dolls."

"But you won that fight."

"Yes. I think she felt sorry for me. I was so scared."

"God, Heather. Why didn't you tell me?"

"We talked about it."

"I don't remember that."

"We talked before."

"Why wouldn't I remember that?"

"Don't get upset, Tommy."

The tears that came were from excitement, Juan, but she wasn't to know it then.

"We left in the back of a van. Other Chinese too. It was still dark when we went on the boat. Grandmother said it came from Hong Kong."

"Mao had died. I remember when you left, we studied it at school."

"My parents saved for the trip. Grandmother said it was time to go home."

"Why didn't you take me?"

"Tommy, don't get upset. I couldn't. How could we?"

"I could have learnt the language. I was good at it, remember?"

"Tommy, we talked about it." She shook her head. "I hated the boat so much. I was sick every day. It felt like years."

I wiped my eyes. "I used to get car sick when I was a kid."

"I thought I was going to die. Grandmother made rice soup for me. I kept being sick and it's all I could eat."

"I always liked her congee."

"I pleaded with her, Tommy. I said I didn't care if I was going to see my parents. I wanted to go back to Crepundia. But she said to trust her. When we arrived it was night, just the same way we left. We all met up on a beach. I remember the sand moved like the ocean. I remember the faces of my parents. They had a candle and it kept going out and so they kept disappearing in the dark and I was scared I would lose them again."

"God, I so wish Grandmother was here, too"

"We went on this long journey in a wagon. Two horses. And on the first morning I saw my mother's face for the first time without it disappearing. She was taller than Grandmother and had the same eyes and nose and mouth as her. But she didn't laugh like her. Although my mother was never one to laugh much."

"She was a crazy old bird, your grandmother."

"It was cold and kept getting colder the longer we rose up in the mountains. I had never been so cold. I think Grandmother thought I was going to die. Every day we stayed in a new farm house. We always travelled at night. I think it was safer, even with the cold. My parents were scared we'd get caught and be separated . . . punishment for leaving. Tommy, there was punishment everywhere in those days. But we got there. A week or more. We got to our village. And I remember sleeping for days. Grandmother always fattening me up. Whenever I woke, every time, she was sitting next to me on the bed with some food in a bowl."

I smiled. "Peking duck."

"Nothing so luxurious, but everything was filling. And when I became strong, I became a farmer like the others in my village."

"God, Heather."

"And some years later, just before Grandmother died, she told me she was sorry for bringing me here."

* * *

After that initial discovery, we always met in my room of the guesthouse.

It was a clandestine meeting, of course. My guide came for me the next morning and was told that I hadn't surfaced for breakfast, and when the manager of the inn came up and knocked on my door I feigned a croaky voice, a cough, and said I would stay in bed all day.

The next day my cough was worse.

And the next.

And every day Heather came as she always did. After the second day, she even brought the dolls. Penny and Dotty and pretty, blonde Carla.

And when she was there, I lay on the bed and stared and stared and felt there may be a God after all—even in this strange land that had thrown all deities away a generation back.

"What were the chances of you finding me, Tommy?"

"One in a billion, my guide tells me. Literally."

She laughed.

"I guess I knew you weren't in Australia. You could have contacted my parents if you wanted, at the beginning at least. So you must have been somewhere you couldn't make contact."

"So China was the only place. My Baby is so smart."

"Well, you could have been dead." I sighed. "But if you were dead, I might as well have been too."

"Oh, Tommy."

Tears came sudden to me in those early meetings. Not gushes, but covert, like Heather's visits. I hid my face sometimes, but she could always tell. So, in the end, I stopped trying to hide them. And she accepted them as part of the conversation.

I looked at the cracked head of Dotty that sat on her lap; and wiped my face. "I can't believe you still have the dolls."

"It's the only bit of my childhood I can touch."

"Of our childhood."

She smiled her almond eyes at me.

"She has a larger head than I remember."

"Don't be cruel, Tommy." She grinned. And her dimples puckered like the eggcups of this lost childhood of ours.

"But her wrinkles are no worse. So you've kept her out of the sun."

She lifted the doll to her face. "Dotty doesn't like to farm. Do you, darling?"

We laughed together.

"I don't remember her ever saying much," I said. "Carla was the one who talked a lot. She was a real saucy thing."

"And athletic. She was everything I wasn't."

"She wasn't smart, if I remember."

She giggled. "Nope, and that hasn't changed."

A tap on the door stopped us in our tracks. I held my finger to my mouth.

The guide spoke through the door to me. "Mr. Tom, could you open?"

I kept my finger in place. "I'm not dressed, Zhen Ying."

"I wait."

"I'm in bed."

There was a short pause. "Mr. Tang say you not come down yet. For days you not come down."

"I have. He just wasn't there when I did."

"Mr. Tang always here."

I shook my head and Heather grinned.

"If you don't come eat, I kick door."

"Okay. I will meet you for lunch at the café."

"When?"

"One hour."

"Thirty minute."

I smiled. "You win. I'll meet you there. But don't wait for me downstairs."

"If not come I kick door down. I swear I do this."

"Mr. Tang has a key. That would be easier."

"He won't give. So I kick."

My little window overlooked the gray-tiled roofs of the town, the sun reflecting like diamonds where the glaze hadn't worn, and I felt a deep hunger and joy flush in my innards all at once. "Zhen Ying, I promise to be there."

And I kept my promise.

* * *

But this first contact between Heather and I became very complicated, as you could well imagine, Juan. This was not the place for such a meeting. China was not the place, then or now, for this first discovery of ours.

I was going to say you can't imagine what happened. But of course, you can.

If it wasn't for my guide. And my Australian passport.

God help me.

And so, Juan, I was shown the border, not particularly politely, and I wasn't welcomed back. And I've never tested their resolve on the matter.

Which has meant, ever since that first time, Heather has had to come to me.

Keep A Diary

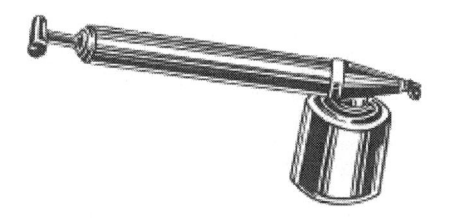

THURSDAY

You were right. It was difficult telling them about the farm—my mothers, that is.

Earlier in the day I visited my Cubilete troupe. They were easy—it was I who would miss them, not the other way around. They took my farming in their stride—a midlife crisis they thought. Like sailors heading off into the blue-green void, tossing and rolling with the escape from their lives; the hunters of fish, trinkets, men—all ploys—the escape the only booty they need. Like a poor magic trick—the Everyman vanishes.

So my Cubilete troupe understood, or thought they did.

My mothers were more skeptical—the discussion long, exhausting, the translator working overtime. Señora Pupo rushed out to get a lobster for dinner since I wouldn't be there the following night. I told them I couldn't stay for dinner, the farm would only let me leave on weekends. The rules couldn't be broken, I told them, Juan. But mothers don't always listen to rules set by others—especially when their children are involved.

It was a carefully audited discourse with them, each of the phrases checked by the other, the words typed by one of my one-fingered prosecutors, the phrase repeated on the audio-translator by the other. I will spare you the process as it happened because of the brevity demands of a diary.

"Why do you want to farm?"

"I want to touch the earth. Make things grow."

"I don't believe it . . . we don't believe it."

I didn't respond since there was no judge to force me.

"How long you farm?"

"I don't know."

"Why you want to farm?" They found a way to repeat the phrase with one touch of the keyboard.

I run like a stray antelope—the lionesses stealthily isolating me from the herd. "I want to grow what's on my plate. You must understand this."

"No."

"I want some time to think. Long hours in the open will help."

Señora Pupo nodded her head. Estelle paused a bit.

"I don't believe you."

I the antelope—lone strides in high grass.

"My girlfriend is in Havana. She will stay with me on the farm."

At this they both nodded.

Estelle typed with her pointing finger. "Tell us about her."

"I love her."

"Tell us about her."

"We will start back slow."

"Why slow? You are a man, not a boy." The pointing finger became the accuser.

We will start back slow like fumbling teens on their first date. I typed this in. Though we were never fumbling before.

"Tell us about her."

"She is beautiful."

"Tell us about her."

The cross examination grew wearisome, the questions not worth repeating—they are self-evident. My Cubilete troupe just wanted to know I was happy—my mothers wanted everything.

Which, in the end, they got.

I the antelope—their jaws took me down at the neck. The deconstruction a slow bloody feast, whiskers a red wet, preening to strawberry pink. Their bellies all-full.

I am tired from it. I will sleep well, I think.

Tomorrow the farm.

And the Everyman vanishes.

* * *

FRIDAY

The joy of it all.

I arrived late this morning—Rafael was unhappy—but the rising sun was an impossible breakfast mate for me today. I promised him this would be my only tardy start. He didn't seem to believe me, though.

Rafael is an odd sod. A weather-beaten gaucho who has lost his steed. He told me he's been at the farm for twenty years. I'm not sure how old he is, the sun plays tricks when it comes to age, but I guess he's older than me. I will ask him when he's in a better mood.

First he showed me around—the long rectangular groves of grapefruit, orange, banana and mango, the ankle-low potato and manioc plots that separate the orchards into an easy view. And the vast, chest-high fields of tobacco—to the shoulder or head of some, the fresh green nose settling over us. Rafael said this was the only corojo tobacco grown in Cuba—no sickness in the leaves—and used to wrap only the most expensive cigars. He said it made more money than all the other plots put together. But the corojo needed the other plants to protect it from the sickness. He smiled at me after saying this—his teeth the color of straw, misshapen and dangling. He closed his mouth when he saw me staring.

I must remember not to stare. Especially not here.

He told me I'd be working with the potatoes. The strip of land was no more than fifty feet wide, rising slightly two hundred feet or more all the way up to the dormitories that sat in a long, perpendicular block and overlooked the land. On one side of my plot was a banana plantation, the other tobacco. Giant green leaves hugged me on both sides.

Rafael took a short hoe attached to his belt and dug into the earth, pulling out a skinny-leaf plant, roots and all. "This weed." He pointed to a fatter-leaved neighbor. "This potato." He handed me the hoe. "Don't dig potato, only weed." So simple the instructions that would shape my life.

I bent down, put my hand into the soil, and pulled at the first weed clumsily. The second came free a bit easier. I looked up at the rutted strip of land that sunk low against the flanking banana and tobacco. I alone would be responsible for removing the weeds from the potato crop. I would start from the bottom right corner and move slowly up the first ploughed ridge until reaching the top, then move down, and so on.

It wasn't a hot day, and a breeze came often and kept my sweat away.

I am tired again. It is late and I need to sleep. I haven't had time to tell you everything of my day—give me time to set the right pace. Perhaps I'll plan my writing as I till the earth. Then bunker in after dinner.

The joy of it all.

* * *

SATURDAY

Heather came and watched me dig the soil today.

She came as she always did. Her beautiful dimples. Her almond eyes smiling. Settling me down as no other could.

She had never seen me farm and it amused her. She sat under the shade of the banana grove and watched me dig in the heat. I knew she wouldn't help, that wasn't part of the deal. But she would be here for me as long as it took.

You know something, Juan, I find it difficult to write about Heather, to capture our time together in a diary format. It's the day-to-day log of it I think is the problem. Funny, the recollections are easier to write about than the real-time events. Why is that? Surely it should be the other way around? But it's a stumbling block I will need to get through.

Anyhow, give me some time—to get through the early fumbling teen stuff that I think best describes it.

Yes, time.

That is the key.

* * *

It was much hotter in the sun than yesterday. Rafael came down in the late morning to see how I was faring. He seemed satisfied with my efforts, inspecting the bamboo basket full of weeds, the roots intact, and even filled my water bottle back at the dorm since the irrigation water wasn't potable. I think he was impressed I was working on Saturday because the weekend was my leave time, but I wanted to make up for yesterday's late start. Rafael had the weekends off as well, so I wasn't certain why he was here, either. I thought it too early to discuss what he did on his leave, so I'll ask him about it some other time. When I ask him how old he is. Perhaps over dinner.

Dinnertime is strange—or 'difficult' may be a better word. It feels like being in a boarding school, with long tables so you're all forced to mix. I understand the concept, but I'd prefer a more familiar routine, my seatmates known quantities, at least at first. Rafael kept a space for me last night. He didn't have much to say, but his presence gave me some comfort. I noticed he found it hard to eat with his teeth in the state they're in, grinding the meat with his back molars after cutting it into little pieces. He seemed more comfortable with the mashed potato and manioc.

The cabbage was a bit too heavily salted, but on the whole not bad. Meat and three veg, all of a different color, my childhood staple. Mum would be pleased.

I'm pretty certain Rafael didn't see me watching him eat—I notice he keeps his head down when he chews. I guess he tries to avoid any distraction, otherwise he might drop a tooth.

The nights are quiet here—the farm out of earshot from the main road. My neighbors seem quiet too. One keeps a radio on, but these walls are solid, double brick I suspect, and the sound is only heard in the hallway. I said hello briefly. They seem nice enough.

Heather hasn't stayed yet. This gives me more time to settle into the place, so probably it's for the best. But I miss her terribly.

* * *

SUNDAY

Hymie picked me up in the morning in his rental. He had spent three days in Valle de Vinales and was waxing lyrical on the beauty of the place. I told him Heather and I might find a way to get there one weekend, perhaps before he leaves, whenever that might be. He seemed to like the idea, though I wasn't completely sure. You see, dear Juan, Hymie has never been enamored with Heather.

We both had a late lunch with my mothers—a pre-arranged feast at the sky-blue casa. Estelle greeted me clicking her palate like a maraca, with wrapped arms and lots of cheek pinching, and made out I had lost weight. Her cousin Marco was a farmer, so she knew about these things. Señora Pupo said to me on the quiet that Marco was the size of a bull. Un toro con ubres—a bull with udders.

A copper pot of Boliche, tomato and cucumber salad, lobster tails, empanadas, congri. Coffee and cake. I noticed the black velvet jacket no longer hung over the lounge chair. I kept quiet about this—I thought it best.

We were deep into the feast when Rosie arrived. She came through the open front door as if invited. Estelle rose and gave her a kiss and dragged the outside chair in and she sat with us as well. Estelle's eyes danced; Señora Pupo's lower, moving with the shuffle of the plates.

I stood and went to kiss her on the cheek, but she moved and I touched her lips with mine. Her little white shorts and little white top. Little white socks. Her skin the color of the congri beans. And the taste of the salt spray from the Malecón on her mouth. After that, I didn't know where to look.

As we all sat together, Hymie perked up his charm, which seemed to annoy Estelle but not her sister. My mothers seemed to be out of sync—like they had fought about something before I arrived. Rosie translated to the table, allowing Hymie to get into his groove of sharp Brooklyn wit. I noticed he didn't use his signature introduction with Rosie—which, unbeknown to him, would have amused her. Or I think it would.

Hymie's interrogation of Rosie was deft, and I felt ashamed that I hadn't already known the answers. She wasn't married, she didn't have a boyfriend, her daughter was six and lived in Holguín with her grandmother. Her occupation was a walking guide in Havana. I smiled at this, and she smiled with me as well. Estelle smiled too. Señora Pupo looked down at the empty plates and didn't smile at all.

We left my mothers when the early evening painted a gray rectangle at the open doorway. Hymie gave Rosie his room number at the Ambos Mundos. My friend is a faithful husband, but I suspect Cuba was testing his faith. Cuba tests the faith of many—it always has. We hugged our leave and Rosie motioned to follow—Estelle practically threw her at the door as we stepped outside. It was light enough for Rosie to see my eyes—she well trained in the reading of eyes, a necessary skill for a walking guide of Havana. And she read mine well. She looked down and brought her lip over her long buckteeth and slid off into the night, probably back down to the Malecón or the Plaza de Armas, maybe back home. And I was ashamed I didn't know where home was.

We drove through the entrance of the farm, the gravel crunching into the quiet. As we turned a slow arc, the yellow-lit windows of the dormitory rooms came into view.

"Tom," he said, "you might be interested to know that adultery in Jewish law can only be committed with a married woman."

"That's interesting, Hymie. But you aren't religious."

"But I am a Jew."

"Yes, Hymie. You are that."

"The corollary being that, technically, a married man who has intercourse with a non-married woman isn't committing adultery."

"What is he committing?"

"I'm not sure, but not adultery."

"That's interesting, Hymie. But you're not religious."

"But I am a Jew."

It is late but I'm not at all tired, and more eager than ever for an early start. I saw Heather today, of course. But again, there seems not enough time to tell you about it. If I do, the detail of it all, I wouldn't get enough sleep. And I need my sleep for the sake of the potatoes under my care.

What magic is this that causes such yearning to dig the earth?

* * *

MONDAY

The window of my room looks due east, straight down at my potato crop, so I wake with an orange-lit alarm clock that also feeds the plants I care for.

Breakfast is easier than dinner. There's a hurry built into it—no time to worry about conversation or loose teeth. This morning, porridge and two bananas, and coffee that comes out of a stainless steel tank the size of a washing machine.

I brush my teeth in line with the others. I don't shave.

I like the routine.

I dig with my hoe, but remove the weeds with my hands.

Heather arrives around ten. The day begins to warm. She sits closer this time, not under the canopy of the falling banana leaves, but nearer to me, so we can talk more easily. Her skin won't burn in this low December sun.

Rafael comes down and we chat a bit. I ask him what I'll do when the weeds are gone—I'm making pretty steady progress? Can I keep looking after the potatoes that I've become so attached to? He doesn't commit, but he likes my eagerness—I can see that. I ask him to keep a space for me at dinner.

Last night I didn't have time to tell you, Juan,—yesterday Hymie and I went to Calle Obispo after seeing my mothers. It wasn't as important as the long lunch, but I seem now to have the time to document it.

We sat in our clumsy square, Yanela and Billy, Hymie and I. I didn't drink and felt left out a bit. Maybe I should drink again, just on weekends. I miss the mojitos and the salsa dance it gives to my head. Billy is keen that I drink as well.

I saw the Lolitas too (I originally wrote 'my Lolitas,' but they were never really mine in any important sense). They didn't show me much attention this time, which was a relief. Billy had ruffled their feathers, so they were preoccupied with his torment—and it was a school night.

Heather never came tonight. She said she wouldn't and kept her word.

I guess I understand why Hymie isn't a fan of hers.

* * *

TUESDAY

My brine soaked skin cures like leather in the sun. I give it more of a dose each day, and it stings now, even when I cover it.

The cricket cap doesn't protect my neck, so I lift up my collar, like Chappelli going in to bat. We played in the backyard, my brother and I, mowed ourselves a pitch, the ball a hard red plastic that cracked when it thinned. I could bat all day, ten innings, score a couple of centuries. Chappelli was my favorite—he could always save the team. Redpath and Lawry bunkered down at the start, but Chappelli scored the runs. My brother was England—he was the younger so he had no other choice. Boycott always played with a straight bat—it took an effort to get him out.

Schoolboy memories come flooding back out here. How could they not?

Heather won't farm because of before. She farmed then—the older teens all did. She reminded me of this as she sat under the shade of the bananas.

Rafael didn't come down today. In the early afternoon I looked up from my digging and he was standing near the top of the crop, quite a distance away. I think he saw me talking to Heather and didn't want to disturb. But even when she left, he didn't come down.

I thought it would take forever to rid the weeds away, but I'm nearly half done. My back aches, so I plan to do some strengthening exercises before bed and when I first wake—to harden the sinews like my skin.

Today I saw a woman come out at the edge of the tobacco field, only twenty feet away from my hunched-over digging. She popped out and startled me a bit. She was a tiny thing; her head, when she bent down just at a slight angle, fell below the foliage. She saw that I was startled and smiled and popped back in and out of sight. A scurrying field mouse in the corojo.

I noticed her again at dinner, but she was sitting with another group of women, all about her age, mid-twenties I would guess, and so I didn't bother trying to chat with her.

I sat opposite Rafael at dinner, but at a diagonal. Leonardo sat directly in front. Leonardo and Rafael. I wonder whether there are any Michelangelos and Donatellos on the farm. Teenage mutant ninja turtles were Christmas presents for my brother's kids, though far too imperialist for Cuba's children, I suspect.

Leonardo has an unpleasant tic, his head nodding to an unheard beat, one eye dancing quietly with itself. My gaze shifting away from these spasms to Rafael's dangling kidney bean teeth and back again. Leonardo was chatty though. He worked in the corojo field, and his skin smelled of green tobacco. I stealthily pointed out the young field mouse who was well away on another table, to see if he knew of her. Rafael gave me a prudish glare at this. Well, it seemed prudish, but he didn't qualify the glare with any comment, since he was preoccupied with grinding meat with the few healthy molars left in his head. Leonardo said he didn't know her name, but she was new. Not as new as me, but here only for some weeks. I hinted to Rafael it would be a pleasure to work in the tobacco field when I finished my weeding, and he gave me another glare, this one decidedly prudish, in between chews. So I left it at that.

The days are full. I wake early, farm, eat and write. There seems no time for anything else.

* * *

WEDNESDAY

I reread my diary, tightened some of the prose. You only get to see the day's rushes—Hymie will get the final edit.

Heather stayed longer today. She was beautiful and we talked and talked. I think she might stay overnight soon.

China was hard for her. The Cultural Revolution was over and her parents weren't separated from each other anymore, but it was still tough.

I've just realized the irony of it all—she coming back to a farm in communist Cuba. Just for me. I'm stupid and insensitive.

I know it doesn't make sense, but that's how I feel.

I'll apologize to her tomorrow.

The talk of the day slowed my digging somewhat, but I intend to finish by the week's end. I told Rafael, and he seemed satisfied. We all sat at the long dinner table together again, twitching and chewing and smelling of tobacco. Leonardo said her name was Eva—that's all he knew. Rafael didn't seem to be as fussed about the gossip this time, perhaps because the chicken stew was easier to gum.

When I first arrived at the table, Leonardo had left a space for both of us, and I took the opportunity to ask him about Rafael. He said he came when his wife and child had died in a car accident. Everyone knew about it. He was a tobacco farmer by trade, but that's all I found out before he joined us.

I smiled at Rafael. He nodded his head and gave a tightlipped smile back at me. And I asked him about his loveless day.

These characters seem straight from Dickens. I like them all and want to see what happens to them.

I feel so blessed to be here.

* * *

THURSDAY

I've gotten into the habit of taking a long siesta in the heat of the day. I swill down my bread and soup then hit the sack. The double brick rooms are cool and quiet, and at the clang of the bell at two, I'm fresh and ready to start over.

My field mouse poked her head out of the tobacco plot this afternoon. She looked around, I think to see whether I was alone, then strolled on over. She wore baggy green overalls and had bits of leaves in her hair. We introduced ourselves and chatted in broken Spanglish.

Eva said people on the farm were talking about me. It seems I'm the only gringo here, Juan. I was muy misterioso. I said I wasn't mysterious and was relieved she didn't prod any further. She told me that sometimes she watches me farm through the tobacco leaves.

"You not see me." She grinned a full set of teeth, pointing at her olive camouflage suit. "I invisible." She twisted her gaze around again at my potatoes. A calm, agitated scan, if there is such a thing. "You farm mucho."

"Sí."

"No me." She scanned again. "I sleep in tabaco." The detritus in her hair suggested a recent doze. "You eat with Raphael. You like him?"

"Sí."

"No me." She pulled her face into a grimace. "Work work work."

I smiled at the girl.

"Why you work mucho?"

"I like it."

"I see you crazy."

"Sí."

She moved back and entered into the shoulder-high tobacco crop. When fully submerged in the foliage, she poked her head out and grinned her full set of teeth again. "Me no crazy. Me sleep." And she disappeared into the tobacco.

At dinner she came over to us. Interestingly, Leonardo's spasms flared up as she approached, but he seemed not to be worried about it. I like this man so much.

"Buenas noches, señorita." The tic tilted his head between each word.

Eva sat down at the table and looked at Raphael, who had yet to finish his stew.

"I eat two plate," she said. "Mucho work, make me hungry." She turned her head to me and winked.

She was beautiful, this mouse of the tobacco.

Raphael gave her a raised up brow but kept on gumming his stew.

"I like food here," Eva said. "You like?"

Raphael nodded.

"Bed, I no like. Too small."

"I miss my big bed. The soft mattress." Leonardo said, throwing up a tic between sentences.

"You, Tom? You miss grande bed?" She looked straight at me with her mouse eyes.

"Not really." Nobody knew of my planned sleeping arrangements.

"And you, Señor Raphael?"

"No," he said with a mouthful of dinner.

"I like grande soft bed. I like sleep naked in grande soft bed."

Leonardo threw up a fit of spasms. Eva giggled. Raphael kept to his stew.

"On Sunday morning at casa I stay in bed. Sometime all day."

"Naked," I said.

"Naked." She laughed. "What about you, Señor Raphael?"

"When I was young, I slept naked," Leonardo said.

"But you still young."

"No, señorita. Not for a long time."

"Younger than me," I said.

"Señor Raphael . . . how you sleep?"

"Silent." He kept on with his food, not raising a glance.

Eva poked her tongue at his turned down head. "Why can't we get big bed?"

"This is no hotel," Raphael said, with his head still low.

I watched her eyes dance around the table in that calm agitated way of hers. She was tiny out of her camouflage gear—coffee-olive and tiny.

"What days do you have off?" I asked her.

"I like so much, I no go home."

Raphael lifted his eyes from his plate to her.

"But no work weekend." She grinned at Raphael. "Weekend sleep."

"Naked?" Raphael said with a flicker of a smile.

"Sí, Señor Raphael. Naked."

* * *

FRIDAY

Heather came early in the morning.

It had been raining overnight, and my knees were painted with the wet earth. I had one long stretch of soil remaining, then I was done. It would take a full day, but with Heather's early appearance, the time would slow, so I was worried I might not get the job finished.

As you might imagine, Juan, we rarely fight.

But sometimes we do if I have to get something done. Not writing—I usually never write when Heather visits, it's one of the reasons Hymie doesn't like her. But if I have to do something complicated, requiring concentration—my tax for instance—or if I'm time constrained, like today, we might fight.

But we never fought as children. Not even a cross word. Not a frown.

Don't get me wrong, I can count on one hand, or maybe two, how many fights, or 'conflicts' might be a better word, we've had over the years. That's not bad, hey? That's not bad at all.

She sat close and moved with me up the ridge. The weeds came out of the wet soil more easily than usual and my basket seemed to fill quickly.

Raphael came down in the late afternoon when Heather was there. He looked at my full basket and then at me and put his hand down and lifted one of the plants out. Tore off a leaf. Showed me the shape—a flint axe-head of the ancients. Picked another out of the basket and tore off another of the same-shaped leaves. Potato leaves.

I looked at him and didn't know what to say. I was so ashamed.

He walked down the ridge, kneeling into the soil every few steps, digging a weed out with his hoe, stood and went further down. Crouching again. Digging and rising.

I didn't speak to Heather even though she spoke to me.

I saw my field mouse looking at me through the tobacco.

Raphael came back up and said I should stop for the day.

I said I was sorry.

Raphael said I needed to start over on Monday. He would come down and show me again. Stay a while. He wasn't angry.

I felt terrible.

I didn't speak to Heather.

I never went to dinner.

* * *

SATURDAY

Hymie turned up late in the morning, so it gave me time to write yesterday's diary. More happened, but I don't have time to tell. Anyway, today is a different day, so I'll write about this instead.

Hymie was my chauffeur—he had organized everything. Our first stop was brunch with my mothers, and when I entered the sky blue casa only Señora Pupo was there. She looked me over and gave me a drawn-out hug.

"You no Marco," she whispered.

Estelle came through the door carrying a sack of rice. The same inspection but more animated. She shouted something unintelligible and held on to my cheeks longer than Señora Pupo's hug.

She shook her head. "Usted está enfermo." You are sick. And I thought she might cry.

We sat at the table with all of my favorites and didn't talk much. No interrogation—they had plumbed my depths at the last one. No pleasant conversation like before, either—in the early days of Havana. Though that was to be expected, of course.

I wanted away, and we left in the early afternoon. Strange eyes don't mix well with congri. And my mothers' eyes were certainly strange. They tried though, and I was touched by their effort.

When we arrived at Calle Obispo it was painted the color of the weekend. We strolled its length and it felt like I was at a circus—under the big top, yet open to the sky. I looked through the timber bars and saw Yanela and her maracas and the dancing shoulders of the bar all-full. Yanela's tired eyes smiled at the crowd inside, the salsa skipping in the heat.

I remained out with the huddle in the sun. Hymie sucked his cigar, his Hawaiian shirt screaming loud—a clown under the big top.

They stood a bit away from us, arm-in-arm. The taller grinned at me. Her hair from a shampoo commercial. Her lips painted lilac. Her tongue.

They didn't move. Everyone was dancing but they alone kept still.

I stayed there and so did they, and I thought about moving on but knew they would follow.

The salsa kept on through the timber bars.

Obispo seemed to close in on me—the faces all strangers. I closed my eyes, sweating. The air didn't nourish. My lungs ate strained soup. Or rice water. Ate not drank.

This is what it's like.

The playing had stopped when Hymie took my arm inside and I followed. The afternoon sun threw down at an angle cutting the bar in two pieces. Yanela and Billy sat at a table in the darker half of the space.

Billy rose up both his hands when we came over. "Tom, you look like a bloody aboriginal."

Yanela stood and we kissed like sisters. "Potato farmer look like potato."

"Don't they have sunscreen at this farm of yours?"

"He's slowly transforming into a Cuban," Hymie said. "A visa requirement."

We all sat together. I realized I hadn't spoken. My lungs kept on eating the soup.

"You drink?" Yanela said.

"Of course he drinks! No fucking Coke today, unless it's up his nose." Billy turned to the barman. "José, mojitos all round."

I looked out into the bright outside at my Lolitas, who were facing away from me with their shampoo hair. Gentle waves of golden streaks. I looked back at my friends—Hymie's clown shirt, Billy's crimson nose—like a clown too. Yanela's moustache.

My lungs started to ease as the mojitos came lime to the table. The air made a gradual return.

I started to talk and slowly get comfortably drunk. Billy said I was seeing through my third eye again, and he touched it with the sweat of his forehead. I missed him and told him so.

I drifted easy into the late afternoon. A mojito dream viewed through my third eye.

"Hymie write book." Yanela said.

"Really?" I slurred.

"We in."

"Really?"

"Have you got a title yet?" Billy said.

"I've told you too much already."

"Are you going to smoke that cigar or eat it?" Billy said.

"I in," Yanela said.

"Really?"

"Let's get more mojitos," Hymie said.

"I bella singer in book."

"Waiter, more mojitos."

"I bella singer work mucho mucho."

"He doesn't want to know about it," Hymie said.

"Give him a match to light that thing."

"I know title."

"Really?"

"He tell me."

"Yanela, he doesn't want to know," Hymie said.

"I know. I know." Her mojito flavored words.

"Don't make me write you out of it."

"La guía para caminar en La Habana."

"Really?" I hugged Hymie with my drunk arms and whispered, "The Havana Walking Guide. Drawn by the sensitive pen of Tiphanie Spade, I suspect."

Hymie grimaced.

"And where is the guide at the moment?" I asked.

"At the Hotel Ambos Mundos, if you really must know."

Alcohol usually isn't my best medicine under these circumstances. But on occasion—and this was one—it can keep the demons at bay. Perhaps Cuba is the difference, its hot breath best mellowed with a cut lime, crushed ice. Or perhaps I just got lucky.

So throughout the afternoon my Lolitas came and went as they pleased. And I didn't much care.

* * *

I didn't sleep at the sky blue casa on Saturday because I thought Heather might stay overnight, and I didn't want her to stay at my mothers'.

I hadn't seen her since our fight.

When she came, she brought the dolls of our childhood. Dotty's large finely cracked eggshell head with ruby lips, still apparently no worse for wear. Blonde Carla with her bendable elbows and knees. And Penny, the golliwog with a red and white striped dress that fanned out below her knees. They were mine in a way—when I had worries, they settled me. Heather always took them out when I was worried.

We lay in the bed and she played with them as we talked. I said I was sorry about getting angry, and she smiled at me with her almond eyes and said not to worry.

She told me that farming was hard. Exhausting and tedious at first, then simply tedious. Farming had usurped her schooling and she hated it for that. I said I wasn't bored in the least but understood her anger.

Heather, by nature, didn't hate anything, but this stolen adolescence of hers had left a scar.

"You are the farmer now, Tommy. But not me."

* * *

SUNDAY

The thrill of waking in Havana with Heather. The orange-lit morning and the warmth. You can't imagine, dear Juan.

It was just like the old days—a warm Sunday morning in Crepundia. We spoke of childish things. Nothing of any importance. We lay together as the sun rose bright through our little window, my skin tingling as she combed my hair, my lids often closed, lolling in the sleepover of my childhood.

God, don't let this end.

* * *

I made my own plans for the afternoon. When I arrived, he was sitting on one of the sunken wicker lounges in his cream linen jacket and pants, a paisley bow tie, his panama tilted to shadow one eye.

Señor Pupo rose and shook my hand. "Nice jacket. It fits you well."

The feel of shifting skin had kept with me all the way from the sky blue casa, down the Malecón, and stronger still as I climbed the rise to the Nacional. The black velvet was not suited to the heat of the day, my underarms were soaked, but today I needed to be one with my hero.

"I should explain the jacket," I said.

"There is no need."

"You know all about me?"

"I recognized you, the man at the window, from the first day you came to play Cubilete."

"But you never said anything?"

"Why did it matter?"

"I feel like a fool."

"Better a younger fool than an old one like me."

I said, "I may make the mistakes of the young, but in my forties I'm no longer of an age to match."

He seemed to understand this.

We sat together as a breeze came up from the ocean, rustling the palms in the large courtyard in front. I waived to the waiter and we ordered some drinks, but I kept dry for clarity.

"You have lost weight," he said.

"Not as much as you."

Señor Pupo sipped his wine. "Are you on the same loveless diet as mine?"

I shook my head. "Quite the opposite."

"You don't eat when love comes?"

"I forget sometimes. And at the farm I use up more energy than before."

"There is no Boliche at the farm?"

I smiled at my hero. My lava skin crawled over on itself, folding pancake layers into a molten bridge between us.

"Tell my wife she puts too much paprika in lately." He grinned.

"I could talk to the Señora for you."

"What can you say that I cannot?" He gave up a gentle smile again. "We miss you at Cubilete."

"Hymie should be an entertaining replacement."

"Sí. He has managed to win frequently since offering his cigars as the trophy."

"The Cuban luck of the dice."

"In Havana we must grab our luck quickly when it comes." He kept his gaze fixed on me. "Your friend is worried about you."

"I guess that's his job. But again I could say the same about Pedro and Héctor. They are worried for you. As I am, of course."

He smiled. "We seem to talk in front of a mirror, you and I."

My skin churned under the heat of the velvet.

"Tom, tell me about this love of yours."

"She is . . . perfect."

"Perfect is good . . . but rare."

"Well, maybe she isn't *absolutely* perfect." I finished my Tukola.

He nodded. "Señor Hymie and I had a conversation—"

"About Heather?" I watched his eyes fall to the terracotta. "Hymie doesn't like Heather much."

"So I saw. Tell me about her."

"I want to, Tony. I want your opinion." I became excited and he saw it as I spoke with my hands. "She is so different from the others."

"You've had many lovers?"

"I'm not young, I've had my share. But none could ever replace Heather." My hands settled in my lap. "So I have a trail of broken relationships . . . broken when she returns back into my life."

"Why does she leave?"

"Because of me." I kept my head low. "You have spoken to Hymie. So you know." I sighed. "But you don't know everything, Tony. No one does."

I waived at the waiter and we ordered lunch—a burger and fries to fatten us up. I talked more of Heather and he listened and I wanted his approval so much. The breeze drifted up from the ocean and kissed us both. And as usual, during this stolen time with my Virgil, I felt blessed to be alive.

I wanted to tell him everything.

But I was a coward, of course. Unrepentant, but a coward.

No one knows everything, though I suspect you have guessed, dear Juan.

And when we had eaten it was my turn to listen.

"You visited your wife again?" I asked.

"Sí. Last week. She was sitting on the chair outside of the house. When she saw me, she turned her head away. But I went up anyway. My rose had gone—I had watched her go."

"This is best. That two-headed foe is too much for you, Tony. Too much for me. Too much for anyone."

"She kept her head turned away from me. But we talked, I to her and she to the bay."

"It's a beginning."

"Sí." He bit into his lip. "You know what we talked about, Tom? Can you guess, my friend?"

I shook my head.

"The weather. We talked about the weather."

And then he began to cry.

I moved over to the couch and held my friend. And we sat there, we two love-soaked men—with our emaciated devotion.

"You know what it feels like to me . . . when I'm with Heather?" I spoke to his panama-covered face. "It feels like I'm a part of the room or the ground, or wherever we are. Like everything is made of one substance, like soft plastic or rubber. We all sit together—the floor, the furniture, the ceiling or sky, Heather and I—all made from the same giant mold."

"Such a love is worth fighting for, Tom." He said this with his head still down at my shoulder. "What more is there to life . . . than amor incondicional?"

"You would fight for this love . . . yes? You wouldn't let this go?" I felt a hammering against my ribs. This is what I came for.

Señor Pupo wiped his wet face and slowly rose level to me. "With every breath, Tom. With every breath."

* * *

I met up with Billy in the late afternoon at Obispo. I was excited—you can't imagine, Juan—so excited about my plans. You asked me to tell you when it happened, when I sorted out those uncertainties of mine. Well here it is, done and dusted. And what a treat it is to document, your idea of a daily diary a masterstroke, the fresh sentiment captured unsullied by further reflection.

A few mojitos was enough to send me into a head spin. Billy said he hadn't seen me like this before.

"He love," Yanela said.

"No, there must be something more than the L word," Billy said.

"Sí, he love. Look at eyes."

"Oh for a life of sensations rather than of thoughts!" I said.

"He's fucking ranting."

"Sí, he love."

"When are we to meet this fair maiden, then?"

"You might scare her away, Billy."

"It wouldn't be the first."

"We could double date . . . a table for five."

"Don't be fucking cheeky."

"Chica pretty?" Yanela said.

"Beauty is truth, truth is beauty . . ."

"That is all ye know on earth, and all ye need to know . . ."

"You know Keats, Billy!" I kissed him on the lips.

"José, no more mojitos for him."

"Sí, he love."

* * *

That evening I went to bed early. Heather stayed again.

We will talk until I doze off—she the last voice I'll hear in this tiny room of mine, with a bed for two, my writing desk, a little dressing cupboard, and the window looking down to the long rectangular crop. All made of rubber. Even the potatoes.

* * *

MONDAY

Raphael and I went just when the light was enough. We went together to the top of the middle ridge, just outside the window of my room. I saw Heather sitting at the desk. I had asked her not to come down today for the sake of my potatoes, and she said she wouldn't. I needed to concentrate.

Raphael dug into the earth, just like the first day.

"This weed . . . this potato. Don't dig potato."

He said he would come later and inspect the basket. He still wasn't angry in the slightest.

The morning was beautiful, the early mist settling over us, the banana and tobacco gray-green in the fog.

When the heat of the day came, I had finished the middle row. Raphael was pleased, digging through my basket and beaming his kidney bean teeth at me. I grinned back and thanked him, but he said there was nothing to thank him for.

In the afternoon my field mouse appeared, popping her head out of the tobacco.

"You no chatter chatter?" she said.

"No."

"So you alone today?"

"Yes. And you?"

"And me what?" she said.

"Are you always alone?"

"I now with *you*." She threw a wide gaze over the field. "Just you and me." She smiled.

"How did you spend the weekend?"

"Eat and sleep."

"Oh yes. Naked."

"It hot. I spend with Raphael."

"I'm pleased."

"We go beach. Look." She pulled her overalls down to show her red-skinned chest. She wore no bra. "You come next time?"

"Perhaps. But I see my friends on weekends."

"I not you friend?"

I smiled at her—this beautiful mouse of the tobacco. "Yes, you are."

"Good. You come Sunday."

She popped back into the foliage and out of sight.

I fondled into the basket of weeds, inspecting the shape of the leaves, ensuring the roots were intact, satisfied with the quality of my work. And when I glanced up at my window, I saw Heather staring down at me.

* * *

TUESDAY

I am trying to eat more at dinner. It really is good food, but I'm so eager to get back to my room, I usually only have time for one portion. And sometimes, in this state of mind of mine, this walking on sunshine view of the world, I might forget to eat at all.

Heather doesn't eat with us—I told her it was against the rules. If she farmed it would be different, but that option wasn't really a possibility—those adolescent scars and all that. She said she would eat at the café just up the road. She liked the walk.

We are slowly getting into a routine, Heather and I, which we both need for this to work.

As happened yesterday evening, we all ate together—Raphael, Leonardo, Eva and I—keeping to the same position at the long slab of a table. The other faces around are still strangers to me, but that's the way I prefer it.

Leonardo revealed tonight that he makes models out of matchsticks—houses, trains, churches, even animals. This is how he spends his nights—my sad hobby, he calls it. Eva said it wasn't sad and wants to sell them in the local market, which brought Leonardo into a prolonged spasm. I'm still unclear what emotion feeds these jerks of his—they don't seem to follow any pattern. When he's alone, I might ask him. I don't think he'll mind.

Eva and Raphael seem to be close now. He no longer hides his teeth with her.

It is late. The writing is shorter because I'm spending more time with Heather.

I'm not sure if this will last. I'm not sure of most things. But I must give this last breath plan of my hero's every chance.

***

WEDNESDAY

The ridges near the tobacco plantation were fine, it was those near the banana grove where I'd made most of my mistakes. There are still lots of weeds down that side, and I fear now not as many potato plants as there should be.

Heather always sat on the banana side of the crop—the chatter chatter side, as Eva puts it. But now Heather seems okay about staying in our room when I farm. And I know she's there, which is enough. Eva says I'm lucky Heather doesn't mind staying by herself during the day. She says, if it were her, she would bug me all day.

I think Eva isn't as lucky as me.

I guess I'm somewhat unique, Juan.

When Eva interrupts my digging, it is different from Heather. I stop my work because I know she doesn't stay long. Sometimes I use it as an excuse to take a break, and we walk up to the potable water tap and fill our flasks. The rainwater tank, a concrete turret low to the ground, rests in the shade of the dormitory. There is a wooden platform that encircles it, and we sit and look down at the other farmers, the wet cement cool on our backs.

I like this time of the day, the farm a goldfish bowl. Most of the farmers seem to work by themselves, the vast tobacco crop an ocean of shoulders and heads, bobbing under the surface, then up again, like seabirds fishing. Sometimes two or three work close, but most are separated by a distance that would certainly be out of earshot.

I asked Eva which was her patch of turf.

"I sleep there, there and there." She pointed to the spots.

"What does Raphael say?"

"He catch me only once."

"And?"

She grinned. "He say if I keep clothes on, he happy for me to sleep."

"A young thing like you should be full of energy."

"Raphael say everyone tired when first come." She poked me in the ribs. "Hey, why you not come after breakfast with all us?"

"I don't like lines."

"You misterioso. Everyone come, even Raphael. You not come after dinner. After lunch. I watch. Everyone come. No you. Muy misterioso." She frowned at me. "Leonardo say you spy."

"For what country?"

"He no sure. I tell him he crazy. I know you not spy. I know you same like us."

"Yes, you do."

She looked at me and winked. "I know you same like me."

She rested her head against the wet cement and I watched her swing a long arc gaze over the field—that calm agitated way her eyes could drift.

"You take siesta today?" she said.

"Yes, after lunch."

"I take siesta." She twisted to look at me again. Her tongue licked the top of her lip and lingered there. "It hot. It good to take these off." She lifted her overalls away from her skin and I saw the curve of her breasts. She displayed them to me.

Or I think she did.

My skin tingled.

"But I no sleep in siesta. I . . ." She wriggled on the timber, flapping her overalls against her breasts.

My lungs breathed in the air easily. No strained soup.

"I room 23." She popped off the platform.

And I watched her scamper down with the slope of the field, straight into the tobacco foliage, without bothering to turn her head.

* * *

In our adolescence we only kissed a few times. This is strange, I know.

In our childhood we never kissed.

This isn't strange—but important. Not critical, though you may argue differently—yet it is my lot.

And tonight—it is everything.

* * *

THURSDAY

Soup and bread. If I miss breakfast, then this is all I get for lunch.

The sunrise was a ripe orange, the skin of a red apple. The sky bled these colors through our picture-frame window, so we propped ourselves up and watched until the sun rose higher than breakfast.

At lunch I'm hungry and want a second serving—Oliver Twist style. Did I mention I sang in the musical Oliver in primary school? Actually, I mimed in it. I was a minor cast member, a street urchin I think, my face painted with black grease, a costume of rags. Beany had a lead part—the Artful Dodger or Bill Sykes or Fagan. Rydges was an urchin like me, and I'm pretty sure he mimed as well. Heather couldn't remember her role, but it wasn't a lead part. She said her Chinese face might have been out of place in a play set in London.

The fruit-painted sky reminded me of Heather's tomato-egg bedroom, so we talked about those days, even about me wetting the bed. She just smiled at this—all these years later and she still doesn't need to discuss it. She remembered it, of course. How could she not? But Heather could always step back and make me feel like I wasn't a burden, even when I know I was.

I think I might have become a burden before she left for China. She wouldn't admit it, in fact, she would straight out deny it. But I think I was, those awkward fumbles, the touching of the breasts and all. Yes, the more I dwell on it, the more I'm convinced.

This puts a different light on things.

She is asleep now, so I can't ask her. But I must press with this, even if she evades the answer. Heather has a way of evading truth when she wants.

I can hear the radio through the wall. It is late, so perhaps my neighbor can't sleep.

My room is the color of dry bone—not at its best at night. I wonder whether I could paint it red. Billy could get the paint, I'm sure—how about it, Juan? Communist red. Fidel would be pleased.

* * *

FRIDAY

"America."

"No, England."

"I'm not a spy."

The four of us sat together at dinner.

"Everyone goes in the morning line," Leonardo said.

"What say you, Raphael?"

"Sí. Everyone." He gummed a vegetable. "But no Tom."

"Eva goes in the morning *and* after dinner," Leonardo said. "You too, Raphael."

"Why is your English so good, Leonardo?" I said. "How do we know *you* are not a spy?"

His face jerked a bit. "You don't." A smile?

"Ah, Leonardo," Eva said. "Where you spy?"

"Cuba." He grinned. "I am a Cuban spy."

Eva turned and looked around the room. "Who you spy on?" she whispered.

"You, pretty Eva."

"Sí. You look at pretty Eva." She laughed and caught my stare. Her tongue lingered again.

Raphael finished gumming his carrot. "We had spy here. Ten years or more."

"How do you know?" Leonardo said.

"Raphael know all," Eva said.

"He told me."

"Do you believe everything you are told?" Leonardo said.

"No."

"So why then?"

"They take him away. When he tell everyone he a spy."

My three friends nodded together.

"Australia. You are an Australian spy!" Leonardo said.

I lifted up my wrists bound with feigned handcuffs. "Finally, the truth. Take me away."

* * *

I watched their eyes as I passed by the post-dinner line. I have to go that way to reach my room—there is no other way. Should I pretend? Should I line up like the others just to fit in?

Their paranoia is understandable. It's an occupational hazard, but it stifles me so.

I must keep to my circle of three. And no one else.

* * *

SATURDAY

We sat together in the cool of the Ambos Mundos' high ceiling lobby. Two sofas formed an L shape, Heather and I on one, they on the other.

They sat close, their thighs touching. Rosie had a new outfit, replacing the white shorts and singlet that I liked so much. Her hair was permed flat. When she laughed I noticed she didn't draw her lip back over her buckteeth like she used to.

Hymie was more restrained—not uncomfortable exactly, but wary. This was all new to him.

I confess I enjoyed watching them. Sometimes Rosie would say something and laugh and catch his arm, lean on him, highlighting a phrase, underlining it with a touch of her hand. He would grin at her with that knowing grin. I know what you are talking about. We have shared this before.

I told Rosie I liked her outfit. It was African she said, from Nigeria or Kenya or somewhere around there. She liked the colors. It didn't matter, it could have been made in Havana and she still would like it. Her buckteeth bright white when she said this. Hymie said with her figure she would look good in anything. She said he was sweet and underlined the phrase with an open mouthed kiss.

Heather said she liked it too.

Rosie sometimes looked wary, I'm not sure why. Well, except for the obvious. What I mean is, I'm not sure what portion the wary looks came from. What bits contributed the most.

They wanted us to come with them to the jazz club in the night; Billy was playing at the Fox and Crow; Yanela would be there as well. I said it might be too late, I wasn't sure. Rosie gave up a cautious look but not Hymie. It's funny, but they never seem to be wary together—they tag team their fidgety looks, a downcast pull at a loose thread, or brushing away some lint that isn't really there.

When they went up to their room, I asked Heather and she said she wanted to go to the club. I said I was happy to get home early, but she wanted to go. She liked Rosie, even though she knew all about her and the rest of it.

"Tommy, it was for money," she said. "It's not the same. I wasn't here then, I understand." And I think she did.

I am writing this on Sunday morning. There was no time last night, and I was far too upset when we finally arrived home.

I have made my blunder and I have to live with it. It was bound to happen, I guess. Eventually, it was bound to happen.

The sun streams into our little window as Raphael knocks on my door. He is going to the beach. I tell him I had forgotten, which is, of course, untrue. Eva will be disappointed, he says.

As a child I used to listen in my bedroom to the sound of the ocean through a seashell. I was young, and wondered how the shell could capture the sea and never let it go. All kids must wonder about this, but I remember dwelling on it. I must have been very young—it was before my bedroom became purple.

I look outside and the sky has no clouds. So I will go. For I want to hear the ocean of my childhood again.

***

The palms sit equidistant along the white sand. Not a house in sight. A long stint in Havana makes it easy to forget you're in the Caribbean.

We sat together on the small white towels that the farm supplies for showering. Raphael had got us two each, but even overlapping them didn't add up to much. I kept my shorts and T-shirt on so that my farm toughened skin was all that would see the sun.

Heather wouldn't come into the water. In all the time I have known her she has never swum.

Raphael had a long lean body, quite muscular for his age. The sand stuck comfortably on his evenly tanned skin, the beach obviously a regular pursuit of his.

Eva stripped off into a bright red bikini. She had run down ahead of us, jumping into the wash, and then strode back up, a slow parade, all shiny in the sun. The wet red of her bikini clung see-through on her skin, her nipples dark crimson, and when she pulled the bottoms up higher, the fine slit of her mound.

We ran down together into the froth of the waves, the instant cold soon replaced by the lukewarm of the Straits of Florida. I swam hard into the surf, my arms strong against the current, ducking through the wash until coming to flatter water, swimming until I tired.

I was way out when I stopped, the water cooler, a darker shade of blue. I saw Eva splashing in the distance, waving, I waved back. I couldn't make out Heather amongst the flotsam of the sand, I couldn't fix to any landmark, the weekend crowd was too thick. I turned around and thought about swimming further, no land in sight. I thought about sharks, like usual when so far out alone, shark bait alone.

I looked for Heather again but couldn't see anyone, not even Eva; the current, subtle at first, had tugged me away from them. I swam across it fast, not panic fast but close to it. I found it harder to breath, a pain tight in my chest, pressing down. I slowed the strokes but the pain kept on, so I stopped just as the tugging sea let go.

The dark blue kept on cold while I waded. I bobbed in the swell, letting the pressure on my breastplate ease away, letting my breath come easier too, not moving, just floating shark bait all alone, drifting under the cloudless sky, sundrenched and afraid. I glided face down, the sunlight etching daggers in the swell, a reminder of dancing light in a swimming pool—though now robbed of all its shine.

And the sound of the vast ocean, a muffled groan, rising up and over me.

In time, I began to lift my arms over in slow long strokes, shifting with the beachwise current, flapping not pulling, until eventually I reached the shore.

I sat on the sand with the sea frothing against my chest, not recognizing the splashing people around me, dark skinned and lanky, children, oblivious and carefree, screaming up in the froth, spilling sand sludge from a bucket, spades digging into the slush, thrown at other kids, lanky and dark-skinned too.

And I stayed there amongst the sand players, musing on my flesh that one day would be eaten away, the putrid long gone between my toes, my eyes, the balls and gunk that sits in the sockets behind, knowing even when all this had gone, these carefree kids would still be breathing in the hot air of the day, the night. And the day after that.

* * *

"We've been through this, Tommy."

"It's important to me."

"Been through it so many times."

"Once again, please. For me?"

"All right. I remember twice at least."

"When was the first?"

"When Grandmother told me."

"On that day?"

"Yes. When she came in with the letter."

"That was a weekday then?"

"I can't remember."

"We didn't get mail delivered on weekends."

"It must have been, then."

"I didn't see you on weekdays. I didn't see anyone on weekdays. I only saw the bottom of a pool."

"Maybe she got the letter during the week."

"Maybe she didn't."

"It doesn't matter. We talked about it, you and I. I remember."

"Why wouldn't *I* remember?"

"This was a long time ago."

"Maybe it was because you were glad to leave."

"Glad? I was scared."

"Maybe it was because I was a burden."

"How could you have been a burden? I loved you."

"Touching your tits."

"Don't talk like that, Tommy."

"Breasts, then."

"You know I don't like talking about that."

"Why?"

"I . . . I don't know."

"Maybe I tried to touch you in other places."

"Don't, Tommy."

"Maybe coming every weekend was too much."

"Of course it wasn't. I loved you."

"Maybe you met other guys at school."

"Don't be silly."

"You must have had other guys coming on to you."

"I don't like to talk about it."

"So you did."

"I don't want to talk about it."

"Did they touch you like I did?"

"Don't, Tommy."

"Did they touch your tits like I did?"

"I'm going, now."

"Did they touch you down there?"

Transcript July 5th 2010

Interview with Tom Peters by Juan Carlos Rebelde

JCR: We have a problem, Tom.

TP: Oh, yes?

JCR: A problem with the authorities this time.

TP: Not the authorities.

JCR: I'm afraid this is serious [Medium pause]. The events at the jazz club generated some attention.

TP: Nothing you can't handle.

JCR: You're making it difficult for me, Tom.

TP: That's your job, isn't it?

JCR: We're losing our way.

TP: We?

JCR: I like to think of this as a partnership.

TP: Touching.

JCR: [Long pause] Well, can you explain the events?

TP: [No audible response].

JCR: I need an explanation, I'm afraid.

TP: I stuffed up.

JCR: That's pretty generalized. What were the circumstances?

TP: It was poorly lit.

JCR: [No audible response].

TP: [Long pause]. I thought it was him. At the club.

JCR: [No audible response].

TP: I thought it was him, okay?

JCR: [Medium pause]. Is that likely, Tom? When you think about it, is that likely?

TP: [shouted] No!

JCR: [No audible response].

TP: But it's possible, isn't it?

JCR: What did he look like?

TP: [Medium pause]. The same.

JCR: Then, I repeat the question. Is that likely, Tom?

TP: [Long pause]. No, Juan, that is not likely.

JCR: [No audible response]

TP: Satisfied?

JCR: [Long pause]. It might not be of any concern to you, but risks are being taken on my side of this partnership.

TP: I don't think you're in any danger, are you?

JCR: [No audible response].

TP: Look, I appreciate everything you've done. I really do.

JCR: [No audible response].

TP: Jesus, what do you want me to say?

JCR: [No audible response].

TP: This partnership. [Short pause] Why?

JCR: That's a good question.

TP: Do you have other such partnerships?

JCR: No.

TP: Why me?

JCR: [Short pause]. I thought you would be a safer candidate.

TP: Being a foreigner?

JCR: Partly.

TP: Should we turn the tape recorder off?

JCR: That won't be necessary, Tom.

TP: Well, it's not illegal, what we're doing.

JCR: [No audible response]

TP: Well, it's not wrong.

JCR: [Long pause] I don't know.

TP: Come on, Juan, it's not wrong if I say it isn't wrong.

JCR: That's one way to look at it.

TP: But the authorities might not agree?

JCR: They may not.

TP: The greater good.

JCR: Precisely, Tom.

END OF TAPE RECORDING.

* * *

MONDAY

"Buenos días, Tom."

"I'm just dropping in my weekend assignment for you."

"You are good boy," she said.

"You're always here so early. Why does Juan make you come at this hour?"

"I choose to. I like to work in quiet."

"So, it's your idea. If you're here so early, why don't you come down and farm with me some time?"

She held up her hand. "It break my nail."

"Excuses, excuses." She took my USB stick and plugged it into the computer. "Tell me something," I said, "do you do the typing of his interviews."

"Some."

"His interviews of me?"

"Some."

"That makes me feel a bit embarrassed."

"Why embarrassed?"

"Well, you know, some of the questions he asks." The printer spat out the pages of my work. "You don't read my assignment do you?"

"No. Just give to him."

"Okay, just checking."

She gave me back my stick. "See you tomorrow, Tom."

"As always."

* * *

Heather came down when I farmed today, so I dug at a slower pace, studied the leaves, their shape, their particular shade of green, felt them rough velvet between my fingers, and when I was sure, one hundred percent sure, I dug them clean out with my hoe, the roots intact, with the precision of a surgeon.

Heather stopped talking while I did this. Or I stopped listening. Each paragraph of our chatter chatter started or stopped with a fistful of green.

"I loved your hair," she said.

"Like Rapunzel you used to say."

"It was more blonde than Carla's."

"You used to brush it, remember? I lay with my head on your lap and you would take that stiff brush of yours and comb into my scalp. God, you can't imagine how I loved you doing that. My skin tingles at the thought of it."

"Grandmother loved your hair. And so did all the girls. We talked about it at play time."

"You never told me."

"I felt special that I could play with it," she said. "Like it was mine."

"Did you tell them?"

"No. They wouldn't have believed me."

I dug into the soil with my hoe, the fine yellow roots a tangled spread in my palm. "You know, Heather, I felt safe when I was with you."

"I always looked after you."

"You still do."

"Not as much as before," she said.

"Maybe." I dug up another weed. "You know something, I think you should eat with us."

"I don't think so."

"I want you there."

"It's not for the best."

"I'll be quick, I promise."

"You're not eating enough. Look how skinny you are," she said.

"I miss Grandmother's dumplings, that's my problem."

"You are funny, Tommy."

"I'm glad you came down today. Real glad."

I looked into the basket, the weeds only a shallow layer, and heard a 'hey' that sung up from the tobacco plot, not far from where I sat. Turning, I saw a rustle in the foliage.

"Heather, thinking back to our time together as kids, I took . . . I feel I took . . . more than I gave."

"Don't be silly, Tommy."

"What did I give you?"

"Yourself. I was lonely. We gave each other ourselves. That's all we had."

"The Mondays were the worst. God, sometimes I couldn't breathe, I missed you so much. Six whole days before I could see you again. God, Heather, you can't imagine."

The 'hey' now louder from the tobacco. Eva's head grinned out through the green; torn strips of leaves tied in her hair, dangling down like olive dreadlocks.

"Hey, you," I said.

She lifted one of the dreadlocks. "No see Eva. How you say camuflar?"

"Camouflage."

"Sí. I camouflage. I invisible Eva."

She stretched her neck out of the plants a bit more and gazed up toward the dorm. I never really knew what she was looking for during these long-winded scans of hers. But they always seemed to be full of purpose.

"You want a break?" I said.

"Sí, Sí."

I looked at Heather. "Is that okay?"

"Sure. Go, Tommy."

"You come too."

"No, thank you. I'll wait here."

"I won't be long. I promise."

Eva said, "Come chatter chatter."

I stood; the soft soil fashioned into the shape of my rear. I must have been sitting at the same spot for some time.

Eva motioned me through the tobacco. "In here. We go secret way."

I turned back to Heather and she sat there, smiling.

I looked up at the sun that still kept low in the sky. I had missed breakfast and felt a hunger tighten deep inside me.

The tobacco crunched as Eva's green-streaked head bobbed deeper into the plot. I followed the rustle of the leaves, twisting a course in the thick of the foliage, trying to keep the scent of the trail. Minutes went by, the course of our path down and away from the water tank. I realized I had forgotten my bottle and turned a full circle, not sure whether to go back or push on.

"Hey." A whisper from the field mouse, somewhere near but unseen.

"I need to get my bottle," I said.

"Over here."

I parted a slit in the drapes of the tobacco, finding a clearing no larger than a double bed, with a mattress of yellow-brown leaves long dried from the sun that lit up the tiny space gold and bright lime.

She lay on the bed, the top buttons of her overalls unfastened, the curve of her breasts, nipples, bared all to the streaming sun.

"This secret place. No one come."

I looked at her but didn't reply. I had forgotten to breathe.

She smiled and her tongue licked her upper lip, loitered there, then tasted the bottom, open mouthed. She saw me looking, my gaze drifting back to her eyes that grinned long into my stare, a race of my pulse, my breath still held. I liked her watching me look, her smile as I watched, as she pulled away the buttons further down, tore them away, spreading open her overalls as they popped off, teasing me as I watched, my breath now shallow pants, easing them down all the way, until her bald mound splayed open for me to see.

* * *

It is late. I haven't had lunch. I haven't had dinner. I now know what hunger really feels like—a great wanting empty that sucks all the juice away from your innards. Hunger is the great wanting.

I had a long shower afterward. The water was cold as it always is during the daylight. Warm at night, warm in the morning, cold the rest of the time. Not freezing as I would have preferred, the pipes warmed by the tropics so the bite is removed, but cold enough. The showers are a lonely place in the day, none of the communal fog, the Latino chatter in the mist, and the tiles look dirty without the haze, cruddy and mildew stained. I had time to study them more, no rush so the next could take my place, scrubbing away the grime in the windowless tiled space, washing away the smell of old flowers. Scrubbing away the smell of low tide.

Heather is sleeping now. Her sense of smell not as acute as mine. I have the nose of a dog.

So I will shower again.

* * *

WEDNESDAY

Yesterday. I should write about yesterday, not today. Today was routine. I rose, I dug, I even laughed, I ate—three meals, you'll be happy to know, breakfast of tostada, dunked into endless coffee of the morning-brewed tank, lunch of vegetable soup and hot bread, three pieces, big chunks of carrot, and dinner of fish and beans and rice.

This food log is written for you, I'm beholden to your request, the true meaning of beholden—obliged. I'm obliged, aren't I. That's the deal, isn't it. A note to the proofreader—please omit question marks, they are not appropriate here. They are not appropriate under the terms of our contract.

* * *

THURSDAY

I'm thinking I should write about the times that we meet. I know you have the transcripts, I have the transcripts, but I don't think they're really complete. What I mean is, I don't think the meaning is complete, or accurate, as they stand, some of the words need interpretation—mine, not yours. I cannot interpret your words, of course, but mine need deciphering. I might go back and look at the transcripts, maybe make some footnotes, or scribble something in the margins. What do you think of this idea?

* * *

FRIDAY

Following up from yesterday's interview, and as an example of what I meant by my diary comment, I would like to say that I'm disappointed with your response to my question of them knowing about the spy. I guess it wasn't a question, it was a statement of fact, but your response frightened me a bit. Frightened may be too strong a word, and I may go back and replace it. But 'frightened' best describes the emotion I feel. It's discomforting, I'm sure you would understand, it is discomforting to know that they know about this. It is discomforting to know what should be secure, isn't secure. But it is frightening to know what else is known, unbeknown to you and I. Especially to the I.

Surely this you understand, Juan.

* * *

SATURDAY

"Do we have a song?" I said.

Heather thought. "I don't think so, Tommy."

"Other couples have songs, you know, songs they play at weddings, or first listened to when they dated."

She smiled. "I can't remember the songs at school. They were probably pretty awful, back then."

"Hymie's is Al Green's 'Let's Stay Together.' You know the one . . . I'll keep on loving you/ whether good or bad/ happy or sad . . ."

"You have a lovely voice, Tommy."

"Eagle Rock. Remember we loved Eagle Rock? We danced to it at school . . . Hey, hey, hey/ good old eagle rock's here to stay/ I'm just crazy about the way we move . . ."

"You dance lovely, Tommy."

"Dance with me . . . Hey hey hey . . ."

"You're funny."

"I love it when you smile. Those dimples of yours. God, I love it when you smile, Heather."

"When I'm with you, it's easy."

"Let's make Eagle Rock our song then. What do you think?"

She nodded. "Okay, then."

"And no matter what, we'll never have another song with anyone else."

"That's easy enough."

"We will never love anyone else."

"I love you, Tommy."

"We'll never let anyone else into our lives."

She smiled with her lovely dimples at me.

"It's my hero's plan . . . you would love Señor Pupo. I want you to be there when I see him next."

"Okay, I will."

"God, you are lovely."

"Oh, don't cry, Tommy."

"Sorry, I get taken away at this point, usually, don't I?"

"I'm here. I'm not going anywhere."

"Sorry, Heather." I wiped at my eyes. "You know something, you know something weird. I can't remember ever seeing you cry."

"Oh, but I have, I promise."

"When?"

"Many times in China. I cried many times when we first went back."

"Did you miss me, Heather?"

"With all my heart. That was what I cried about most."

I wiped my eyes some more. "I won't love anyone else, I promise."

"You don't have to promise that."

"I want to. Do you want to?" My nose ran. "Do you want to promise that too?"

"Tommy . . . that's the easiest promise to make in the world."

* * *

SUNDAY

An afternoon spent with Hymie, my mothers, and Heather. Rosie stayed away, I think because of what happened in the jazz club last weekend.

Hymie didn't want to elaborate on how they were doing; I sensed unease in him. Perhaps the crutch of not technically committing Tohranic adultery no longer gave him the support that it did. He seemed to walk with a limp.

They all tiptoed on eggshells with me. Señora Pupo dished up the stew in hillocks on my plate. Estelle never commented on my weight, never made a motion to cry, never mentioned the farm, but preferred just to sit and watch me eat. So did Heather. She said I ate the stew like Grandmother's Peking Duck, closing my eyes with every mouthful. It made her smile.

For brevity I'll translate my mothers' banter and Hymie's schoolboy Spanish. As you know, Juan, my language skills are much improved since my first arrival in Havana.

"Do you like me wearing the jacket?" I asked.

"It looks nice on you," Señora Pupo said.

"I love the Boliche. I miss it so." I closed my eyes as I talked. "But I think you're putting too much paprika in."

"Too much paprika?"

"Yes. A bit too much. What do you think?"

Estelle said, "Sí. Too much." Her eggshell talk.

"He loves you so much, Señora Pupo."

"Sí," Estelle said. "Too much paprika."

"You need to give him a second chance, both of you."

"Are you sure you want to talk about this, Tommy?" Heather said.

"I'm sure."

"It's such a miserable day, the rain," Hymie said.

"I had lunch with Señor Pupo last weekend."

"Sí, the rain is too much," Estelle said.

"I used to play Cubilete with him, you know."

"Too much paprika, yes," Señora Pupo said.

"Sí, too much."

"Brooklyn weather."

"Tommy," Heather said, "are you okay?"

"I had lunch with Tony!"

Silence fell down on the table.

"You really shouldn't shout, Tommy."

"I'm sorry. I shouldn't shout." I had said this with my hands over my face. And looked up at the table. "But I think this is important. I had lunch . . . with Tony . . . at the Nacional."

Señora Pupo lifted her gaze to me. "You call him Tony."

"Of course I call him Tony."

"Did you tell him this name?" she said to Estelle, who shook her head. She looked back at me, hard. "You know my Tony?"

"Sí, I know him well. Él es mi héroe."

They sat and watched me, these eggshell treaders. I had their full attention, now, as I presented the case for my respect for him, for my adoration, for *el hombre del amor*, for this man of love. I stammered with some of the words—sacrifice, I needed the dictionary for this word, I raced up the stairs to get it, to my little sky blue room, the bay out front, where you first arrived in the reflection of the wet street, I became excited when I found it, in the book I finally found it, I stood and pointed to the ceiling covered sky, the dictionary in my hand, sacrificar, sacrificar, Heather stared, she didn't speak, she couldn't speak, sacrificar, to love is not easy, it can . . . I looked for the word, turned the pages, I'm sorry it tore, the page tore, I promise to patch it, but here it is, ruina, ruina, it can ruin, it can spoil, yes, too ripe, the fruit can be too ripe and spoil, like a pear, I spoke to her, she looked and smiled and her dimples, God you can't imagine, with brown spots, you can dig them out with a knife, keep digging away, the fruit is sweet, but it can go off if you let it, not even if you let it, sometimes you can't stop it, you can't stop it spoiling, I said this to her dimples, her beautiful dimples, and she cried, and the Señora, she cried too. And they cried together.

* * *

We talked on the drive home—no eggshell talk, straight talk. I'm too tired to document it, and really it isn't that important, other than to say that it was straight talk.

We were talked out when we entered the gate, the sound of sliding gravel, the yellow-gray lit road.

I turned to my chauffeur. "Have you come up with a Tiphanie Spade yet?"

"Not exactly."

"Can I make a suggestion?" I said.

"Can I stop you?"

"Heather."

"Heather?"

She looked displeased. "Tommy, I don't think—"

"No, listen, it's perfect. She's here, she's beautiful and personable. She'd be a great Tiphanie. How about it?"

"Reliability may be an issue," Hymie said.

I grinned at my friend. "We will make this work, I know it."

"Tommy, we are home."

"We are home. You are such a pal, Hymie." I slapped his thigh. "Make sure you say hello to Rosie for me. Tell her I'm sorry about last week at the club. I . . . you know, make mistakes. Try to explain for me will you? Tell her—"

"Why don't you tell her yourself?"

"Maybe I should. Maybe I can next weekend. Will you still be here next weekend, Hymie?"

"I'm not sure."

"Maybe I will then, before you go. I'll see you before you go?"

The car had stopped. At least, I couldn't hear the sound of the engine.

"We're home, Tommy."

"We're home," I said.

God I love this place.

* * *

I want to tell you about the nights. I am writing in the early morning, before dawn, the sun is not yet up. I am writing because it is clear to me, and I haven't told you before. I haven't told you about them, these nights, not when I cast off to sleep, it's never at the beginning, it's when I wake, it's always when I wake in the depths of the night.

I wake warm. It's black. There are no lights outside. The ground is lit only by the moon, and so it is black. Well, mostly black. Even if the moon is round, the clouds can cover it, even with my curtains open, fully open, it is black. I cannot see. Do you understand? I wake holding her soft. She is soft. Sometimes she wakes with me. Sometimes she doesn't. Sometimes we talk, though the talk doesn't matter as much. It's the touch. It's the touch in the black. Sometimes, we just hold each other, we don't talk, I hold her, in the black, in the warm, and there is nothing like this, nothing can replace this, and it only happens, it only happens in the middle of it all. In the middle of all this! Do you understand? Oh God, you can't imagine this, the big rubber mold all around and the touch. Do you get it—this warm touch only happens in the middle of it all.

* * *

MONDAY

In the morning I weigh in. I look at the scales; the weight is recorded. Like a prizefighter, a tall bantamweight. But I'm already in the middle rounds and ahead on points by my scorecard—not yours, I know this, but I'm in the middle rounds and I feel strong and ahead. I swivel and shimmy, the bookies look worried, I wasn't expected to last the distance, a gash over my eye maybe, but I can see clearly, the razor not needed, a couple of staggers, a couple of long stints on the ropes, but I've never hit the canvas. And I don't intend to.

* * *

TUESDAY

"You no like?" Eva said.

"It doesn't matter whether I like it or not."

"Sure it matter."

"Not to me."

The blistered wet of the cement tank cooled at my neck. Eva looked down and waved her hand at something; a fly, or a mosquito, but I didn't hear a buzz.

"You did it with Raphael?" I said.

"Why this matter?"

"Some people are saying you did."

"Crazy people. Why this matter?"

"I guess it doesn't."

"I did it with *him*." She waved her hand in the same direction as the silent insect, and I realized I was to focus my attention further away than I first supposed. I squinted down into the tobacco but couldn't make anyone out.

"Maybe it matters to Raphael," I said.

"No to you?"

"It did matter to me, but not now."

"We same."

"In some ways. In some ways not."

"Sí, we same." She looked down to where she waved before. "You no come to beach."

"I couldn't."

"Because of chatter chatter?"

"I have other friends on the weekend. It's my only chance."

"You come Sunday?"

"I don't know."

"Raphael like you."

"And I like him." I turned and grinned at her. "And I like you."

She cast a wide arc gaze that spanned the full vista in front, then turned back to me, and whispered, "You like this?"

I watched her pull the lowest two buttons of her overalls away. Watched as her finger entered inside.

My breathing stopped. "Jesus, Eva, don't."

She put her finger further in, moving deeper into her palm.

My lungs ate at the air.

"You no like?" She looked around to check we were alone, then spread her legs to show me the view, her hand and hips moving against each other, watching me look, "You no like?" said softly, her eyes closed now, moaned as she fingered herself, hips rising with each moan, thighs parting, then opened a wide eyed gaze, looked around, and eased it out, reaching over with the hand, a smile, wiped my lips, and further into my mouth.

"You no like pretty Eva?"

I slid and fell off the platform onto the dirt, picked myself up, not bothering to brush away the dust, hobbled down the slope, something in my ankle torn, hobbled down and away from her.

And my lungs ate at the soup, all the way down into the bright of the day, and further still.

* * *

"It's swollen, Tommy."

"I'll keep it up with the bandage on."

"I don't know. It's all bruised. It might be broken."

"It's okay."

"I'll look after you."

"Really."

"It's what I'm here for."

"Maybe I should have an accident every so often . . . to keep you here."

"I'm not going anywhere. Did you show Juan Carlos?"

"Just the nurse."

"You stay here with me until the swelling goes down. No more farming."

"We can sleep in."

"Sure, like we used to. Pretending we're asleep when Grandmother walked past."

"In the winter, with the little bar heater, God, Heather, remember the little bar heater?"

"I do. And we can watch the sunrise."

"You were always my heater in the winter, Heather."

"Stay in bed and watch the sunrise."

"My Sunday morning bar heater."

* * *

WEDNESDAY

I woke in the black of the night, in the quiet black when we heated each other up, and talked because there was no rush to sleep. We would wake with the sun, then look without touch, watch it come up on the weedless potatoes, then I slept, we slept, until a tap at my window, Eva's face at the pane, hands like big ears to cut out the glare, she wanted to come, but I slept, pretended as with Grandmother, I lay there and we talked and talked and I stayed away and Eva stayed away as well.

* * *

THURSDAY

I don't have the transcripts of our talks today, but I want to comment while my mind is still clear—my disappointments with you. Yes, plural.

It is Thursday. I cannot farm; my ankle is an eggplant. Thursday is Cubilete day. I cannot farm so this is my chance to play with my friends. Call it workers compensation. I know I was strictly not working, but the laws surely are the same as back home, I was at work, on my break, and I tore my ankle, tore the ligaments according to the nurse, but even if it isn't fully covered, even if there isn't any compensation, which I completely understand, all I ask is to replace today with a weekend day. To be precise, replace today with Sunday. I would swap beach day for Cubilete day in a heartbeat. And what did you say? What did you say to this <u>sound</u> idea? I don't like underlying prose, it shows weakness, but sound should be underlined here. Sound is a word you like to use, isn't it, my dear Juan, sound is your favorite label to describe an event, a happening, it is sound or unsound, so what did the little tag say for this idea of mine? Unsound. Actually you didn't say unsound, you just said no. I should not have talked about the spy incident first. That was my mistake. I saw it agitated you, another one of your words worth underlying—*agitated*. With my experience in such matters, and I think you would agree I am no novice, this was a silly mistake. What interests me is your preference to talk about the Nabokov twins, it seems a fascination of yours, in fact I think I mentioned the spy incident just to get you off the topic of those girls. 'Gals' as Hymie would call them. Anyway, I'm drifting; the point I was trying to make is that sound and unsound should not be predicated on matters unrelated. I did not eat yesterday, superficially, I agree, this was unsound. But, as I described to you in my diary and my interview, I did not eat because of what happened with Eva. I did not eat because I needed to distance myself from Eva. And so, unsound becomes sound, predicated on matters not readily apparent but nevertheless relevant.

I talked about the spy stuff to get you off the topic of those fucking Lolitas. *Sound.* Comprender?

* * *

FRIDAY

It wasn't quite dawn—our bedroom lit with just a splash more than moonlight. We were sound—a deep slumber that no one should be taken from. It was the time when the grass would frost if it could, but we were warm under the covers.

I woke with a kiss on the cheek.

I cuddled into her.

Her lips touched mine. A giggle.

Her tongue and mine. Tongue?

Jesus.

My cock ached.

The sweating fervor. The smell of her breath. The taste.

A giggle.

I tried to find a way, my fingers slinking to her hairless wet.

Her tongue.

Her little hands fingering my meat, guiding me.

Jesus.

A giggle. My giggle.

My hips and thighs taut. Her hot breath and her tongue and my head and shaft, hard, sucked by the warm mouth of her cunt.

Oh Jesus. What bliss is this?

Harder. She said it with her tongue and gripping hands. Harder.

Oh, Jesus.

Harder.

A giggle. Not sure whose.

Something strange crawled into the space.

Or from above, but not far.

Something wasn't right in the darkness.

Chatter chatter.

I felt short of air. "Eva?" My eyes strained to focus. "Eva is that you?"

I sat up and switched the light on.

The light stung my eyes.

And Eva was sitting at the edge of my bed.

Jesus.

I looked down at Heather, who stared up at me scared.

"How long have you been here, Eva?"

Heather put her head under the covers.

"Fuck, Eva. Did you see us?"

"Don't shout, Tommy," Heather said, still hidden.

"Were you watching us, Eva?"

She laughed with that strange look of hers—a scanning of the room for something that wasn't for me to see.

"You must not tell anyone, Eva!"

"Tommy, don't shout." Heather's head rose from the covers but her scared face kept on.

"Eva, you must not tell anyone. Please, promise me!"

"Don't cry, Tommy."

"You must not tell anyone!"

I started to drink the soup of the air.

"It's all right, Tommy. She won't tell."

Footsteps came down from the corridor.

"Go away, Eva!"

"Don't cry, Tommy." Heather turned to the field mouse. "You'd better go, Eva."

And the mouse looked at me with her big brown eyes in that strange way. But did as we asked.

* * *

I couldn't sleep after.

My neighbors on both sides complained about the disturbance, which was their right. The night supervisor would make a report. Which was his right. I didn't eat breakfast, which was my right.

I couldn't stand the stares if they came. I wouldn't know if it was just from the disturbance or from what Eva had told them. She just had to tell one person, not in my inner circle, but one of her young buddies. Then all was lost.

"Why do you worry what others think, Tommy?"

"I have a soul."

"Is it religion?"

"It's beyond religion."

"I understand, Tommy."

I held my hands to my face. "I feel very strange."

"I feel strange, too."

I kept my face hidden. "Maybe you should go away for a while?"

Heather sat cross-legged at the foot of the bed. "Tommy?"

"Just for a while."

"What we did wasn't really wrong, Tommy."

I kept my head in my hands.

"Maybe talk to Señor Pupo," she said. "He might know how to help."

"I couldn't."

"Or maybe, Billy? Billy would understand."

"Billy might understand, but does that help? Is Billy a voice of reason?"

"It was going to happen."

"That doesn't make it better. You don't understand this struggle of mine, Heather."

"I do, Baby. But it was bound to happen. It's all right."

I felt an ache in my chest and rubbed at it, but it didn't seem to help.

"You need to eat, Tommy."

"I feel so strange." I looked at her. "I feel strange when I should feel on top of the world."

"I know. It's all right. Do you want me to brush your hair?"

"Don't you think that means something? Why don't I feel on top of the world?"

"I do," she said.

I sighed. "Just for a bit. Maybe for the rest of the day. Let me clear my head."

"Okay, Tommy."

I smiled into her almond eyes. "I love you, Heather."

She giggled. "I know you do, silly."

* * *

I sat at my desk in full view of it, seen through the window of my room.

It started at the edge of the potato plot, the tobacco edge, and moved up toward the dorm. Not smoothly, but in haphazard jerks, a twister that, when made to stop, flung its carnage every which way before moving up some more.

Eva's breasts looked small in the distance. First I thought she had a shirt on, tan in color, tightly fitted, but they moved as she ran, these small breasts of hers, as she rushed, struggled, holding with one hand her slipped-down overalls, the other thrashing closed fisted, striking as they pounced over her—Leonardo I saw, and others I knew.

In the distance Raphael looked on as well, but at a good gap from the storm, and I watched him drop his eyes down, staring at the soil instead, chin on his chest.

Unlike him, I kept on looking.

Leonardo was large against Eva, a giant clutching her, arms wrapping her chest, pulling her overalls up that kept slipping, dodging her fists, the others lifting her legs, one for each leg, carrying her splayed out, before she kicked free the overalls that dropped at her ankles, her bald naked exposed, and her cries as it all came within an earshot of the window of my room.

As I watched, the scene settled me, made me feel blameless. A twisted vindication of my actions.

This selfishness of mine is hard to admit. It makes me feel sick.

When the twister came up to my window, just outside the pane, I saw her face—she could not see mine, the sun shining silver on the glass—

saw her tears, soil-stained, the scratches on her arms, a line of fine red on her chest, Leonardo's eyes, his broad arms against hers, lifting her up like a sack of tobacco, tobacco that he had helped to harvest, lifting her with the others, dodging her beating legs, her eyes thrashing too, before it all flashed past my window and out of sight.

When I stood and moved over to the window to get a better view, they had gone. And I watched Raphael turn, kicking at the soil, and walk back into the shoulder green of the crop, and out of sight as well.

* * *

I walked to the table with a thick limp, Leonardo greeting me with a facial spasm of gargantuan proportions.

"Our Australian spy returns," he said.

Raphael rose and helped me to my chair. Eva stayed seated. And I sat without managing eye contact with any of them.

"You are late," Leonardo said. "We have pudding tonight." He threw up a gentle tic. "And it won't last."

"I needed to see the nurse about my leg."

"You must eat," Raphael said.

"I might have some fish."

Raphael stood and brought me back two portions, and a dollop of pudding on the side. I smiled at my friend, making brief eye contact for the first time.

I watched Eva, who sat next to me, out of the corner of my eye. She had kept quiet and played with the food on her plate.

"Raphael tells me you're a good swimmer," Leonardo said. "Where did you learn?"

"Spy school."

"You are funny. I might come to the beach on Sunday and watch you."

"I'm sure you have better things to do."

"Sadly, I don't."

"Anyway, I don't think I'll be going."

"The ocean would be good for your ankle."

"It hurts too much."

The table fell silent for a bit. Then Eva said something I didn't understand, the others turning to her for the briefest of moments.

"You not eating," Raphael said.

"I like my fish cold," I said.

Eva spoke in tongues again, their heads not moving this time.

"We are a sorry lot tonight," Leonardo said. "It is Friday, we have pudding, and we are just a sorry lot."

"Sorry lot is a very English turn of phrase," I said.

"I must have picked it up from a travelling Englishman."

"He must have stayed a while, this traveler of yours," I said.

"What can I say, I have an ear for language."

"A trained ear."

"Callar!" Shut up! Eva sung up loud to the room.

The heads turned now, and further down the table.

I stood, a thorn cutting deep into my eggplant ankle. I kicked the air with this worthless limb of mine, a Santiago claw, almost falling then staggered to balance, leaning against a seated man whom I'd never spoken to before or now, and moved with my fat limp away from the table, through the long rectangular dining room, and back to my room.

* * *

SATURDAY

"Don't cry, Tommy."

"I'm sorry."

"He can't come now."

"Why in the night? It was always the day."

"You should have told me, Tommy."

"It was always hot, the sunlight bright. So why now does he always come in the night?"

"You should have told me."

"He delivered ice-creams in his truck, so it was always hot. It had to be."

"Why didn't you tell?"

"He gave them to me."

"Try and sleep, Tommy."

"Chocolate Paddle Pops in the bush."

"It's okay, I'm here now."

"Banana, too."

"He seems to only come when I'm here, Tommy."

I sat bolt upright. "No, Heather!"

"Sleep, Baby. It's so late."

"How could I have told you?"

"You didn't tell me, Tommy. You told him."

"Juan?"

"You tell him too much, sometimes."

"He's much smarter than me."

"I would have looked after you."

"But I was ashamed."

"Grandmother would have known what to do."

"You can't imagine how ashamed."

"Don't cry, Tommy. He's gone."

"I can't sleep."

"I wish I had the hair brush."

"You can't imagine what it did."

"It's so late, Tommy. Try and sleep."

"What he did."

"He would be long dead now."

"But I was safe with you."

"My golden haired boy."

"It was enough just to be safe with you."

"I would have fixed him right."

"Safe every weekend. Why can't I be safe now?"

"But he comes when I'm here."

"No, Heather, he comes all the time! Don't you understand, he comes whether you're here or not! He comes whenever he wants."

"Don't get upset, Baby. Sleep, now."

"But I'm safe with you. Right?"

"Sleep, Baby."

"Will you talk to me 'til I sleep?"

"Of course I will."

"I'm tired, now."

"I'm combing your hair."

"So tired."

* * *

SUNDAY

I didn't go to the beach, but I've been thinking about my near drowning, mulling on it, the flesh and bone thing, or the flesh really, the lack of it, what it means this slow shedding of the flesh of mine that must come to us all, which is comforting in a way, not morbid at all, well morbid yes but not morose, these thoughts aren't unsound either, it's the casket in the living room thing, what the Buddhists do, or maybe another culture, how they keep their coffin, their own empty coffin, in the living room of their house, to remind them, like tying a string on your finger, a constant reminder, when you eat in the lounge room, playing with the children if you have them, or laughing with whoever, laughing with the casket lid open, yes, that's it, a room of fall down laughter with the open lid casket in the background, lined with white velvet, empty but waiting, for that day of reckoning, forget the God part, the reckoning I'm talking about is not about God, don't worry about that, the reckoning is about the end of breath stuff, what this means, what it means to disappear into the soil, which must be the case, even those fancy caskets must leak eventually, even the top of the range, the timber must rot eventually, it might take a thousand years or more, but eventually we must go back into the soil, and what this all means, not what it means then, I know what that's about, rather what this means now, what this means today.

* * *

The jazz club stirred, restless, and there were many staring eyes. Even those who weren't here before were caught up in the drama.

Billy said, "Do you want me to walk off the stage?"

"He can't come in," the man said.

"I will walk off this fucking stage, right now."

"Billy, he'll have to go. He can't stay. He is banned."

"Right in the middle of my fucking session."

"It's not my decision."

"Then you better learn to sing."

"Billy, be reasonable."

"And if it's not yours, whose fucking decision is it?"

"Isaac's."

"Isaac wouldn't know if his ass was on fire."

I said, "It's okay, Billy." I stood back a bit.

"No, it is not okay. He is my friend and my guest."

"Take five minutes break," the man, who never looked at me, said.

Billy wiped at the wet from his forehead. "These bastards have got me, Tom. My album just out. They know it too." He kept his voice up so all could hear.

"It's okay, Billy."

"Thanks all for coming tonight, we're just having a short break. Five minutes," the man said to the sunken down eyes.

"And where the fuck is Isaac?" Billy said.

"He just left."

"He's a gutless prick."

"Billy, take five, cool down. But he has to go."

"Come next Sunday, Tom. I'll talk to that monkey Isaac. I'll fix it. Promise you'll come."

"It's okay, really."

"Let's get together in Obispo."

"I'll try."

"And you make him stand! Can't you see he's hurt? You don't even offer him a chair, you bastard."

"Five minutes, Billy."

"Fuck off."

Transcript July 12th 2010

Opening of interview with Tom Peters by Juan Carlos Rebelde

JCR: Come in, Tom. I'm sorry to call you in without notice. Please take a seat. [Medium pause] How are you feeling?

TP: [No audible response]

JCR: I notice you're still limping. How is your leg?

TP: [No audible response]

JCR: Is there a problem, Tom? You seem to be agitated about something. [Medium pause] You have a problem with the recorder?

TP: You do normally ask.

JCR: I'm sorry. Do you mind me recording this as we normally do?

TP: I'd like Heather to come with me next time.

JCR: I have no problem with that. [Long pause] So can I tape the interview?

TP: Okay.

JCR: Can I get you anything?

TP: No thanks.

JCR: It's not too long before lunch, but I think I would like an empanada. My secretary brought them in, she had a big family dinner yesterday, her mother's birthday, plenty of leftovers, and she knows I love her empanadas.

TP: I'm okay.

JCR: In that case, I might hold off until lunch.

TP: You do that.

JCR: Well, let's start then. [Short pause] I'm not sure if you knew, but I worked many years ago in a laboratory at [short pause] well let's just say in a laboratory of a government department, a government institution, in Havana.

TP: I didn't know there are institutions that are non-government in Havana.

JCR: Well, you might be right about this. But it was more government than most. Anyway, I was involved in some experiments. On mice.

TP: Why doesn't that surprise me?

JCR: We had strict rules at the institute, which you may be surprised to hear, but we had strict rules on looking after the mice.

TP: What type of experiments?

JCR: Unfortunately, I cannot go into the details. But let's say they were of a psychological nature.

TP: What a surprise. Tell me, how many legs did these mice have?

JCR: A little joke of yours. I like this. It's a good sign.

TP: I'm a real comedian.

JCR: Anyway, we had these strict rules about the care of the mice, and one of my jobs was to see they were enforced.

TP: Another surprise.

JCR: It was a menial task. I was quite junior in the lab.

TP: You had nothing to lose but your chains.

JCR: Oh dear, Karl again. You really are quite obsessed by him. Anyway, back to this task of mine. You probably don't know that mice, when they are sick, show some physical warning signs. You can't talk to them so you need to look for these signs. Are you following me?

TP: You liked this job?

JCR: I liked being involved, but perhaps I questioned the aims [short pause] of the experiment.

TP: Best not to question. The greater good.

JCR: Anyway, when the mice are sick they become hunched over, their fur is different, it sticks up, seems finer. And of course, they lose weight. [Medium pause] Weight is a good indicator because I could measure it, watch what it did over time. In fact, in these experiments, it was the only thing I did to monitor them. Someone more senior made other measurements, the real experimental data, but I just weighed each one every week. On Monday, in fact.

TP: Like today.

JCR: Exactly. [Medium pause] But the lab had a strict rule. If the mouse lost more than twenty percent of its body weight, it would need to be removed from the experiment. This was non-negotiable.

TP: Removed?

JCR: Well, euthanized.

TP: Killed.

JCR: Humanely.

TP: How?

JCR: We broke their necks. [Long pause] It does sound brutal, but it's quick and painless.

TP: For you.

JCR: It is the standard way in labs all around the world.

TP: Good for them.

JCR: Anyway, the method of culling is not something that you or I can change.

TP: Strict rules.

JCR: Exactly. [Short pause] This long-winded story of mine brings me to the reason for this visit.

TP: My Monday morning weigh in.

JCR: Exactly. [Long pause]

TP: My fur is sticking up.

JCR: Like a porcupine's.

TP: I'm hunched.

JCR: It seems that way to me.

TP: And you want to break my neck.

[Medium pause]

JCR: I'm afraid so, Tom. I'm afraid so.

MONDAY

I am not a mouse. The contract is broken.

* * *

TUESDAY

"He wants you out," I said.

"Did he say that, Tommy?"

"It's the same thing. It means the same thing."

"If I leave, can you stay?"

"It doesn't matter."

"You are so thin, Tommy."

"Not for long."

"Maybe it's for the best, Tommy."

"You always say that."

"Sometimes you do too. And sometimes it's true."

"Not this time."

"My Baby is so thin."

"This flesh of mine, the putrid rot has begun. Why wait for the open casket to fill?"

"I'm worried about my Baby."

"I don't want you to go."

"Don't get upset."

"I thought this could work."

"I won't go today, Tommy. They can't make me go today. Wipe your eyes."

"I thought this could work, I really did. When we made the plans."

"Okay, so it's harder than we thought. It always is. You're so thin, and there are other problems."

"My hero, he said I should fight for this."

"Problems like your writing."

"With every breath. He said with every breath."

"Your *writing*, Tommy."

"Juan said he likes my writing."

"You aren't doing much of it, and it's my fault."

"He said he loves my writing."

"And the problem at the jazz club. That was bad."

"It was dark. I thought it was him."

"I know, Baby."

"It was him!"

"It couldn't be him. He'd be dead now."

"He was there, Heather. I saw the tattoo."

"He comes when I do, Tommy."

"Not always, Heather. He comes at other times."

"Baby, don't get upset."

"He was there, I'm sure of it."

"Try and stay calm."

"My arm hurts."

"My poor Baby. I'll stay as long as I can, I promise."

"Why do they do it in the same place. It hurts so much."

"Try and keep still when they do it."

"When I roll on my arm, it wakes me up."

"You got to keep still though, Tommy."

"Someone is coming."

"I'll stay as long as I can, Tommy. I promise."

**

WEDNESDAY

It was you, Leonardo. How clever you are, with your face that jumps between smiles, your matchstick dogs, horses, Fidel heads I bet, how do you do the beard, do you shave them, whittle them into curly hairs, does he have the cigar, or my sponsor, my dear Juan, how do you do his glasses, does the matchstick bend to make the frame, his fat stomach, do you do his fat stomach or lie, I bet you lie, spy school stuff, hey? It was never Raphael, I knew that, Raphael is a true farmer, it is the plants he cares for, his friends, lovers if he's lucky, it was supposed to look like it was Raphael, the head gaucho, supervising my digging, it was meant to look like it should be him, not the face that twitches, stutters, gentle smiles, so clever, so strong, his arms don't spasm when needed, no Santiago claw with Leonardo, when he wants he is as strong as an ox, which he needs to be with me. Holding me down.

* * *

THURSDAY

My arm hurts. Did you know it hurts so, a deep lingering hurt that reminds me of what is happening? And what is going to happen.

* * *

MONDAY

The morning line is slower than I'd thought it would be. It flows like a low-lying creek, just before drying up. This is my first experience with it—cake, coffee, fruit, porridge, then the migration of the wildebeests. Everyone is here, you are right, Leonardo, even you, but you're not strictly in line, you follow it with your eyes, you are in line with us all, but you don't ever make it to the end, like us. The yellow-scored treasure end of the line.

Eva kept me a space. She took my hand and pushed us in at about a third from the front. She said something to the girl she pushed ahead of, the etiquette of the line still unknown to me. The girl protested but Eva's agitated calm eyes warned her away. She held my hand, the line bulging where we stood, like a mouse in a snake's belly, and you smiled at this, Leonardo, twitched and smiled, which is okay, I guess.

I seem to be the center of attention this morning. The whispers follow the bulge we make, fingers point, which is also okay. I used to hear the whispers when I passed the line, so why not within? It doesn't worry me. I'm one of them now, and they seem relieved. And they seem to like me more, but perhaps it's my imagination.

* * *

TUESDAY

Heather doesn't stay every night now. One in two, or three. She said she'd stay as long as she could, but it's beyond both our control.

Our talk is more intimate these days—rushed, serious talk, with little of the Catherine wheel excitement found in the middle of it all.

Intimate talk.

Talk of loss. Departure. Loneliness.

I revert to Billy's balance sheet of life. The negatives fill the page.

Heather focuses on the gains. She says I'm not listening. I'm too negative. Go and see Juan Carlos. Work out a plan for the future.

Intimate talk.

Though, not for these pages.

Transcript July 21st 2010

Interview with Tom Peters by Juan Carlos Rebelde

JCR: I read your diary, Tom.

TP: [No audible response]

JCR: It's much shorter. Some days are missing.

TP: [No audible response]

JCR: I thought we could talk about a plan. [Short pause] It's Heather's idea. And a good one.

TP: [No audible response]

JCR: Firstly, you can stay here as long as you wish.

TP: [No audible response]

JCR: You are safe here.

TP: [Long pause] Safety is most important to you.

JCR: If that's a question, then I would say, on the whole, no.

TP: Inconsistent, aren't we?

JCR: Perhaps.

TP: [No audible response]

JCR: Do you have any writing plans?

TP: My assignment takes too much of my time.

JCR: Perhaps we can reduce that. If that would help?

TP: No. I have no story in me at the moment.

JCR: No rush, Tom.

TP: No rush.

JCR: [Long pause]. When will Heather be back?

TP: Excuse me?

JCR: I said—

TP: I heard you. [Short pause]. I haven't told you everything, you know.

JCR: [No audible response]

TP: Guilt. It's such a powerful emotion.

JCR: [No audible response]

TP: Don't you think, Juan?

JCR: [Long pause]. Yes. But it's sometimes misplaced.

TP: I'm sure it is. Best not to be guilty over one incident that happened many years ago. [Short pause] But if it's a repeated offence, then it's a bit hard to shake.

JCR: [No audible response]

TP: And of course, you weren't to know it, but you haven't helped any [short pause] with the guilt.

JCR: [No audible response]

TP: You have niggled at the topic. Unbeknownst to you.

JCR: [No audible response]

TP: I told Heather you're too smart for me. But you weren't so smart on this one.

JCR: [Long pause] It isn't a competition, Tom. This partnership of ours isn't a competition.

TP: No. I'm being unfair. [Medium pause]. We talked about it, yesterday. Heather and I. We don't usually, it's too messy, this stumbling block of ours. This persistent guilt ridden stumbling block. [Long pause]. Jesus, Juan. I—we—have been so surprised you haven't worked it out. You, of all people. I've deceived you, a bit, of course. Changed the subject, tinkered on it, or just lied. But, you have been able to dissect the truth from fiction before. [Short pause]. But not this time.

JCR: [No audible response]

TP: It's the guilt I'm sure. Such a strong emotion has kept this one secret of mine intact.

[Long pause]

JCR: Are you sure this guilt is not misplaced?

TP: Yes, Juan. I'm sure. [Medium pause]. But I guess you do deserve to know. Turn that thing off.

END OF TAPE RECORDING.

FRIDAY

Sadness has taken over for a time. Sometimes it seems more than I can stand. I long for sleep in the cool of the day, long for the relief of lying on the mattress, a single cotton sheet on top, and wait for sleep to take me somewhere away.

Before, when I farmed, when I farmed without the limp, I had such a longing to be awake. That hit of bright electric awareness—a wide-eyed, open-mouthed love of being awake. How strange that life can turn so swiftly in the other direction—tar black even in the bright of the day. Why they call it blue, this joyless life, I have no idea? For it is black.

And so, in an attempt to free me from this dank sadness of mine, I join the evening line.

* * *

SATURDAY

I think about my rotting flesh more and more. You say it will pass, but I have my doubts.

* * *

SUNDAY

I sit outside, just below my dormitory window, looking down at the tilled earth. My chair is special, like on the deck of a cruise ship, my eggplant ankle elevated on a pillow, bandaged to keep the swelling down. No need for ice anymore the nurse said. I'm on the mend.

It's a warm clear day.

And I have visitors.

"Thank you for the chair," I said.

Leonardo threw up a tic and smiled. "My pleasure."

"I feel like I'm in a Thomas Mann novel. Maybe I'm Hans in The Magic Mountain. A sanitarium in the Alps, but without the need of a blanket."

"We don't like rest here too much." Leonardo said.

"No. This damn ankle of mine. And harvest time will come soon. I'll start back tomorrow."

"Raphael will be pleased."

"I'm not so sure about that." I looked up at him. "I said some awful things to you."

He twitched and grinned. "You did."

"Of course, they weren't true."

"Mostly."

"No, Leonardo. Of course they weren't."

"If you say so. But my skin is thick."

I watched his eyes wander down to the corojo. "How long have you had that tic?"

"What tic?" His face gave up a spasm. "Ah, I make you smile. Raphael will be pleased about that too."

My mothers came as well—a bus ride taking up three chairs, one reserved for a copper pot of Boliche. We sat outside with the plates on our knees; Señora Pupo with her hat tightly fastened, Estelle with her pine face uncluttered. Just like home at the sky blue casa. But with no shifting of lava skin this time.

I could not refrain from asking. "Have you seen Señor Pupo?"

"No," Estelle said.

"Una vez." Once, the Señora said. She kept her stare at her plate of Boliche.

"Bueno," I said.

"Why good?" Estelle gave me her best disapproval face; the time for eggshell talk had gone.

"Dos veces," Señora Pupo said. Twice.

Estelle's eyes snapped toward her. "Where?"

"Hotel Nacional."

"Bar Galeria. Muy bueno!" I said.

"Ridículo," Estelle said.

We ate our Boliche and I wished I had the velvet jacket on, though probably it would have lost its powers by now.

"Have you moved into my room?" I asked Señora Pupo.

"Yes, but she move when you come home," Estelle said.

"No. You deserve the space. I will not hear of it. But, if you don't mind, I will eat dinner with you from time to time."

"Sí. Vamos a engordar." We will fatten you up, Señora Pupo said.

* * *

MONDAY

She looked through the tobacco at me but I kept on digging—pretending she wasn't there.

The sun hadn't let up all day, and I continued to sweat heavy on my potato face. I stared down at the plant that managed to grow despite my clumsy failings, a green flourish, weedless for the most part, though they had made a reappearance in my absence. I eased my hand under the soil, exploring the first time, felt shyly amongst the roots, tangled spider web roots, until my fingers touched a tiny spud, gently in case it cracked, or hatched, and further down to find one smaller, marble size; and within a finger's breadth another.

* * *

WEDNESDAY

I limped my fat ankle along the ridge.

Eva sat at the edge of the tobacco. With the shift of a cloud the sun smacked her face—a hand rising to shield her eyes.

The plants all looked healthy to me.

"You good farmer," she said.

I bent down on my good leg and picked up a weed.

"I no good farmer," she said.

And put my hoe back into its place.

"I no good."

She had sat in the same spot for some time now, and I looked squarely at her with the light in her face. "Do you want to help me, Eva?"

"Sí."

"Come and I'll show you."

"I watch you. No show." She scampered on over with her mouse legs.

"Kneel down next to me," I said.

She helped me down, taking the weight off my eggplant ankle.

"This weed . . . this potato . . . don't dig potato."

"Why I dig potato?"

"Good question. But it can happen if you don't concentrar."

"I concentrar. I concentrar good now." She bit into her lip.

I gave her my hoe. "You have a go."

"Lo siento . . ."

"There's no reason to be sorry, Eva. Not with me."

"Okay. I no sorry." She dug into a clean patch of soil. "You sorry?"

"No. I was, but not now."

"You concentrar good, like Eva. I watch . . . you leg bad, but concentrar good."

We dug into the earth together, following the late afternoon that settled cool on our faces.

"Where you mother?" She asked this out of the blue.

"She's dead."

"Eva, sorry. Tom need madre."

I looked at her and she moved her gaze away, though her eyes strayed not as before.

"How she dead?"

"Cancer."

"Where cancer?"

I pushed my finger into her stomach; she didn't resist my prodding. "Ovary."

"Ah, ovario."

"You know about this?" I said.

"Sí. Eva enfermera."

"Really, a nurse? When you're not a farmer that is."

"I bueno nurse. No bueno farmer." She poked her finger into my side. "Tom bueno writer . . . no bueno farmer. We same, sí?"

I spoke to the banana trees. "I was there when she died."

"This good."

"I'm not sure about that, but it wasn't a painful death."

"That good."

"The doctor gave her pain killers. Morphine."

"Ah, morfina."

"Dr Pap and his big needle of smack. I remember the smell of it. Her skin and the bed and the pan where she pissed. It all stunk of morfina. That junky smell—what does Burroughs say—junk turns the user into a plant. My mother the rubber plant. That got me over my needle fear, though. I had to give it to her, every four hours, when Dad was at work. Dr Pap showed me how, in the muscle he said, deep in the ass. She had no fat so it was easy."

"Not in arm like here," Eva said.

"No, it was always in the bum. Not like here."

The bell sung up to bring an end to the day.

I said, "We all have to die, I guess."

"Sí." She patted the soil with her hand. "But better madre vivo."

"Of course it's better if she was alive!" I realized I shouldn't have shouted. "But it happened a long time ago."

"When happen?"

"I was still at school . . . when I was fifteen."

"Ah. Eva sorry." She spoke like me to the bananas. "Tom need madre. Tom es un niño pequeño." Tom is a little boy.

* * *

THURSDAY

I received a letter from Hymie. He's negotiated a contract with my publisher for the Brazilian short stories, and an advance for anything written in Cuba. He said that Tiphanie Spade was pissed off because it might be tough when trying to cut a deal for her Cuban novel. But

Hymie said he had to be firm, business is business, and anyway Tiphanie was a bit of a brat.

I'm not too sure about my writing in Cuba—these stories reveal too much for my liking. So I might let Hymie know that Tiphanie has nothing to worry about.

Hymie attached a photo of his wife's fortieth birthday, her face full of cake and smoke and candle wax, waving at the camera with puffed up cheeks, grinning goggle eyed, the kids nearby but out of focus. On the back of the photograph *wish you were here* was scrawled in Deborah's flowery script.

As I looked at the photograph, I wondered how Rosie was going, whether she still wore the African dress, whether her daughter was seven yet, whether she could wake the same as she did before Hymie arrived, with his Hawaiian shirt and fat cigars and hotel room with a TV and minibar and a big bed that could easily hold another couple, because she never left his side. And I wondered whether she would do it all again, if given the chance.

* * *

SUNDAY

"You miss chatter chatter?"

"Heather. Her name is Heather."

"Why you angry at Eva?"

"I'm not."

"Sí, you angry."

The water tank brought its chill to my neck. "I'm not angry, I promise."

Her little legs dangled from the timber bench. "You sad Heather go?"

"Sí. And sad about other things."

"I sad. You sad. I tell you . . . we same."

"Perhaps you were right all along."

She kicked into the empty space. "I visit today."

"Who?"

"Hombre."

"Boyfriend?"

She shrugged.

"Ex-boyfriend?"

"What ex?"

"An old boyfriend."

"Sí, old boyfriend."

"I know all about them . . . the ex's are the farmers' lot."

"What lot?"

"The farmers' plight . . . fate . . . the farmers' destiny."

"Ah, *destino*."

"You like him, this boyfriend?"

She shrugged.

"Does he like you?"

"Sí."

"Does he love you?"

She kicked into nothing again. "He no sure." She dug into my ribs with her finger. "Farmer destino, sí?"

"Sí, pretty Eva. Sí."

She pointed to a strip of the tobacco plot. "We cut soon."

"You?"

"Sí. And others. Sell to cigarro."

"Where will you sleep when it's gone, Eva?"

"With plátano."

"With the bananas?"

"Ah, you laugh."

"I guess it's been a while."

"You nice smile."

I poked her like she did to me. "What's the name of this boy of yours, then?"

"What one?"

"Your boyfriend."

"Sí, what one?"

"Jesus, Eva."

"No, Jesus. Alonzo y Edmundo."

"What do you want with two boyfriends?"

"Me don't. It them."

A cool gust managed to find us.

I said, "You are lucky, you know that?"

She put her head on my shoulder and gave up a sigh. "Eva no lucky. And Tom no lucky."

The wind changed direction and brought with it the breath of cigars from the field below.

"What other thing?" she said.

"What?"

"What other thing you sad from?"

We both kept our gaze at the tobacco, but her resting head meant I only needed to bend ever so slightly to whisper in her ear.

* * *

MONDAY

Raphael took me down to a small cleared strip of land between the corojo and mango groves. It looked like it had just been plowed.

He bent down and picked up a palmful of dirt and handed it to me. "What you think?"

I felt the soil that crumbled between my fingers. "It seems dry."

"Sí. This shit soil."

He walked down the strip and I followed him like a limping disciple. Every thirty feet or so he would bend down again to sample the soil in his hand, always with the same conclusion. "Esta es la tierra de mierda." This is shit land.

When we reached the base of the plot, at the fence that separated the farm from the main road, he turned to me. "I give to you shit land."

I laughed and he smiled with his kidney bean teeth, yellow, red and brown like the soil.

"You no like?"

"I'm not that sure. What did it grow before?"

He kicked into the dirt. "Corojo. Bad corojo."

A truck rushed past with a gush on the road in front.

"Corojo isn't easy to grow, you taught me that."

"Sí, not easy."

"I'm not a good farmer, Raphael. You taught me that too."

"Sí, you shit farmer." He put his arm around me. "Gringo not grow corojo. Gringo grow mandioca." He flashed his teeth again. "Mandioca grow in good soil. Mandioca grow in shit soil. Mandioca grow in shit house if want." I felt his laughter against my chest. "But mandioca make soil good, make strong. Mandioca look after corojo."

He strengthened his grip on my shoulder and we started back toward the direction of the dorm, tramping over the dry shit soil that was now mine.

* * *

THURSDAY

I wet the soil with an old rusty can and plant the manioc on the peak of the ridge, an angle to the soil, pushing the stem that was freshly cut from year-old plants just up the way—further in the dirt than skyward, one at a time, three feet apart, these little naked beach flags of stems that, when given a chance, will sprout starch-rich roots, fat tuberous roots near the undersurface of the soil, watered on and off, then ready for harvest to feed the farmers who planted them.

* * *

WEDNESDAY

We sat at the long dinner table in our formation of four. The smell of warm stew filled up the space between us.

"I go home tomorrow," Eva said.

"For how long?"

She grinned at us. "Forever."

I looked at this pretty field mouse of the tobacco. Her black bobbed hair, her brow that nearly touched in the middle, thick as her finger, and her eyes—brown and large and beautiful—these eyes that could smile and dance and tell tales and more.

"Back to your big soft mattress," Leonardo said.

"Sí."

"Back to home cooking," he said.

"Mi madre no sabe cocinar." My mother can't cook. She held her gut with both hands. "I eat mucho in farm. Eva fat."

"Eva mucho sleep," Raphael said.

"Naked," I said.

"Sí, naked," they all sung up. The table lit with bright eyes and warm stew.

"Raphael, how will the tobacco grow without Eva?"

He grinned at me. "Like your potato. Better."

She twisted her gaze to scan us all—one by one. "I visit you."

"Come for dinner," Leonardo said.

"I come pudding night. One month. You here in one month?"

"I certainly will be," Leonardo said.

"Sí, Sí," Raphael said.

"You here, Tom?"

"With you gone, Eva, it will be hard for me to stay." She beamed at me with those eyes of hers. "So, when I finish the planting, I might go too."

We looked over at the wildebeests that had started to shuffle into the evening line.

"I must get back to work," Leonardo said, and threw up a gentle tic as he stood. "Don't be late."

"You keep spot at front for us. We see you soon," Eva said.

"You'll get me in trouble. People will say you are my favorites."

"Sí, we are," she said.

"Sí, Sí," Raphael said with a mouth of soft carrot.

Leonardo smiled and twitched at us. Turning, he said something I couldn't make out to one of the wildebeests, and took her by the arm in that gentle way of his, making her laugh, and she sung up a reply and laughed some more, his head tilting with that heavy tic of his, laughing and jerking, as they went off, arm-in-arm, to the evening line.

"Tom, Raphael, you visit me?" Eva said.

Our eyes said of course.

"We go beach," she said.

"Sí, sí."

"We go beach, Sunday? Hey, Raphael. Hey, Tom. We go beach Sunday?"

I reached over and held her hand. "It'll be all right, Eva. You're going to be fine."

"Sí, Eva be fine," she said. And lowered her gaze.

"Next week we come," Raphael said.

She looked up at me. "Tom, next week?"

"Okay, next week."

"We picnic." Her wide brown eyes skipped a tune. "I make picnic, no mother."

"It's a deal."

I looked around the long rectangular room at the shifting herd, the faces well known, some a flushed cherry color, a sting on their skin I could see, others the color of Raphael, the color of soil, their stories bound by the leather of their hide.

As we shuffled over like the others, Eva took my arm and whispered, "Tom, you leave forever, like Eva?"

* * *

It was night but I was in the bush-land of my childhood, and there the sky was a texta blue, a bright light aquamarine without any haze or cloud or anything, like it was colored in, and the sun was high and scorching, so it must have been summer, we had our gray uniforms on, and we were skipping into the bush, the undergrowth crunching under our clinkers, skipping like we were off to see the wizard, the wonderful wizard of Oz.

"I saw a snake," Rydges said.

"Come on, we'll miss the traffic," Danno said.

"I tell you it was a brown."

"It was probably a turd."

"We need to get ammo," Beany said.

"I got us plenty of ammo," I said.

"When, Tom?"

"When I was here last."

"You were here without us?"

"Yeah, I come here all the time."

"Why didn't you tell us, Tom? I want to come next time."

"Me too."

"It wasn't a turd, it moved."

"It might have been coming out of your ass."

"When did you come here last?"

"Two days ago."

"Fuck, Tommy. Why didn't you tell us?"

"I hope it bites you on the ass, Danno."

Danno stopped skipping and he bent over, peeling his shorts down and his hands splayed his cheeks open for us to see. "Bite my brown eye." He laughed and Beaney laughed and so did Rydges.

"I come every week."

"To chuck rocks?"

"I come every week."

"I'm coming next time," Rydges said. "I'll bring a bag of lollies and chips if I can come."

"I come every week."

"Hey, look who it is."

She stood in the middle of our path, with her gray school dress and her twisted pigtails and her eggcup dimples.

"Hey, Heather."

"Hi, Tommy."

"They love each other," Rydges said.

"Tommy loves Heather," they all chanted.

"And Heather loves Tommy," she said, smiling. "Can I play too?"

"Girls can't play," Danno said.

"Let her," I said.

"Girls can't play . . . they're too slow."

"What happens if he tries to catch us like last time? Girls are too slow, Tom. You see them in British Bulldog."

"They can't even tackle."

"Let her play, Beany."

"Sorry, Tom. She came last in the egg and spoon race. If he comes, she's caught for sure."

"I don't want you to get caught, Heather."

"It doesn't matter, Tommy."

"It does, too. I don't want you to get caught."

"Let's go. We'll miss the traffic."

And they skipped off into the heat of the trees and when they were gone, hidden from sight, I skipped off too and followed them into the bush. It seemed ages before I found them, a fork in the path, one arm just ten yards from our rock throwing spot that fell down a straight drop to the road, the other leading somewhere else. They were all sucking on paddle pops, I could taste them as they fashioned them into sticky points.

"Over here, Tom," Rydges said. "Get an ice-cream . . . you can choose any flavor you like."

"I don't like ice-cream."

"Bullshit. Everyone likes ice-cream."

"I don't like ice-cream."

"Just down that path, Tom. He's there waiting for you to come."

"I don't want to go."

"Mine is caramel."

"You can have it, but I'm not goin'."

"But he's waiting, Tom. He said for us to come and find you."

"I don't want to go."

"He said you can have any flavor you want. If you don't tell anyone."

"You'd have to go down to the station if you wanted to tell."

"I'm not goin' to the station."

"Nor me."

"Mine's banana."

"He's swell, isn't he," said Rydges. "Any flavor you want."

"I'm not goin', I tell you."

"Come here, Tom." His deep voice came soft from behind them on the other limb of the path.

Rydges and Beany and Danno turned and smiled and slinked to the side to allow his way past. He was holding his esky, a St. George dragon painted on the side, his footy team, he always brought it, I didn't like the Dragons, I liked the Bunnies.

"Come, Tom." His voice deep and soft.

I looked at his furry red arm, sun bleached hair thick and curled, the blue eye and the twin fins and the big belly with blue stripes and warts on his face. Big blue warts on his grinning face.

"Go on, Tom," Rydges said. "He's got chocolate, I know you like chocolate."

"I don't like ice-cream."

"Come here, Tom." He barked the instruction, not soft at all, and he turned back down the path that he came from, the ice-cream path, and I started to follow his legs and his King Gee shorts and his big black boots. But never his face. I never looked at his face. Ever.

"Tommy."

I turned, and Heather stood just a few steps away at the beginning of the short path to our rock throwing spot.

"Tommy, you don't have to go, you know."

I watched the blue whale turn back towards me and he dropped his esky as he came.

"Girls can't play," Danno said. "They're too slow."

"Tommy, you don't have to."

"She'll get caught, Tom, she's bound to get caught."

Heather smiled at me and the sound of the traffic purred out of sight and the blue whale kept on coming towards us.

She held out her hand. "Come with me instead, Tommy."

"Yep, she's goin' to get caught. Last in the egg and spoon she was."

The blue whale was just feet from me now—so close I could see the pupil separate from the white of his eye.

"Come on, Tommy."

And she grabbed my hand, reaching up, her little fingers and palm, and the touch felt warm, not sweaty but smooth and soft, satin soft.

"That's it, Tommy. This way."

And we ran holding hands.

"This way, Tommy."

"They're wrong, Heather. You're fast."

She grinned. "This way."

And we laughed like we did when I dropped a dumpling or we beat Grandmother in mahjong or just when we woke together for no good reason other than that.

And we kept laughing, as we jumped, high into the clear texta sky, the red stripes of an ice-cream truck drifting into view, and the road with its rushing vehicles that seemed so far below, but started to swell larger and larger, and we turned to each other still hand in hand, grinning, as we fell down to the streaming traffic.

* * *

FRIDAY

"Isaac, come over here you bastard."

Our reserved table sat with an uncluttered view of the stage, a bottle of Havana club on the house, and eight full glasses.

Billy waved up again. "Isaac, come the fuck over."

Isaac came with his goatee and beret all hip in the haze.

"This, my friends, is our gracious host for the evening." Billy stood and rested a hand on Isaac's shoulder. "Let me introduce you all. On this side are the best cubilette players of Havana . . . but what cubilette is I have no idea. At that end are Havana's finest sisters, I'm sure you can see the family resemblance. Of course, you know our little maraca girl . . . and Tom, do you remember Tom?"

Isaac nodded and feigned a smile—managing to avoid looking my way.

"I seem to remember you meeting Tom on a couple of occasions at least." Billy winked at me. "You probably remember the last . . . like Hurricane Katrina it was, right in the middle of my set. Do you recall, Isaac?"

"It's cool."

"You are such a good sport. I tell you, my friends, he is the Mother fucking Therese of the jazz world."

Isaac tried to move back to the safety of the stage, but Billy wrapped an arm around him like packing into a scrum. "You might not know, Isaac, tonight is all about Tom. It's his big night!" Billy arced his gaze to the other tables, then back into a calmer pitch. "I must keep my voice down . . . don't want to scare the patrons. But Isaac, you more than anyone have the right to know. You see, Tom has just escaped from the authorities. And we—and by we I include you my little goatee friend—are his rescue party."

Isaac stared open mouthed at the table.

"No listen him, Isaac," Yanela said. "Billy loco."

Billy laughed up loud, his great gray mane flapping around, and dropped to kiss Isaac with his forehead. "Tom will be a good boy, don't you worry. And we might need another bottle before the night is out. These ladies are really putting it down."

I looked over to my mothers who sat at the opposite end of the table—away from my hero. They were on their second glass of rum, and the Señora had already begun to ride her chair like a bull. Héctor sat heavy opposite them and topped up their glasses with every sip, puffing on a Partagás cigar. I wondered how many Hymie had lost to him with his winnings.

Señor Pupo sat next to me surprisingly calm. I think it was enough for him he was here. It would be easy for me to chat to him, my mothers cast away from our English banter, but it didn't seem the right occasion. I had watched my hero and the Señora throw glances at each other when they first arrived, timid at first, then, with rum flavored courage, a more protracted stare. I might wander around the table later and steal the Señora's seat, play a game of Cuban musical chairs, and see what happens.

And I might get a chance, after the rum of the evening took hold, I might just get a chance to talk to Señor Pupo about more pressing matters. Heather had said I should talk to him—that he would understand. Maybe I'll walk with him, stagger more likely, when the evening comes to a close, back to his place, maybe for a nightcap at the Galeria, and seek his guidance. Seek his approval. Seek his absolution.

Billy sat at his piano up on the stage. "Ladies and gentleman, thank you for coming to the Fox and Crow tonight. My apologies for my lack of Spanish, but the only language you need to understand comes from these . . . comprender?" The instruments in Billy's band sung up their introduction. "This evening, I have a friend of mine who will join us for a few songs . . . not too many because she'll steal the show . . . stand up, Yanela . . . there she is, take a bow, that's it . . . a special treat for you all a bit later as we cruise into the night. And before we get stuck into it . . . I want to say a big hello to Tom . . . there he is down there . . . wave, go on, he's a shy one . . . Tom's a very good friend of mine and a famoso writer—look at his face, he hates me saying that—who is back with us after a brief stint farming potatoes . . . or carrots . . . or something in the dirt. I myself don't like gardening much . . . what about you guys . . . no, too early a start for musos . . . but someone has to feed us. So to you, Tom, we dedicate this first song, a Gnarls Barkley classic . . . and welcome the fuck back."

* * *

SATURDAY

Heather came today—an unexpected surprise.

She came as she always does.

I was writing my diary and she sat on the bed with Carla, Penny, and Dotty and played while I talked—her pigtails tightly wound, tied with those big red ribbons of hers, flapping dog ear ribbons, her gray school dress sitting just above her knees, her little white collared shirt, socks bunched low on her ankles, black leather shoes, old clinkers, I loved those old clinkers, with the buckles much easier to manage than tying laces, not that the girls ever had difficulty tying their laces. I remember Mum taking me to the shoe store, complaining about some staining or defect in the leather of my clinkers, I remember this well. Boys have this problem, the shoe salesman said to my mother, it's from the trough, you know, the urine. Piss stains on my clinkers. I don't remember what they looked like, but my mother accepted it without debate, and of course I knew it was true. Be careful she said—try and aim, Tommy. I laugh now, about pissing my name in the school dunnies, Beany in raptures, running to class late, Rydges always last.

I must phone Dad tomorrow, fill him in on how things are going, catch up on my aunt's knee operation, she would've had it by now, my nephew's soccer career in the under sixes, his rock collection, chew the fat.

Heather sits tiny on the bed, as she always does, for when she stands the top of her head just makes it to my nipples. So it's best she sits. She bends Carla's waist, her knee back straight. She's quite a good sort, is Carla, with her little sleeveless top, checks of black and gold and red, tiny pink shorts, short shorts, the Swing'n sixties that moved edgier into the seventies, that brought twist'n turn Barbie ready to party.

Heather came as she always does. But she didn't speak. I know you would be worried if she did, wouldn't you, Juan?

God she is beautiful, with her eggcup dimples and those long twisting pigtails and her almond eyes. So I'll just talk and talk, turning my chair and little desk to face her, my fingers touch typing but looking at her, always looking at her, until that time, which I suspect won't be long, she finally decides to get up and leave.

* * *

SUNDAY

The Malecón curves, moss colored, along the lap of the wash. Pastel colonials slowly shedding their paint follow the curve, yellow lamp-lit in the dusk, the gray of the sky, the gray of the ocean, the road too, charcoal gray, wet from rain, the ocean splash; and the crimson Cadillac, yellow Dodge, that flashes up brash against it all. I hobble along this curve of the Malecón, still with a limp.

She sits facing opposite to the others, away from the ocean toward the path, swinging her long stick legs, coal black, shiny, her white shorts, socks that peek just over the tongue of her sneakers, white too, the African colors forgotten. She smiles her buckteeth at me, but swiftly covers them with her upper lip, embarrassed—though, why?—and manages to grin with this wrapped up smile of hers, and swings her legs higher, as a trapeze artist might, gaining just enough height before the final jump into the outstretched hands of a trick.

I sit with her and we talk for a while, about the weather, bad for business this damp, the nights best when warm, sweaty warm, a rush of blood warm. And her daughter, Izzie, a nice name, Izzie, whom she saw back in her hometown last Wednesday, in Holguín. She shows me a photo, thin Izzie, dark as her mother, curly haired tied up in a bun the African way. And her long bus trip, with a lunch stop, two toilet stops, the slow trip back for the weekend of double shifts, sometimes round the clock, though not with weather like this. And Estelle, she sees her sometimes, professionally, a cash in hand rental, but visits too if she needs a break or wants some woman company. She likes Estelle, the

Señora disapproves, which she understands, that generation can find it strange, especially the women, but not Estelle.

We stand and I walk with her down the wet gray esplanade, close but not touching. She says I look well, muscular, which I laugh at. She asks where I'm staying, I point it out, the street between the pink and green, just two blocks up from there; she likes the Vedado, more quiet than Vieja, not for business though, she smiles and doesn't hide her teeth at this, it's too slow for business in the Vedado.

We cross the Malecón as two couples skip towards us, laughing, arm-in-arm, fooling around between primary-colored Chevys, Plymouths, friends it seems because the cars slow when they see them. We enter the road that opens between the pink and green colonials, identical except for their color, and slowly stroll together up my quiet-lit street, hands protecting our faces from the rain that falls slantwise against us.

Transcript Sep 6th 2010

Interview with Billy Whitton by Juan Carlos Rebelde

JCR: Thanks for this quick chat, Señor Whitton.

BW: No hay problema.

JCR: When a client of ours leaves, we like to formally record the interview with the next of kin, or whoever is accompanying the client home. I hope you don't mind?

BW: Still no hay problema.

JCR: Excellent. Sometimes relatives tell us they were not told what to expect. What to do. It can be embarrassing for us.

BW: Cubans just don't appreciate what they have. They should see the NHS back home, it's a fucking squalor compared to here.

JCR: Its funny, we haven't met before, but I feel I know you quite well.

BW: You know my music?

JCR: Alas no. I am more of a classical fan than jazz.

BW: Classical, jazz, rock, salsa. It's all food for the gods.

JCR: Indeed.

BW: Perhaps I could drop my album off to your secretary?

JCR: Please, don't trouble yourself.

BW: No hay problema doctor. No hay problema.

JCR: I just want to confirm that Tom will be staying with you for a while.

BW: He will. Two bachelors together, just like the odd couple.

JCR: Oh, I'm sorry to hear you're now a bachelor.

BW: I'm always a bachelor, but I've recently parted company with a young lady.

JCR: Oh, just the one? [Medium pause] Forgive me, a little whim of mine. [Medium pause]. But will Tom be staying for the week.

BW: As long as he likes.

JCR: Very generous of you. Very generous. [Short pause]. You understand his condition?

BW: I had a cousin with the same affliction.

JCR: Excellent. Well, not for the cousin of course.

BW: Another bit of whimsy doctor. You crack me up. I must get you that album. Gratis of course.

JCR: You are too kind, but please, don't go out of your way. [Short pause]. Here is a pamphlet that describes some signs that we might like to hear about, if they occur. You can phone us at any time. Twenty-four hours.

BW: They say Cuba is poor. But where in the world would you get such fucking service, hey doctor?

JCR: You're too kind.

BW: God knows, I might need your services here one day.

JCR: I think that's unlikely.

BW: My cousin, it's in the blood. On my mother's side. Dad's an alcoholic. Mum's side is crazy. How the fuck can I be expected to survive with genes like that.

JCR: I'm sure you do just fine.

BW: Never heard voices though.

JCR: That's good.

BW: I saw a ghost once.

JCR: Look at the time, I must be getting on.

BW: My memory lapses from time to time, but that's the booze.

JCR: So Señor—

BW: Billy, please doctor. Only the judges call me Señor.

JCR: Well Billy, that's about done then. Unless there's something you want to talk about regarding Tom, before you go.

BW: Perhaps some advice on how to be around Heather. How I should behave, if she comes back that is. When I was a kid my brother had an imaginary friend. Little Donald. Don't sit on little Donald he would say. We always had afternoon tea on Sundays, very British of us, and mum would always pour little Donald a cup, my brother didn't even have to ask, she would pour the extra cup and I would stare at her as if she was crazy. So doctor, I guess my question to you is, do I buy Heather a mojito?

JCR: Well Billy, we are quite a liberal society in Cuba, but even here, serving alcohol to children is frowned upon.

BW: [Response unclear]

JCR: I'm afraid that was careless of me, this recent discovery of mine [Brief unintelligible words] Quite unprofessional to breach confidentiality. Very stupid. [Short Pause] But I would ask you to keep that to yourself, Billy.

BW: [Response unclear]

JCR: And to answer your question, it won't be necessary to pour any drink. Just try and understand as best you can.

[Long pause]

BW: There is no hay problema with me doctor. [Medium pause] Actually, maybe just one final question. [Short pause] These signs you talk about, the madness—such a nasty word—when do you think it will happen next, to Tom? My cousin Eric would go off the deep end at any full moon. You could write a fucking Chinese calendar based on his conversations with the almighty. Jesus used to sit next to him at the dinner table, though he didn't eat much. [Laughter] So, any idea when it will happen next, to Tom.

JCR: Oh. [Medium pause] Whenever he chooses.

BW: Excuse me?

JCR: Whenever Tom decides to stop taking those little yellow tablets of his. [Medium pause] You look confused, Billy. I see you don't understand. Tom's madness is completely controlled by his medication. That's a toss of the coin, and he is one of the lucky half. [Short pause] But when he decides to stop them, we'll look after him at the farm. Let me see you out.

[Long pause]

BW: Why the fuck would he stop taking his tablets?

JCR: Oh, Billy. That's an easy one. For that L word of yours, Billy. For love.

HOSPITAL DE LA HABANA

GROBART GRANJA / GROBART FARM
HOJA FRONTAL / FRONT SHEET

MÉDICO/DOCTOR: JUAN CARLOS REBELDE
NOMBRE/NAME: TOM WILLIAM PETERS
DIRECCIÓN/ADDRESS: CALLE 16 NO. 273 E/ JE I, VEDADO, HAVANA 10400
FECHA DE NACIMIENTO/DATE OF BIRTH: 2 FEB 1962
ALERGIAS/ALLERGIES: NIL
GRUPO SANGUÍNEO/BLOOD GROUP: AB NEGATIVE

ACKNOWLEDGEMENTS

This book is dedicated to all those who helped—the readers of each draft, the editors, and the places from which the story was carved.

ABOUT THE AUTHOR

PTG Man lives in Sydney, Australia. He is the author of two other novels, *The Scent of Daisies* and *A Very Human Place*.

Made in the USA
San Bernardino, CA
08 October 2016